MONSTERS
IN THE
HALLWAY

BEAVER'S
POND
PRESS

Cover design created by Jane Gardner of Queens, New York using an old photo of the Eau Claire County Hospital (asylum) that was torn down in 1999 for a housing subdivision. Only the cemetery remains.

ISBN 13: 978-1-59298-721-4

Library of Congress Catalog Number: 2017913014

Printed in the United States of America
First Printing: 2017
21 20 19 18 17   5 4 3 2 1

Book design by James Monroe Design, LLC.

Beaver's Pond Press, Inc.
7108 Ohms Lane
Edina, MN 55439–2129
(952) 829-8818
www.BeaversPondPress.com

This book is dedicated to the lost life of my father, Palmer James Kosmo, who spent twenty-seven years in mental institutions, and to my mother, Virginia Fischer Kosmo—an amazing, powerful woman who could not be stopped. My sister, Sandee, and I owe everything we are to her. I pray she is up there reading my story.

PART 1

CHAPTER 1

EAU CLAIRE, WISCONSIN—MAY 5, 1959

It all started with a dead Boy Scout.

Detective Lieutenant Joe Stroud had just melted into his well-worn brown leather easy chair in his living room, killing time before heading to bed. He was flipping through retirement magazines imagining how he was going to walk away from the force next month after thirty years on the job. He could almost feel the warm Florida beach sand filtering between his toes and a frozen coconut piña colada chilling his right hand, when his wife, Bette, burst into his daydream.

"Somebody spotted a body up at McDonough Park on the north side. Gordon says it looks like a murder."

"Murder? What the hell? There hasn't been a murder in Eau Claire for thirty years. And that was a bunch of bootleggers fighting over territory during prohibition—my very first case."

"Yeah, yeah. I know," Bette said. "Ya better get a move on it. Gordon sounds about ready to explode."

1

"Well, you know Gordon," Stroud added. "He tends to be a bit of an alarmist."

If it really was murder, Gordon had reason to be alarmed. This would be trouble, trouble that could derail Stroud's retirement.

He and Gordon were the only full-time detectives on a police department of thirty-nine sworn officers. Most of the force had served less than five years, and their training largely involved walking the beat and riding around in one of the department's eight overused squad cars. Parking tickets were major crimes. However, just about every cop had real battlefield experience coming out of World War II. While that didn't offer a lot of investigative skills, it meant they weren't shocked by much—before today.

Stroud didn't bother changing into his semiofficial dark-blue detective suit. His red-and-black-plaid wool lumberjack shirt and tattered blue jeans would suffice for rutting in the mud. He climbed into his personal car—a rusted, coffee-brown 1950 Ford Country Squire station wagon and drove eight miles to the park planted high atop the bank overlooking the south shore of Dells Pond. He traveled quicker than the posted twenty-five miles per hour speed limit.

Dells Pond was not a small rain basin in some backyard. It was an enormous lake created in 1880 when lumber barons diverted the Chippewa River and flooded a lush green farm valley, inundating fields, barns, and homes. The massive pond was where they stockpiled floating white pine logs before sending them cascading downriver. For more than fifty years, Eau Claire was the lumberjack mecca for Wisconsin's thriving timber industry, and Dells Pond was the bank where millions of logs were deposited to wait their turn at nearby sawmills. The pond was so deep and treacherous with submerged buildings and waterlogged trees that even experienced divers dared not venture far below the permanently murky surface.

In early spring, adventurous—make that foolhardy—kids danced across the "rubber ice," so named because as the giant expanse of pond ice softened under warming temperatures, it flexed under foot and ice-cold water squirted to the surface in steaming fountains. Those who ran quickly would get very wet.

Generally the ice held. Except for the day in March 1953 when Danny White skipped Sunday school at Saint Luke, ventured to the pond alone, and was never seen again. His body was never found.

Danny's death terrified parents. But for the young, it only seemed to heighten the fascination and the electricity they tasted jogging across the rubber ice. However, they did tend to stay a tad closer to shore.

Stroud approached the playground and picnic area overlooking the densely wooded banks of Dells Pond. Lumberjacks once toiled through the harshest winter weather in this spot. Most days now, it was usually filled with youngsters. But not now. It was a crime scene—an eerie, dark scene illuminated by the light of a half moon and bobbing beams from half a dozen police flashlights.

"Hey, Gordon," he said. "What we got here?"

Detective Sergeant Gordon Richardson still looked like the Marine who stormed Omaha Beach in Normandy, France, on D-Day. He stood a tall five-ten without an ounce of anything but muscle and bone. He brandished the strong face befitting a Greek statue that never betrayed emotion.

In the war, he had witnessed guys being blown apart alongside him. While standing next to Gordon one dark night, his best friend took a sniper shot mid-sentence, right through the forehead. The compulsion to light up a cigarette proved fatal. There were still nights when Gordon would awaken sweating like a hog headed to slaughter. He wondered why he survived.

Despite all his grim experience, Gordon's face was now pasty white. The man who had witnessed violence beyond comprehension sloshing through the muddy fields of Europe appeared ready to gag on his words.

"There—under the table."

Stroud followed Gordon's eyes.

"Oh shit. It's just a kid. A Boy Scout," Stroud murmured aloud more to himself than Gordon.

Stashed beneath a severely weathered wooden picnic table that was etched with time and hundreds of hand-carved names, many in pairs surrounded by crudely scratched hearts, was a young boy clad only in a mud-smeared khaki Boy Scout shirt emblazoned with a proudly earned Life Scout badge.

"Gordon, this boy looks younger than he actually is. My son was in Scouts, and it takes quite a while to become a Life Scout. That's just one step before Eagle. He's got to be sixteen or seventeen—just a really small kid for his age."

"I found this billfold in the pants," Gordon said, "and it looks like his name is Roy Pettit. Shit, I wonder if he's Bart Pettit's kid. That worthless piece of shit is serving time for murder."

"That's right. He murdered Johnny Anson at the Sinclair station in Chippewa Falls."

Gordon shook his head. "Looks like the kid was trying to rescue the family name by joining the Scouts, then this happens. Some days it seems like there is no justice."

Stroud imagined the kid full of life and hope only hours earlier. Now the lifeless shape was more department store mannequin than human. His pants, underwear, and shoes were tossed in a haphazard pile a few feet away, barely concealed amidst remnants of tall brown milkweed plants left over from the previous season, waiting to be pushed aside by new growth.

"The lame attempt to hide his body and clothing tells me our suspect may have been interrupted. I bet there's a witness out there, but they may not even realize that what they saw is important.

Who found the body?"

"Miss Anonymous," Gordon said. "Some gal, sounded kinda young, called the station. She said there's a body in McDonough Park, then hung up."

"We need to find out if she or anyone else saw somebody around here this evening. Somebody spooked our guy, and just maybe they saw him run. Get some guys going door-to-door," Stroud said.

Gordon nodded.

"And Gordon, keep two guys here, and don't let anyone get within a hundred yards. I mean not one person gets in here without my approval. Not even the chief. Well, except Doc Mobley. He should be here any second to take a look. This kid was attacked by some sexual deviate. Look at those purple marks on his neck. He was choked, but we need Doc to confirm it. Stand by—I'll be right back. Gotta get some bags from my car for evidence."

Stroud scooped up a pile of rumpled napkins, waxed paper, candy bar wrappers, and paper cups. *Probably tossed by kids on end-of-the-year school parties,* he thought. He also grabbed three large white feathers. *Maybe they floated down from one of the birds flashing overhead, trying to make sense of the senseless scene.* The only promising lead was a large fingerprint, too big to belong to the dead boy, planted on the kid's shiny brass Boy Scout belt buckle.

"Hey, boss," Gordon interrupted. "Just got a shout-out on the radio. Paul grabbed a nut who escaped from the insane asylum across town last night. Milbrandt says he's the killer, and he wants you on it right now."

Since 1949, the City of Eau Claire had been organized under a manager-council format. Percy Milbrandt, who previously served as mayor, had been elected council president, a position equivalent to mayor. Most folks still called him "mayor" anyway.

"We have to finish up here first. Milbrandt's gearing up for election, so ya know he's gonna be all over this one. He wants to pop his buttons to the newspapers about how fast he solved the kid's murder. But we gotta do this right, no matter what anybody says, especially that guy. How the hell did he get his nose in here so fast?"

"Dunno. If I had to guess, though, I'd say he got a call from his buddy Chief Schimdts."

"No doubt."

It was well after midnight when Stroud returned home and collapsed into his easy chair. There were no more thoughts of sandy beaches or cool drinks. A dead boy haunted him. He wanted to set it aside and hit the hay, but there was no way to erase the image of that dead boy tossed under a table like some unwanted picnic scraps.

This was one of those nights when diving into a giant bottle of booze to drown your monsters felt like a good idea—an idea that led down a rat hole where the only drowning victim was the drinker. Stroud had realized that at a very early age. He loved a glass of beer, though, which was another good reason not to wash away your troubles with it. Not much joy in the taste of that beer.

So he settled for a tall water, straight. He sipped mindlessly as he tried to get a handle on what came next. Only one thing was certain—retirement would have to wait.

He slowly turned his head from side to side, scanning the room like a searchlight throwing its gaze across a troubled sea, reaching out to lost sailors. His search was for answers: Who would murder a Scout, a boy who just wanted to be a better person?

Stroud's gaze fell on the oil painting his father, Herman, had sat for on a Paris street at the end of World War I. Stroud loved that painting. Not because it was a great piece of artwork; it was not. He constantly fought off Bette's demands to take it to the basement.

He loved it because it reminded him of what his dad had looked like, as memories tended to fade.

Any problem Stroud encountered, his dad always had the answer. Stroud desperately wanted to talk with him tonight. Old Herman Stroud had been a cop for more than forty years, often the only one in town during the insanity of Eau Claire's lumberjack days, when law and order were more words than reality.

Stroud wondered if his dad had ever seen anything like a sexually assaulted, dead boy. How would he have dealt with it?

As he stared at the painting of his dad, Stroud could almost feel his father offering advice. *You can do this son,* he heard as plain as if the painting were alive. *Just talk to the people. It was somebody he knew and trusted. You can do it.*

Stroud leaned back and slept. Bette tapped him on the shoulder shortly after five in the morning.

"Sorry to wake you, honey, but you said you wanted to get to the office early."

CHAPTER 2

MAY 5, 1959

Every senior in the Eau Claire Memorial High School class of 1959 was obsessed with the future—except Jason Korsen. Jason's life derailed shortly after he walked into Pearle Landfair's English literature class.

"Jason, you need to go to the office," Mrs. Landfair said. "Your mother is waiting for you."

What? Jason thought as he turned around and headed for the office. *I doubt Mom has been back to the high school since she graduated. Why is she here? Now what have I done? My grades are all good. Haven't pissed off any teachers lately.*

Jason smiled to himself as he recalled the other time he met his mother in a principal's office. It was fourth grade, and Mrs. Baker had tossed him out of her class after he pulled Sandy Engebretson's pigtails.

"Troublemaker," his teacher told Principal Barfield.

Jason's mother, Ginger, laughed out loud when Mrs. Baker

then said, "He's my best student, so he gets his work done before the other students. But then he starts talking and causing trouble. And even worse, he writes with his left hand. That's a sign of demonic possession. And with his father's *problem*, that concerns me."

Ginger stopped laughing, revealed that she herself was left-handed, then jumped to her feet poised to unleash her own demons.

Principal Barfield sent Mrs. Baker back to her room and reassigned Jason to Miss Oberg's classroom with instructions to give him extra work.

"Keep him busy," he said.

Jason realized this trip to the principal's office wasn't about being left-handed. Nobody cared about that any longer. But this principal could be the problem. Jason was convinced Principal Haugen hated him—had hated him even before he was born. Haugen had a history of childhood fights with Jason's dad, Peder. Haugen said Peder was a classic bully. Peder said Haugen was a loudmouth sissy.

As if on cue, Jason turned the corner and stared into the massive trophy wall outside the front office. His eyes fixed right on the giant golden statue on the fourth shelf. When days got tough, he always got a boost reading the plaque:

1929
Wisconsin State Champion
Speed Skating
Peder J. Korsen

As a boy, Peder was an outstanding speed skater. He lamented a failed try for the 1936 Olympic games, where his friend Jimmy Hendrickson finished fifth in ski jumping. Eau Claire named their ski jump after Hendrickson, and he dominated one whole section in the high school trophy wall. But Peder's trophy had its special place in the trophy wall too.

Maybe Principal Haugen will give us Dad's trophy so he doesn't have to look at it every time he goes into his office.

When Jason approached the secretary's desk, she nodded. "Go right into Principal Haugen's office." She pointed to an open door.

Jason saw his mother seated on a soiled imitation-leather easy chair with Principal Haugen planted next to her in a matching chair. Principal Haugen gestured to a blond wood side chair as Jason entered. Neither Ginger nor Principal Haugen wanted to make eye contact with him. Nobody said a word.

More than the silence, his mother's appearance stunned Jason. No matter what rocks life tossed at anyone's head, Ginger always offered a smile and a word of encouragement, usually humorous. But not this day. No smile. No comment. She sat there staring at the floor.

Ginger never left home without spending at least an hour primping herself, but this day it appeared she may have combed her hair with her fingers. She wore no makeup. Her dress looked as though she had slept in it.

What's going on here? Jason wondered. *Can this really be some kind of retribution for Dad using Haugen as a punching bag?*

What more retribution did Haugen need? Haugen and the whole town got the last laugh about Peder's "problem," as Mrs. Baker had called it. He had been locked away in an asylum for the better part of the past nine years. He had been released once, only to return after he set the house on fire while Jason, his sister, and their mother slept. This time, there was no release date in sight.

Some folks viewed growing up without a father as something short of normal. It had never occurred to Jason that he was different than any other kid. Then again, he had nothing to compare his life against.

After losing his father to mental illness at age nine, Jason had essentially no men in his daily life—unless you were talking about the neighborhood grocer, druggist, or barber who freely shared time and advice. There were Boy Scout leaders, but they came with mixed consequences.

Jason chose to view his situation as an opportunity to develop responsibility and early independence. And he had two powerful role models in his mother and grandmother, with whom he lived. Grandpa Ernie had died shortly before Peder's first hospitalization. Ginger and Grandma Libby were a pair of dominant forces at a time when women were expected to know their place—in the kitchen and serving their husband's every wish and command.

Now in 1959, the Korsen household consisted of two mothers; Sidney, the annoying younger sister; and Jason as "the man of the house." Clearly, they didn't qualify as the typical nuclear family. This nonnuclear family also fell below the poverty line, although they were not about to admit it, especially to themselves.

"Jason, we have some very bad news." Principal Haugen seemed uncharacteristically warm and apologetic.

Oh God. Tell me it's not Grams. Jason realized this was something more than the principal's childhood memories. This was something far worse.

"You are so young to have to deal with such bad news," Principal Haugen continued, "but I need to tell you that your friend Roy Pettit was found dead in the picnic area at Dells Pond this morning. The police think it was murder."

Jason sat in stunned silence, trying to comprehend. *How could this be? Why would anyone murder Roy?*

Jason immediately thought of Roy's family. Roy's grandpa, Bartholomew Tyrone Pettit I, was a high-powered executive with American National Bank and a popular city councilman. Now old Bart was undoubtedly spinning in his grave. His son Bart II tarnished the Pettit name and tossed his own family into ruins when

JIM KOSMO

he was sent up the river for life for killing Johnny Anson, a high
school dropout who worked nights at the Sinclair station in Chippewa Falls. It was supposed to be just a stickup, but Johnny made
the fatal mistake of taking too long to retrieve forty-seven dollars
from the cash register. Bart II pulled the trigger in panic when a
car pulled up at the gas pumps outside.

Roy's mother, Ruth, was a likable, church-going lady who
tried her best to raise her two boys, Bart III and Roy. But the stain
of being married to a murderer combined with her limited skills
left her struggling as a minimum-wage cleaning lady at the White
House Motel. Roy's big brother was Bartholomew Tyrone Pettit III,
but somebody branded him Batshit Bart when he was a boy, and
it stuck. He earned the title early in life, when he couldn't avoid
killing just about anything that moved—including neighbors' cats
and dogs and any animal or bird that ventured within range of
the antique single-shot .22 rifle he inherited from Grandpa Bart I.
Simply killing helpless critters was never sufficient. He feasted on
torturing them more than a cat taunting a wounded mouse. Oddly
enough, he came to love the Batshit name, thought it made him
sound like a tough guy. Best of all, it really pissed off his old man.

Batshit disappeared from town for a year, and had reappeared
just three weeks earlier. It turned out he had spent the year getting
free meals and housing at the Waupun State Penitentiary, where
he was girlfriend for his 275-pound sweaty cellmate. Now Batshit
Pettit was living large with no visible source of income. Eyebrows
were raising. Jason knew Roy took serious crap in school about his
dad and his brother.

"It's worse," his mother stammered through her tears, breaking into Jason's thoughts.

What could be worse?

Ginger had not shed a tear since Peder first went to the asylum. But today she was clearly shaken. She couldn't seem to find

any more words.

"The police arrested your dad. They think he killed Roy," Principal Haugen completed for her.

"What? Dad's in the hospital. He couldn't do that."

"Apparently, he escaped from the asylum yesterday and was seen at the church during your Boy Scout meeting."

Without even thinking, Jason's hand went to his mouth as he started biting his fingernail. *So that was Dad*, he thought. *But is he a murderer?* It was almost too much to absorb.

Jason knew his dad had serious mental issues, but he was positive he did not murder Roy. Yet Jason feared that the police were eager to pin the murder on his father simply for being a "nut."

Jason didn't realize how correct he was. As news of the crime would be revealed around town, one fact became abundantly clear—everyone was convinced Peder Korsen had molested and murdered Roy Pettit. The council president saw the crisis as the perfect answer to rescuing his faltering election campaign. Local newspapers reveled in exposing every sordid detail of the biggest story to hit town in decades. Most people just wanted that crazy guy locked away forever.

Jason knew there had to be another answer. His father didn't do it, but someone did.

What about Batshit? Jason thought. *Everyone knows Bart's up to no good. Maybe Roy figured out what Bart's up to, and they got in a violent fight. Wouldn't be the first time two brothers did that. Or who knows—maybe their old man got into a nasty feud with one of his prison buddies, and that guy got out and came after the family. Lots of options. So why are the cops so fixed on Dad?*

If no one else wanted to find Roy's real killer, Jason would do it himself. But how does a high school kid do what the police can't do? Where do you even start to find a murderer when everyone in town thinks he's already been found?

Or maybe Jason already knew who the murderer was. There was someone else.

Sudden pain shouted from the tip of Jason's index finger, jerking his mind back to Principal Haugen's office. This time, he had bitten the nail so short it bled. Again. *What a stupid, humiliating bad habit,* he thought. He constantly tried to stop biting his fingernails, but the best he came up with was mastering the technique of automatically balling his hands into tight fists in a lame attempt to conceal his embarrassment.

Jason glanced up and locked eyes with Principal Haugen, who smiled. To Jason's relief, the smile reflected more compassion than ridicule.

Jason's mother continued watching the carpet. She wasn't really there.

"Jason, why don't you take the day off?" Principal Haugen said. "Go home and help your mother sort this out. Come back when you're ready."

Ginger slowly rose from her chair as if a puppeteer were gently pulling up on her strings and guiding her to the doorway. Jason fell in behind. He didn't even look at the principal as they drifted out the doorway, floated down the hallway, and climbed into the shiny black Plymouth, where Grandma Libby Hunter had been waiting for more than an hour. Not a word was said on the ride home.

What next? Jason thought as he stared out the window. *Why does all the crap keep falling on us? What did we do to deserve this? God, Mom tries so hard, but things just keep getting worse.*

It wasn't always that way.

PART 2

CHAPTER 3

1946–1948

The Korsen family had once been poster material for the ideal American household with Mom, Dad, one boy, and one girl living in a brand-new suburban house complete with the proverbial white picket fence and one of the first television sets sold in Eau Claire.

The Korsens moved to their big new house when Jason was five and Sidney was a newborn. Unwilling to wait out the construction schedule, Peder and Ginger situated the family in the damp, newly poured concrete basement of what was to become Ginger's suburban dream house. While they hunkered down in the damp bunker, Peder slapped plasterboard on stud walls to carve out two bedrooms, a bathroom, and a large open area that served as living room, kitchen, dining room, and laundry all wrapped around a big lime-green furnace.

Brown woolen army surplus blankets tacked to the wallboard served as bedroom doors. Peder had acquired the blankets free from his uncle who had slipped across the border into Minnesota to work at Faribault Woolen Mill Company, a historic factory that had kept soldiers warm in every war since 1865.

There was no ceiling in the basement dwelling other than rows of yellow studs and the underside of the main-story floorboards, which resembled a torture board of nails poking through. The only exit was up the stairway next to the furnace. Multicolored frayed-rag rugs were tossed about liberally in a futile attempt to lend some manner of homey atmosphere, but it was clearly a musty cave lacking only an invasion of bats. In that first year, baby Sidney barely survived two bouts of pneumonia that spawned her lifelong battle with asthma, and Peder fell ill to scarlet fever.

Ginger would permit nothing but new appliances in her castle, even if it was just a basement. The featured attraction was her brilliant white Maytag wringer washing machine with a violent agitator. It was a vast improvement over rubbing wet clothes across a rippled washboard in the laundry room sink. The shiny new machine also eliminated the need to twist clothes by hand, as its twin rubber rollers wrung water from garments.

On the very first load, she got distracted, probably by something little Jason was doing. Her hand became entangled in Peder's white "going to church" dress shirt as she was feeding it into the rollers. Her left hand was sucked steadily into the crushing white rubber jaws. For someone who rarely revealed emotion, she turned red with alarm, jerked the machine across the room with the strength of coalminer, and howled a fearsome cry.

Jason unwittingly became a tiny hero. He ran to the wall and jerked the power cord from the socket. No one was quite sure how he knew enough to do that. Maybe he just followed instructions for once in a lifetime. Whatever it was, it earned Jason a free pass on most mischief for the next few months.

Having grown up in the Italian section of Chicago, Ginger's

culinary creations leaned heavily toward divine pasta dishes. Peder, however, was strictly a meat-and-potatoes guy. He had difficulty with any meal that didn't include the combo. Occasionally, he did manage to choke down spaghetti smothered under a river of rich red meat sauce, Jason's favorite dish.

Whatever Ginger cooked, the family digested the aroma long before anything appeared on the little yellow Formica kitchen table shoved up against an unpainted temporary wall. Peder had positioned the electric range under a window, hoping to send food fumes outside. It didn't work, especially in the winter, when temperatures frequently tumbled far below freezing. Opening the window only unleashed a waterfall of frigid air cascading into the underground bunker. Ginger lit fragrant candles and said they would mask the odor. That didn't work either. In time, their olfactory glands became so saturated they couldn't smell anything.

As if numbing their nostrils wasn't sufficient, their eardrums reverberated constantly from Ginger's turquoise Columbia phonograph. She enjoyed Mario Lanza, Bing Crosby, Al Jolson, the Andrews Sisters, and others on occasion.

But mostly it was a steady diet of Frankie Laine, a guy from her old Chicago west side neighborhood, on black vinyl platters spun constantly on the phonograph. She especially loved pummeling Jason's little ears while singing along with Frankie's haunting version of "That's My Desire" over and over and over. It was Lane's first major success in a career that would garner twenty gold records. Jason enjoyed it—the first fifty or sixty times.

During the day, Ginger always wore one of three simple, loose-fitting housedresses that differed only in color. All were cut from the same Butterick pattern and stitched together on her new Singer sewing machine. She customized them by adding oversized side pockets suitable for carrying a full load of wooden clothespins.

After surviving in their subterranean bunker with two small

kids for more than a year, Ginger and Peder crawled to the surface and moved into the skeleton of Ginger's dream house. The yellow wood bones of newly erected walls begged for drywall. The kitchen and two bedrooms were mostly ready for inhabitants, which was good enough for Ginger and Peder. Peder hired some carpenter friends, but he did most of the work himself. Being the son in a long line of skilled Norwegian craftsmen, he was very handy. Eventually, it was a great house where Jason spent his grade school years trudging more than a mile to Longfellow Elementary School.

Just before Easter, shortly after the Korsens climbed out of the basement, some entrepreneur at the tire factory where Peder worked was selling baby chicks dyed various pastel shades. Peder bought one in each color—pink, purple, green, yellow, and blue. Most of the guys brought some little stained birds home. But within a day or two, wives across town were demanding that the noisy, messy fowl go away.

Peder was always in search of a way to create his own business and escape the drudgery of rotating shifts at the tire factory. He conjured up a scheme to build a chicken coop in the backyard, collect the other families' noisy Easter chicks as free inventory, and raise the tasty birds for sale.

The Korsens weren't in the country, however. Their house sat on a city lot 75 feet wide by 150 feet deep. Nevertheless, Peder was convinced that after a year of practice in his backyard laboratory, he could buy a small farm and launch his poultry business. He collected every book he could find on raising chickens and running a small business.

Within a week, 122 baby chicks took up residence in the Korsens' suburban yard. Like most city folks, they had absolutely no idea how quickly the chicks would swell to adulthood. The little guys shed their pretty pastel colors and cuteness within days. By summer, the yard was teeming with a flood of fully grown chickens blasting an unbearable cacophony, especially when the roosters started crowing at five o'clock in the morning.

It helped that the flock supplied the neighborhood with fresh eggs and meat. Sunday became chicken and dumplings day at the Korsen house, with plenty of leftovers for Peder's lunch the following week. It also helped that the little buggers devoured all the Korsens' table scraps. And chicken crap made great nitrogen-rich fertilizer for Ginger's garden. At least that's what Grandma Libby, the family's very own master gardener, promised. The little eating machines especially loved protein, including every insect that had the misfortune to venture into the yard.

Still, neighbors started crowing louder than the roosters. The guy next door seemed to fit in perfectly with the roosters. He was beanpole-thin with slits for eyes, a pointy beak for a nose, and a distracting knob on his throat that jumped when he spoke. He became enraged when he complained about the noise.

Peder responded in kind. Well over six feet tall and north of two hundred pounds, mostly muscle, he shook a massive fist in the skinny guy's face while admonishing him, "Mind your own business." Mr. Chicken Neck summoned the police, who quickly discovered there was no law against raising chickens in the city.

So, the Korsens went on buying chicken feed, collecting eggs, and slaughtering one of the feathered flock every Sunday. Along the way, Jason discovered that it was absolutely true that on rare occasions a chicken would run around with its head cut off.

Angered by Mr. Chicken Neck calling the cops, Peder planted a chain link fence right down the center of the driveway the warring neighbors shared. In a time long before zoning laws were given serious thought or enforced, Mr. Chicken Neck's house had been placed almost on the property line. The new fence left just enough room for Peder to squeeze past into the garage, but it totally blocked Mr. Chicken Neck's access. The spite fence lasted several years until Ginger had it removed as a peace gesture.

Peder's chicken coop was a piece of art, a perfect scale model of the family home. The chickens, however, seemed to prefer hiding in the tall grass, crawling into the garage, or slipping into Mr. Chicken Neck's yard. They usually did not return from visits next door.

Over the years, Peder lost interest in chicken farming, so Jason became keeper of the flock. It meant that he fed the birds daily and cleaned up their messes. More importantly, it gave him possession of the chicken coop. It became a little club house, a secret den perfect for boys to refine the manly art of smoking cigarettes.

One day while his parents were away, Jason invited two buddies, Bennie and Rex, to join him. Rex and Bennie were a few years older than Jason and didn't come by often, but the chicken coop was the perfect big-buddy magnet. For Jason, it was just good to hang around with older guys and let everybody, particularly the local bullies, know he had big friends. Rex especially had a reputation as a very tough guy who appreciated any excuse to demonstrate his pugilistic prowess. Best of all, Rex knew stuff—like how to smoke, drink beer, and talk to girls.

"Oh yeah," Bennie said. "Ol' Rex knows those special words that make the girls' panties fall off."

"What?" Jason sputtered in alarm. "How's that even possible?"

His buddies doubled over laughing.

"I can't tell ya about that till you're at least thirteen," Rex managed to say.

"But what if I say the words by accident?" Jason continued.

Rex and Bennie bellowed even louder.

"Don't worry about it, kid," Rex said. "Da're magic words. You can't say them until you're thirteen."

More, even louder laughter erupted.

Jason was somewhat relieved but also truly puzzled. What

words could these be? And how could words possibly pull down a girl's panties?

Rex whacked a wooden match against the side wall. The trio lit up, snuffing out thoughts of girls and their delicate apparel.

"Hey, it's bad luck to use a match three times," Benny said.

They all laughed, and Rex tossed the spent fire stick into the chicken shit pile. Unfortunately, the match was still hot. It quickly ignited the stack of tinder-dry straw Jason had carefully shoved into the corner. The straw pile literally exploded into flames and dense black, acrid smoke.

The trio rushed to the door, but the makeshift wire lock Jason had fashioned to prevent Sidney and other intruders from entering jammed. Anxiety rapidly gave way to panic as the wire twisted tighter. Finally, in desperation, the trio counted to three, drove their shoulders through the finely crafted little door, and escaped.

Choking and gasping for fresh air, they tumbled into the large black boots of two burly firemen who had just arrived with a crew aboard a pair of big fire rigs and a rescue truck. Apparently, Mrs. Lanner, two houses away, spotted the fire and thought the Korsen house was burning.

Terrified that her little boy was about to die, Ginger flew across the street from the Stygars' house, where the neighborhood women were enjoying morning coffee and a daily gossip session. It was a close call for Jason—not because of the smoke and flames but because of his mother and that nasty leather razor strap she cracked better than a mule-train driver's whip. She ripped it off the nail where it hung near the back door, looked sternly for an eternal minute, then set it back.

In practice, the strap was mostly threat, except for the time Jason went through the ice playing on Dells Pond with Danny White. That strap may have saved his life a couple of years later.

Danny was one of those kids who always did exactly the

opposite of whatever his parents or teachers expected—to their constant frustration. He was a Scout and an above-average student, a fact that seemed to annoy and confound every adult he knew, but it also earned him exceptional leniency for his mischievous ways. He relished risky behavior, seemingly defied gravity, and paid no mind to fear of consequences.

Most classmates were intrigued and amused by Danny's bizarre behavior but stood aside in fear of contamination. Thus, Jason was one of Danny's only friends. That friendship earned Jason three nasty red welts on his buttocks when his mother learned of his "rubber ice" adventure with Danny. Memories of the strap sent Jason to Sunday school the day Danny chose to head for Dells Pond, never to be seen again.

Just the sight of the stupid strap hanging by the back door was sufficient warning, although Ginger dealt out far greater pain with her words that day of the fire.

"Jason, I can't tell you how disappointed I am. I thought you were a better person than that."

Needless to say, the chicken coop and all the feathered creatures were banished from sight before Peder made it home from work that day.

Two weeks later, Peder was washing away his worries with a heavy dose of beer during a late-night visit to the Hilltop Tavern. At the end of a long night at the bar, he thought it was fortunate he had his 1939 Plymouth in the parking lot, because he was in no condition to walk. As the streets and trees wobbled and weaved before him, he sped down Birch Street, sliding around the corner onto Starr Avenue where he slammed into a giant oak tree, coming to an abrupt halt.

The next thing he remembered, his eyes fluttered open to the sight of two giant oak trees towering over his crumpled car and a flood of sticky red syrup sliding down his face. The oak trees had saved him from slamming into the Shell Oil Station and almost certain death, but they ripped off both fenders on the left side, shredded two tires, smashed the radiator, and snapped both axels. And the force of the collision had smashed Peder's head into the steering wheel, ripping a nasty gash across his forehead and knocking him unconscious for a brief time.

Dripping blood, Peder crawled out of the crushed car and stumbled three blocks down the street to home. Ginger summoned Arrow Towing to scoop up the mess and ordered her sheepish husband back to the scene after scrubbing him up and changing his shirt. Halfway there, he encountered two cops, who tossed him in their squad car and charged him with reckless driving. Driving under the influence was not a major emphasis at that time. Nobody checked blood alcohol count.

Before he was fully awake the next morning, Peder was standing in front of a judge. Peder boldly proclaimed innocence, whereupon the judge ordered him to return the following Monday with his lawyer and witnesses.

As Peder strode defiantly out of the courtroom, he came face to face with Ginger. She grabbed his arm, spun him around, and pushed him back into the courtroom, whereupon he entered a guilty plea. He was fined fifteen dollars and court costs of six dollars and forty-five cents.

Ginger considered not paying the fine and letting "the criminal cool off for ten days in a cold jail cell," but she ponied up the cash. Towing and storage charges added twenty-five dollars, and repairs piled on another $140, even with a free radiator. The numbers may sound more than reasonable today. But in 1948, a new car cost $600, the average worker earned $5,000 a year, and a typical two-bedroom house was $8,000.

Years later, Ginger would recall the accident as the day she thought Peder started on his plunge down the mysterious rabbit hole of mental illness. His doctors never discounted the theory, nor did they affirm it. Nobody really seemed to know what ignited insanity for Peder or anyone else. Did it creep into one's head unnoticed or come with a sudden blast? Was it genetic, traumatic, or environmental?

Jason came to believe his father's propensity for tilting back little brown bottles of beer surely was a major contributor, if not the primary factor, for his mental illness. For years, Peder had proudly acclaimed his amazing ability to consume more alcohol than anyone on the planet without suffering the normally expected effects. And it was true. The guy could suck down half a case of beer without appearing to be impaired. What amazed Ginger was the mere fact that he could dump that much liquid, alcoholic or otherwise, into his body.

Whether due to the accident, the drinking, or some unknown trigger, Peder never regained his past enthusiasm for life, his wife, or his children. His descent began.

CHAPTER 4

1949

Monsters visit every little person at some point. But in December 1949, monsters visited the Korsen home. These monsters weren't under Jason's bed. They were lurking in the hallway just outside his bedroom.

They surrounded his dad, staring blankly with piercing, fluorescent eyes and grim, foreboding expressions. As massive as Peder was, he looked tiny next to the four monsters. They weren't so tall as they were bulky with even bigger bulging muscles than Peder's. Two wore long white coats. The other two were outfitted in crisply pressed police uniforms.

Jason got out of bed and maneuvered his little left eye to peer through the sliver of space left by the almost-closed bedroom door. Then he froze motionless in the darkness, praying the monsters wouldn't sense his presence.

One of the monsters broke the silence. "Okay, Peder. You need to come with us."

"It's all right, Ginny," Peder yelled to Ginger, who was hidden away somewhere in the next bedroom. "Paul's an old buddy from high school."

Even at eight years old, Jason could feel tension floating down the hallway. *What is he talking about? Where are they taking my dad, and why? That monster sure doesn't seem like any 'old buddy.' This doesn't make any sense.*

"I need to shave, shower, and change clothes," Peder said.

"Go ahead, Peder," the main monster, Paul, said. "We'll wait right here."

Peder normally spent very little time in the bathroom, but this night he lingered more than an hour. When the water wasn't running, Jason could hear a one-sided conversation filtering through the closed door. Jason assumed his dad was talking to his imaginary friend again, something he did often.

Paul called to Peder through the door now and then. But mostly the monsters just hovered in the hallway—motionless, in absolute silence.

Nervously, Jason slipped back to bed. He slapped the tiny World War II airplanes dangling from clear fish line above his bed, poised in a perpetual dogfight. With the hit, the left wing from a Nazi Messerschmitt fluttered across the room. He got out of bed again to retrieve the piece. Then he grabbed a twisted, nearly exhausted tube of model airplane cement from the night table. He stuck the tiny plastic wing back in place.

It wasn't the first aerial incident over Jason's bed. His mother frequently whacked them with her feathery dust stick, but she always attacked the Nazi planes, never the P-51 Mustang or the British Spitfire.

"If you're going to keep an air force in your room, you need to start keeping them clean," she spouted every time.

While Peder's muted conversation filtered through the wall,

Jason stared out his bedroom window. He watched a white-tailed deer slide across the yard in stealth mode.

How does that giant animal move so quietly? he wondered. *I would never have known she was there except for a lucky glance. Uh-oh, now she knows I'm watching.*

The deer froze for a moment, looked toward his window, then returned to rutting in the snow, ripping up his mother's dormant iris bed to feast on a frozen salad.

A tiny movement in the corner of the window drew Jason's attention away from the deer. *Hey, there's Spidey, my pet spider.*

The little popeyed, fuzzy creature had built a spectacular piece of artwork that occasionally snared an invading fly. At first Jason thought it strange that such creatures linger indoors all winter, but it was obviously a brilliant survival plan.

Spidey was never completely satisfied with her web. Or perhaps she just suffered from an abundance of nervous energy as she awaited a tasty fly to appear. She was always busy, constantly weaving new strands into her beautiful web. When the web vibrated from a fresh catch, she slid down it with more grace and dexterity than the Flying Wallendas. She devoured most of the fly, leaving a few parts untouched.

"Apparently legs and wings are not tasty," Jason whispered to her. "But I wish you would clean up after yourself."

Just then, Jason realized he was talking out loud, not unlike his father. *Maybe Dad's imaginary friend is a spider? I should ask him when the monsters leave.*

Finally, Peder emerged from the bathroom dressed as if ready for church in his prized steel-blue dress suit. Even in his bedroom, Jason's nostrils were tickled with the powerful scent from an excessive splash of Old Spice aftershave lotion. Peder flashed an insincere smile framed under his wavy coal-black hair pasted in place by more than a little dab of Brylcreem. His rugged Nordic profile was dominated by a large crimson-stained nose that had always made Jason wonder if his dad could have been the model for the Indian head nickel.

"Peder, I hate this," Paul said, "but procedure requires that you wear this jacket."

This news brought Jason back to spy into the hallway. Talk about a strange jacket. The sleeves were far too long, with a light-brown leather strap dangling at the end of each one.

Peder reluctantly shed his suit coat and slipped on the jacket without protest. The two monsters dressed in white coats pulled his arms down and fastened the leather straps into silver buckles. The two monsters each grasped one of Peder's elbows while the other two, in police uniforms, took up positions in front and behind him. The little troop marched straight down the hallway and disappeared out the front door. It was mystifying and terrifying all in one.

After Peder vanished, Grandma Libby appeared almost every day or the family went to her house. Jason's mother and grandmother talked in hushed voices, but never a word to Jason. Nobody talked to him. It was as though he were invisible. Christmas, his ninth birthday on December 30, and New Year's Day passed almost unnoticed.

Sidney was only three and oblivious. Jason tried to get his head around it but couldn't. He knew enough to realize it was not good when cops drag your dad away in the middle of the night and suddenly your mother is exiled to her bedroom, where the only sign of life is an incessant, mournful melody of sobs echoing down the hallway day and night.

"Is Dad in jail?" he asked one day when she made a rare appearance.

"Jail? Oh no. He's . . ."

She burst into tears, wrapped her arms around him, and collapsed into the burgundy velveteen couch, nearly crushing her little boy. She tried to compose herself, stammering and attempting to speak every few minutes, but words just wouldn't come out.

After what felt like an hour, she swept her tears aside, cleared her throat, and said with authority, "Absolutely not. Your dad is sick. Paul took him to the hospital."

Hmm, Jason thought. *Were they afraid he would fall down? Were his arms broken? What's the deal with the stupid jacket?*

"Is it polio?" Jason asked.

That was the worst thing he could imagine—which was saying a lot, living in the 1950s. The crippling killer virus held the world hostage with overwhelming mass hysteria. Beaches closed. Theaters, restaurants, churches, and other public places struggled to survive the lack of attendance. Health officials even cancelled the Minnesota State Fair, which pulled the Korsen family to St. Paul every August.

The dreaded "Polio Scoreboard" terrorized readers every day on the front pages of the *Eau Claire Leader* and *Telegram* daily newspapers. They looked much like baseball box scores, but these scores revealed the numbers of new polio cases and polio deaths reported in the Eau Claire area during the previous twenty-four hours.

The constant attack of the stealth killer was coupled with a paralyzing fear of impending nuclear annihilation by the Russians. The combination created an oppressive, ongoing atmosphere of doom that was almost more than the human psyche could endure. As it was already, fresh, grim memories from the Great Depression and World War II haunted every adult, lending credibility to any worst-case scenario and tossing the entire nation into the steely grip of mass mental depression.

In school Jason and his classmates practiced "duck and cover," cowering under their desks to hide from the initial shockwave. (Some genius apparently thought desks could block a nuclear blast.) Other misguided souls sought to gain a modicum of control by building concrete dugouts, or "fallout shelters," in their back-yards. They were under the grand illusion that they might ward off the deadly clouds of radiation tumbling from the sky during the coming nuclear winter—but with no thought of how they might exist for decades underground.

After surviving in a soggy basement for a year, the Korsens decided that they had seen enough concrete. They elected to forego adding a fallout shelter, choosing instead to take their chances with the Russians.

None of these responses did anything but fan the flames of mass hysteria, create wealth for a few opportunistic concrete con-tractors, and ignite burgeoning growth in development and pro-duction of ever more powerful and costly weapons.

Polio was actually a more treacherous villain than the Rus-sians. It hovered invisible in the air, poised to pounce without warning. No one knew when, why, or how it came—only that it was virtually out of control. People kept their children in the house at night and made certain everyone took a daily nap. Get-ting enough rest was about the only advice doctors could offer. Not very reassuring

"Polio? Oh no, it's not that kind of sick," Ginger said. "His brain is sick. He needs to go away for a while until they can fix it."

His brain is sick? I never heard of somebody having a sick brain. I don't even know how to ask a question about that, Jason realized as he searched his own brain.

Jason had no way of knowing that his life had changed for-ever the night the monsters appeared in the hallway. Except for a brief early reprieve, his father would not feel freedom for twenty-seven years.

CHAPTER 5

1950

Unable to cure him in Eau Claire, Peder's doctors soon transferred him to a new facility. He moved 180 miles south to Mendota State Hospital in Madison for more aggressive treatments, including hydrotherapy, electroshock, and subshock insulin therapy.

Mendota State Hospital, operating since 1860, was the primary state hospital for treating mental illness in Wisconsin. Formerly the Mendota Asylum for the Insane, it assumed the more comforting title of Mendota State Hospital in 1945. Today, it is the politically correct Mendota Mental Health Institute. Peder was part of a record year with 2,528 patients in 1950.

Dr. Reynolds conducted the intake interview when Peder arrived in Madison.

"Peder, do you know why you're here?" the doctor inquired.

"Some people don't understand who I am and what I can do," Peder replied.

A powerful, confident guy who generally dominated any conversation, Peder struggled to adapt to his lack of control at the hospital. His confidence was nowhere in sight. As he sat with Dr. Reynolds, tremors took control of his body. His eyes were blank black marbles. He struggled in silence as he rapidly opened and closed his right hand, as if punishing some invisible rubber ball. The only sound was a rhythmic click as he mechanically snapped his lower jaw left and right. Then he slowly lifted his eyes, held Dr. Reynolds in a firm stare, and spoke.

"They think I'm crazy. I may have to kill them if it continues."

"What is it that you can do, Peder?"

"Great people talk with me, and I relay their messages. My house is connected to them by a special radio. I know things others cannot understand. I have heard voices, and the newspapers report my thoughts. I'm working with England, France, and other countries as well to bring peace to the world. That's why I was given the Diamond Award for Peace."

"You won the Diamond Award for Peace?" Dr. Reynolds feigned interest in this delusion.

"Yes. If people would only help me, they would be benefitted."

Dr. Reynolds scribbled on his notepad:

He has other various paranoid delusions. There is no marked intellectual deterioration. He answers the usual questions satisfactorily, and his replies to questions are in keeping with his education. He is oriented and has a partial insight into his condition. He believes he is above the average intelligence and has ideas other people do not have. He fancies his house is connected up with radio, that he can hear voices from the radio that are directed to him, and that the newspapers report his thoughts. He admits homicidal tendencies and feels he has to protect himself against people who talk about him. It is quite

evident he has hallucinations of hearing voices and delusions
of a paranoid nature.

The doctor listed Peder's official diagnosis as dementia praecox (also known as schizophrenia) paranoid type.

Shortly after dinner two days later, Peder was reading a book
in the dayroom when he suddenly leaped to his feet, fired his
book against the stark white wall with a resounding smack, and
launched into a screaming tirade.

"You can't keep me here! It's not legal! I want my own clothes
right now!"

Dr. Reynolds arrived in minutes, spoke calmly to Peder, and
slowly quieted the situation. He administered a shot of amytal
sodium into Peder's left shoulder and took him to his room to sleep.

Nothing significant happened until January 9, when Doctors
Alfred Carlson and Adolf Bergstrom took charge. They described
Peder in his chart:

Physically, he is a large, robust man without any remarkable
physical defects. He was administered the Shipley Institute
Test that determined he suffers an intellectual impairment at
a level designated as 'probably pathological,' and he exhibits
below-average ability with abstract problems; although, he
does exhibit a superior vocabulary. On the ward since admis-
sion, he has shown borderline adjustment, being more or less
complaintful. At times, he appears on the verge of an acute
excitement.

At interview, he shows a superficially cheerful attitude,
but beneath this is a strong paranoid trend. He relates numer-
ous grievances, which are in the nature of delusions. Some of
his ideas along this line go back to the time of the last war, dur-
ing which he apparently wanted to build a house and now feels

the wartime restrictions were directed especially against him. He also has delusions about the radio, claiming the programs were interrupted in order to make comments about him.

Doctors Carlson and Bergstrom prescribed hydrotherapy, treatment for a minor infection on his right ankle, and electroshock for the brain.

Nurse Mary Monahan—a tall, slim veteran RN with short-cropped dirty-blond hair and a very pleasant manner—was summoned to take Peder into what appeared to be an oversized bathroom with four-inch-square faded yellow wall tiles and a giant checkerboard floor of black-and-white linoleum. There was a severely scratched stainless steel table with matching stool just left of the door—both bolted firmly to the floor. Two bright fluorescent light fixtures, possibly stolen from a police interrogation chamber, painted the room with stark white light that carved crisp, sharp-edged shadows. The only other item in the room was an extra-large bathtub, almost a pool.

A cloud of humidity filled the room as the heavily chlorinated pool of water saturated the air with a bitter aroma. It invaded Peder's nostrils, igniting distant visions of a high school swim meet.

"Peder, please put your robe on the table and climb into the tub. Careful, please," Nurse Monahan said as he climbed in. "We'll bring the water up to your neck and completely submerge your body. The water is warm. This should be very relaxing. Please let me know immediately if anything concerns you. Lie back, and let your body and your mind rest. Think about the best day you ever had: Where were you? Who was there? What was the weather?"

The swim meet was stuck in Peder's head, and that was a pleasant enough memory to focus upon. He didn't really care who was there. The weather was irrelevant because the pool in his memory was inside the YMCA, where the weather never changed.

It was always very hot and intensely humid, even on the coldest winter days. The air was always imbued with a pungent concoction of sweat, chlorine, and rubbing alcohol.

Nurse Monahan approached the tub with a large rubber blanket. "I'm going to place this on top of the water and around your neck. It'll help hold the temperature at ninety-seven degrees."

In the twentieth century, mental hospitals employed various applications of hydrotherapy. Fortunately for Peder, he avoided the cold-water treatment used on those sad souls showing signs of "excitement and increased motor activity."

And if you think waterboarding was invented by the CIA in Iraq, think again. In the 1700s, it was a popular treatment for the insane. Physicians promulgated the theory that the treatment "cooled" the brain and terrorized patients into submission. Undoubtedly true, but it failed to cure them.

The procedure involved bringing a blindfolded subject into a room, whereupon he was tossed unexpectedly into a giant tub of ice water and taken to a state of near drowning. Proponents believed the extreme shock treatment startled the patient's brain into recovery, not unlike later electric and drug-induced shock treatments.

Although the near-drowning approach was mostly abandoned, some hospitals continued to use a cold-water treatment, submerging the subject in approximately forty-eight degree water. The belief was that the cold water slowed blood flow to the brain, decreasing mental and physical activity and thereby shocking the brain into recovery.

All forms of hydrotherapy were mostly discontinued in mental hospitals in the 1970s. About the same time, relatively similar methods became popular at resorts and spas wishing to decompress frenetic, stressed out, allegedly sane persons. Thus, the hot tub was popularized.

After three hours, the relaxing nature of hydrotherapy began to wear off for Peder. Shriveled and agitated, he splashed violently, ripped away the rubber blanket, and demanded to be released. Nurse Monahan ended the session and returned him to his tiny stark-white room.

He endured a dozen warm-water treatments lasting two to four hours each throughout January. Eventually, Dr. Bergstrom determined there was little, if any, improvement. He moved Peder on to electroshock treatment.

Electroshock therapy (ECT) was first introduced in Europe in the 1930s. Medical scientists theorized that the brain could be repaired by inducing seizures or convulsions. The theory was based on empirical observations that epilepsy and schizophrenia never appeared in the same person. Although that later proved to be invalid, the treatment took hold. Psychiatrists and the news media quickly claimed ECT was the miracle cure for mental illness. It was introduced in US hospitals in 1940.

Psychiatric doctors and the news media were so enraptured by ECT and passionate about touting the miracle cure that people began seeking it for any mental distortion, not just schizophrenia. It was prescribed for depression and was particularly popular for treating women who suffered "baby blues," or as we know it today, postpartum depression.

No one really knew how ECT impacted the brain. Much of the early enthusiasm for the treatment was based on self-serving in-house hospital studies reinforced by the psychiatric society's insatiable passion to discover medical methods to treat brain disorders. Without the modern-day benefit of magnetic resonance imaging (MRI) equipment, there was no way to observe a live brain before, during, or after treatment. Electricity frequently was delivered in high, "unmodified" doses without anesthesia or muscle relaxants. It often led to memory loss, fractured bones from violent convulsions, and other serious side effects, including death. It is well to keep in mind that psychiatry, like medicine in general, can be an ugly profession. There have been many grisly procedures and treatments and many years of misguided theories. Though horrific, experimentation with various brain-shocking techniques paved the way for successful treatments of brain disorders. In later years, the procedure was greatly refined and combined with precise doses of anesthesia. Thanks to lessons learned while treating thousands of human guinea pigs, ECT continues as a treatment, though in far lower doses more precisely targeted for specific disorders.

Thus, Peder became an involuntary mental health treatment pioneer. In early February 1950, he was subjected to his first of sixteen treatments. Electrodes were taped to his temples, and a blast of electricity was fired through his temporal lobes into the region of the brain responsible for memory. He lurched into spasmodic convulsions and lost consciousness.

When his eyes popped open, he was dazed, nauseated, and fighting the worst hangover of his life—and he was quite the authority on hangovers. He managed to smile kindly at Dr. Carlson, who was sitting there nearly breathless with anticipation in his long white surgical gown, cradling his head atop his steepled fingers.

Perhaps Peder's smile was merely a reaction to the magnified brown eyes peering at him through Coke-bottle lenses encased in tortoise-shell frames, topped off by a massive jet-black caterpillar eyebrow crawling across an endless forehead. Whatever the reason for the smile, the doctor interpreted it as confirmation of a successful procedure. Never mind that Peder had no idea where he was, who he was, or what was happening. His memory board had been wiped clean.

Peder was barely settled into his chair for dinner in Mental

Ward Six when his gremlins launched a new attack. He flipped over the dining table, startling half a dozen other patients and dumping green salad, mashed potatoes, and fried chicken into their laps.

"Somebody poisoned me! There's itching powder in these potatoes!" he screamed as white-coated attendants raced to his side.

Peder was a powerful man. The attendants themselves were brawny guys as well. They struggled mightily to bring him under control but eventually took charge. They jabbed him with a hypodermic needle filled with a potent sedative.

"Evidently he has not improved any from shock treatment seeing as he still expresses the same bizarre ideas he did previously," wrote Dr. Carlson. "The outlook in this case does not appear too good. In the near future, he will be considered for insulin therapy."

Throughout April and May, Peder endured forty subshock insulin treatments. Similar to electroshock, insulin therapy sent the brain into hypoglycemic shock under the theory that the blast would jolt patients from their mental illness.

For each procedure, two of the brawny male attendants held Peder in place, strapped his arms and legs to a narrow treatment bed, and fitted him with a red rubber mouthpiece to avoid breaking his teeth or biting his tongue. The first insulin-induced coma was a relatively low dose of one hundred units. The dosage increased up to 450 units in later sessions.

During the procedure, Peder flushed, perspired profusely, salivated, and suffered seizures just like those from ECT. There was pronounced moaning, twitching, and violent thrashing. Medical staff restrained him as best they could to avoid his injuring himself. Generally, treatments lasted an hour before they were "terminated" by injection of intravenous glucose. Care was taken following recovery to avoid injury from hypoglycemic aftershocks.

Among the unintended consequences of insulin shock treatment were a 5 percent fatality rate, irreversible brain damage, and a high incidence of obesity. Obesity occurred due to a profound, almost raging hunger following treatment. Patients would gorge themselves with food, especially items of high sugar content.

This type of bulimic response occurred in reaction to many forms of brain-shock treatment, especially lobotomy. Neurosurgeons determined that the frontal lobe controlled the portion of the brain that stimulated or suppressed appetite. Damage or destruction of the frontal lobe or its exiting fibers often resulted in irrational, voracious consumption leading to significant weight gain.

Peder avoided death and obesity. But once repeated sessions of insulin shock and lightning blasts of electricity scrambled his frontal lobe, his mental capacity appeared greatly diminished. However, his doctors were pleased with themselves when he became docile and compliant and told them what they wanted to hear. They failed to realize—or didn't care—that he was a different man.

Peder's brain required time to heal from the medically induced concussion. Six months after his arrival, he was functioning well physically, even if he had little memory of his past life. The medical staff applauded themselves for their accomplishment, assuming they had performed a miracle.

They sent him home.

CHAPTER 6

1950–1953

"He's coming home," Ginger announced.

Jason found the news better than pulling down straight As on his report card. Everyone pulled out their favorite shirts and dresses, as if heading to an Easter parade. Grandma Libby even set aside her harsh feelings for Peder and polished her car for the ride to the asylum to rescue him. That evening, they celebrated at the White House Restaurant, where Jason, who thought "meat" was only hamburger, discovered filet mignon.

Everything went well for a few months. Better than well. Peder went back to working at the US Rubber Company factory. Peder's old friends returned, and life was better than a *Leave it to Beaver* episode. Normal was their new normal.

But it didn't last. Before long, Peder was talking to people who weren't there, and he constantly fretted about someone lurking in the family's attic.

One day when no one else was home, Jason crept up the

creaky, wooden stairway and peered into the attic. In his ten-year-old mind, he thought that if he could chase away whoever was up there, his dad would be okay.

Nobody was there, of course. Not even a squirrel. Jason was truly baffled. If no one was up here, then what was his dad talking about? All Jason discovered was a huge unfinished space with nothing but exposed wood and yellow fiberglass insulation dangling everywhere, like massive spider webs. By the time he slowly came down the stairway, he was covered in the prickly yellow stuff. He proceeded to deposit it on just about every piece of furniture in the house. His mother never said a word, but the look she cast in Jason's direction that night spoke loudly enough. She knew. She always knew.

On Friday nights, Ginger frequently escaped for dinner and a movie with her friends Katherine and Dorothy. She took Sidney to Grandma Libby's and left Jason with Peder.

Jason enjoyed Friday nights with his father. It almost made him forget his father's brain was sick. The two would play catch with a baseball or football until dark. They'd then head to the Hilltop Bar.

The Hilltop Bar was the unofficial annex of the tire factory where Peder worked. Guys flopped on bar stools to recover from a tough shift. The distinctive aroma of rubber still hung in the air over them, like steam from a boiling pot.

Each time Peder and Jason walked in, they received the same greeting.

"Hey, Peder," the porky bartender would say, caged behind the long bar that stretched almost the full length of the west wall.

A dozen guys would spin about and smile. So would the triplets—the ladies who lived at the end of the bar. Or so it seemed; there they sat every time Jason and Peder came in the door. Jason called them the triplets because to him the three women looked identical. Peder laughed and said they weren't related. Jason wasn't convinced, though—especially once he learned their names were Anne, Amy, and Abigail.

At first, Jason loved going to the Hilltop. They'd have hot beef sandwiches and all the free pop, potato chips, and candy he could consume. Best of all, he could watch the amazing little theater in a box that showed football games, boxing matches, and movies.

Television was a brand-new concept available mostly only in taverns, instantly transforming every corner bar into an entertainment center. There was only one channel, KSTP from Saint Paul, and reception was fuzzy most of the time. The little black-and-white screen frequently showed nothing but a blizzard of snow, or the picture rolled like a Ferris wheel spinning out of control. Somehow, reception always went out just at a critical point of a movie or just as the ball flew through the air in a game. Miraculously, it never went out during a commercial.

Not only did Jason have to deal with reception issues but he also had to deal with the triplets interrupting him. They wore more than enough makeup, with thick lips that would outshine a newly polished apple. They could never sneak up on anyone without their overpowering, supersweet aroma betraying their presence. Their perfume stood out even in competition with the bar's nauseating concoction of odors from stale beer, whiskey, peanuts, popcorn, rubber, and sweat.

Each night, Anne squeezed in on the bar stool next to Jason. She'd smile and push her long fingers through his blond hair. Her flagrant attention made Jason uncomfortable. But mostly, it annoyed him. He tried to ignore her as much as possible and just watch the Friday night fights. Fortunately, Anne usually would shift her attention from Jason to Peder before long.

Then one Friday night, it dawned on him. As Anne untangled her fingers from Jason's hair and moved them straight to Peder's,

Jason realized why his father brought him to the Hilltop. He was the girl magnet—nothing like a cute kid to break the ice. Jason was young, but old enough to realize he was being used by his father.

That sick brain must be the problem, he reasoned.

Jason had become convinced that all Peder's bad habits came from his sick brain. Or was it the other way around?

A week later, Peder grabbed his jacket for the Friday night trip to the Hilltop, but Jason lingered in the living room.

"Come on," Peder said. "It's time to go."

"I don't wanna go there anymore," Jason said.

"What? I thought you liked watching the games and getting all the free stuff."

"I've seen enough. Just wanna stay here."

Clearly upset, Peder sat down across from his son. "Okay, what's the problem?"

"Nothing." Jason tried to think fast, as he wasn't about to reveal the real reason. "I just got lots of homework."

"It's only Friday. You got all weekend."

Jason searched for a response. "Yeah, but Mom wants me to go shopping with her tomorrow, and we got choir practice and Sunday School."

"Fine. I get it," Peder said with a huff. "You're old enough to stay home. Just don't leave the house, and keep the doors locked until I get back."

Peder figured there was more to his son's reluctance to join him at the Hilltop. But he preferred to let it go, lest it spill over into Ginger's purview.

Instead, his solution was to go out the next day and buy one of the first television sets sold privately in Eau Claire. It was a monstrous Stromberg Carlson entertainment center with television, radio, and a phonograph that played Ginger's Frankie Laine records. His high school chum Okey, who had jumped into the new radio and television business, delivered the big set. Okey and Peder climbed atop the roof to install the thirty-foot-tall antenna.

Jason was thrilled to have his own home theater without having to deal with the triplets or any of the raunchy aromas at the tavern. However, his luck was not any better than the bar's; he still had to endure the electronic snow and spinning pictures.

Three weeks later, Jason was enjoying life, watching the Friday night fights, sipping a bottle of root beer, and devouring all the potato chips Peder had left for him when his mother came home early. Suffering from a toothache, she had decided to call it a night.

Ginger walked in the door, surprised to find Jason alone in front of the television.

"Where's your father?"

Jason shrugged. "Probably the Hilltop."

Ginger stomped out the back door. Two hours later, she returned with Peder. Apparently, they had said everything that could be said on the trip home because now not a sound was uttered by either.

He staggered into their bedroom, and she curled up on the living room couch with one of grandma's quilts. Her red eyes stared through the wall.

Ginger never went out on Fridays after that. As more months passed, conversation between actual people grew to be less and less a part of their lives.

To complement his other bad habits, Peder chain-smoked Chesterfield cigarettes. It was unusual to see him without a smoldering tobacco stick attached to his right paw. A gray cloud hung over everything, physically and metaphorically. This ever-present cloud stained the walls and ceilings with a dirty yellow hue. Little Sidney coughed incessantly from her asthma.

This cloud of smoke and uneasiness nearly became a shroud one crisp November morning in 1952. Peder departed for the early shift at the tire plant just before the sun peaked into town. A short time later, a shrill scream echoed down the hallway, rupturing Jason's deep slumber in the predawn darkness.

"Jason, Jason! Get your sister. Hurry, hurry, hurry! The house is on fire!" Ginger cried.

Her desperate screams penetrated Jason's bedroom door as she struggled to feel her way through the house rapidly filling with smoke. She had ventured into the basement and tried in vain to extinguish the flames, but a bucket of water only seemed to add fuel to the blaze.

Opening his bedroom door, Jason was devoured by a gray monster cloud. Choking on the acrid smoke, he stumbled into his parents' room, where Sidney was sound asleep in her tiny bed. As the smoke burned his eyes and he began to choke, he grabbed Sidney, jerked her out of bed, and dragged her as quickly as an eleven-year-old could pull a nearly unconscious six-year-old down the hallway, toward the sound of his mother's frantic cries. They stumbled out the front door, where subzero air snapped them awake.

Ginger darted from the house, practically running down her children as she scooped them off the ground with one arm squeezing each. She raced across the yard to the house next door, where Mr. and Mrs. Chicken Neck ushered them inside and served up two steaming cups of hot chocolate for the children.

After summoning the fire department, Ginger ventured back to the house in a futile attempt to rescue Tippy, the Korsens' over-sized black-and-white cat who loved to snap the brilliant white tip of his long tail in your face. Two steps into the door, and she fled, lucky to escape alive from the growing inferno. Tippy wasn't so fortunate.

A long freight train at the crest of the Madison Street hill delayed the downtown fire trucks. By the time they arrived, the window in the side door was alive, pulsating in hypnotic, brilliant orange flames. In a strange way, it was beautiful. Time hesitated as the little family watched dancing flames and swirling smoke rip through their wonderful home. It was a three-dimensional scene painted from a palette of black, varying shades of gray, and periodical bursts of dancing orange.

Firefighters saved a large portion of the house from burning. The basement was completely gutted, as was Ginger's kitchen. Damage was surprisingly minimal in the rest of the house, but the smoke effects were still severe. Everything was embedded with an acrid odor and encased under a thick film of sticky blackness. The place became a foreboding black dungeon encased in a clear sheen of now-frozen water. Icicle necklaces dangled from the roof edges and every window ledge.

All anyone could talk about was the fire and their miraculous survival. Everyone except Peder. He not only didn't discuss the fire, he appeared almost oblivious to it.

Days later, a fresh blanket of snow covered the neighborhood. Crystals twinkling in the morning sunlight concealed the blackness as the family, except Peder, who was working, approached their scorched home. Stepping through the doorway, they instantly traveled from high noon to darkest midnight. The smoke-stained windows filtered the sunlight, making it appear more like moonlight. In fact, being in the house felt like walking on the moon.

The smell was still pungent. Even with the windows and doors open, it was difficult to be inside more than a few minutes. Their clothes were instantly in need of decontamination.

Jason stood in what had been the kitchen. Nothing was recognizable. There was no color but black. Jason noticed a dark melted lump. On closer inspection, he guessed it had been their plastic Aunt Jemima coin bank. He gingerly picked it up, but it suddenly ruptured into pieces in his hands, sending brilliant flashes of red plastic across the dark kitchen. Silver coins stuck out of the melted plastic blob.

In the living room, Jason's eyes darted right to the glass bowl that had once been home to Hermy, his pet turtle. The bowl was completely dry and coated in soot, but the rocks, the gravel, and the tiny bridge he made for Hermy were untouched. Hermy, however, was nowhere to be found. Jason never learned if his turtle had just vaporized in the fire or if a fireman or his mother had moved it out of sight.

The family went to live with Grandma Libby while the house was being repaired. Jason could hear muffled whispering. Grams, an absolute teetotaler, was unhappy with Peder's frequent late-night trips to town.

Almost every night, Ginger hovered motionless at the back door for hours, framed like a stern Mona Lisa peering out the window into the blackness. In the middle of the night, a sudden burst of activity would shatter the silence as Peder would stumble through the door, push past her, and fall into bed. With him finally at home, she'd collapse on the living room couch, clutching a quilt Grandma Libby had stitched together from slices of exhausted shirts and faded blue jeans.

When he was with the family, which wasn't often, Peder just read the newspaper, listened to his radio, or went for a walk alone. He was different. He seemed sullen, silent, withdrawn. He spewed constant angry chatter into the air at some invisible being. Even when he went to one of three nearby taverns, old friends became uneasy as he spurned their attempts at casual conversation and instead just talked to his imaginary friends.

Then came a startling revelation. The state fire inspector delivered a copy of his official written report to Ginger, revealing that the ignition point for the fire was in the basement—and it appeared to have been set intentionally.

Ginger and Libby kept Jason in the dark once again, but he

couldn't escape their whispers hinting that Peder's mystery friend may have told him to set the fire. Every conversation was wrapped in fear as Libby considered the danger her daughter and the children faced. Libby constantly urged Ginger to get outside help.

"Before he kills us all," Libby added.

Jason wanted to believe the fire had been caused by an errant spark or just his dad's carelessness in abandoning a smoldering Chesterfield on the stack of firewood too close to the furnace. But he knew better. As happy as they had been to have Peder back, Jason couldn't escape the nagging thought that his father had tried to kill them.

Is that what a sick brain does? he wondered. *I guess it's good to know why he tried to burn the house down, but knowing why doesn't make it go away. How do we ever sleep at night, wondering if he'll get sick again and do the same thing? Can a sick brain heal? Is he better?*

Two months after the fire, they moved out of Grandma Libby's house and back to their refurbished house in early January 1953. Life almost seemed good again. But as Jason crawled into bed every night, he couldn't get the fire out of his head. Jason thought maybe his dad seemed better now. Maybe it was just being with Grandma Libby that had upset his father. They never liked each other.

But then the smoky cloud hovering over the Korsens' life suddenly spiraled into a storm. Peder's chatter with invisible people had continued, and not only at home.

Peder was feeding molten rubber into a tire mold when Amos Solvine, department supervisor, stepped behind him. Solvine, two years out of college and son of company president Adolf Solvine, was eager to demonstrate his authority.

"Come on, Peder," he snapped. "You're falling off the pace here. We got a quota to meet. Your daydreaming and playing with imaginary friends are costing us all bonus money. Pick up the pace or go home."

Peder clenched his fists, spun about, and cast an evil stare down on the diminutive foreman.

"Who the hell do you think you are? I been making tires since you were in grade school, you piece of shit. What do you ever do around here but make noise? Damn lucky your old man's in the office, or you'd still be looking for a job."

As every eye in the department fixed on the growing feud, Amos wasn't about to give ground, even if Peder outweighed him by nearly fifty pounds of muscle.

"One more word, and you're going home."

"Screw you!" Peder shouted.

With that, he delivered a powerful roundhouse to Solvine's jaw, dropping his supervisor to the concrete floor.

Solvine suffered a broken jaw and severe head injury. He was in the hospital for two weeks. In response, the factory president said strict action needed to be taken against Peder. Even Peder's own union representative agreed.

Ginger agreed as well—for the safety of her family. Peder was a large, strong man. He had always had a reputation as a tough guy, but he had never threatened his family physically. Not unless the fire inspector was to be believed . . .

Despite all Peder's faults, Jason had always viewed him as a very gentle man. His fondest memory of him was the day they got matching brown leather jackets and dress hats, which they proudly wore to church. (Though even for the photograph in their new jackets, a smoldering cigarette dangled from Peder's right hand.)

Life was once again locked in varying shades of gray, much like the piles of ash that had been the Korsen house. Peder was gone again to the asylum, this time not to return.

CHAPTER 7

1953–1954

After visiting several doctors, Peder was branded "incurable" by some perverted good fortune. That meant he wasn't a good candidate for the next great cure: lobotomy. Lobotomy went a step beyond electroshock therapy. Doctors drilled holes in the head to access the frontal lobes of the brain. They then inserted a hollow needle with a retractable wire loop at the tip. They extended the instrument and rotated it once in a circle, slicing a small core of brain tissue. Four to six cores would be removed. The procedure was so highly acclaimed that it earned Egas Moniz of Portugal the 1949 Nobel Prize for medicine.

Moniz's American protégé, psychiatrist Walter Freeman, performed an estimated 3,500 lobotomies throughout the United States from 1936 to 1967. Even within the psychiatric profession, Freeman was an incendiary figure. Doctors vociferously challenged his aggressive procedures. There was a near-violent battle amongst medical professionals as to whether mental illness was organic, as Moniz and Freeman believed, or whether it resulted from psychological damage, as Sigmund Freud and his disciples asserted.

Occasionally, lobotomy succeeded. But frequently, it produced irreversible brain damage, and many patients did not survive the procedure. "Successful" lobotomies often resulted in "surgically induced childhood," whereupon patients were encouraged to work in coloring books and play with dolls and teddy bears. This was only slightly worse than Peder's electroshock experience. Many patients never advanced beyond this childlike behavior, or they exhibited extreme lethargy and lack of initiative. But they became obedient, cooperative, and nonthreatening.

Three months after being readmitted to Mendota State Hospital, Peder's doctors discontinued all treatments, aside from calming drugs. They wrote into his chart,

> *This patient came back from over two years on conditional release with practically the same symptoms. He is flat emotionally. He laughs to himself frequently without cause. He admits he still has paranoid delusions. He was not given ECT or insulin shock treatments because it was felt that he was a chronic schizophrenic and that such treatments had proved unsuccessful previously. He is content to sit on the ward and has no desire to go home. It is recommended that he remain committed indefinitely.*

Upon learning there was no discharge in sight, Peder launched into uncontrolled rage. He tossed anything that wasn't nailed down—which mostly meant books, papers, and a lamp—against the wall. A pair of giant orderlies, probably cloned from the same factory that spit out the earlier pair, wrestled him into a straitjacket and hauled him off to M4, the high-security ward.

There they stashed him in the seclusion room, more aptly defined as solitary confinement. At least it had a bed, if you could call it that. It was a slab of scratched, white-painted steel. They eased him onto the bed, bound his ankles with a wide black leather strap, and secured his legs and arms.

It took only a day and an extra dose of medication before Peder became catatonic. He returned to his room at M2, where Dr. Jerome Goodrich found him seated on his bed, staring at a blank wall.

"Peder, are you feeling better today?"

No response, not even recognition that someone had entered the room. For nearly thirty minutes, the two souls sat three feet apart without perceptible motion or sound other than Peder's labored breathing.

"They don't know who I am," Peder finally spoke in a firm but measured voice, startling Dr. Goodrich.

"Tell me, then, who are you?"

"God sent me to help people throughout the world find peace. I am able to speak to everyone through radio and television, but there are some who wish to prevent me from speaking. They are trying to kill me. I must stop them. They hide in the bodies of people I know."

"You are safe here, Peder. We do not let those people in."

"They are too powerful. You cannot stop them. Don't you know that most of the people here really are crazy? God's enemies can take possession of their minds."

"I won't let that happen, Peder. You are safe here."

Oddly, Dr. Goodrich's persistent, confident reassurance appeared to work. Peder relaxed, and his breathing settled into a normal pattern.

A week later, Dr. Goodrich wrote,

He sits comfortably, not in any state of anxiety or tension, fre-
quently smiling, pleasant, and affable. However, his behavior
on the ward has been reclusive, and he is introverted, flat in
affect, and illogical in his thinking. He states that his present
omnipotence extends all over the universe and that his pres-
ent thoughts center on union politics and religious debate.
He speaks constantly about world faith. He is no problem in
management and has been eating and sleeping satisfactorily.
He was prevailed upon to help pick beans, and he cooperated
reluctantly. In view of these findings, we recommend he be
transferred to a county institution.

Peder was shipped to the Trempealeau County Asylum in
Whitehall, Wisconsin, forty miles south of Eau Claire. Technically
speaking, he was close to home. But he might as well have been 400
or 4,000 miles away. Doctors discouraged relatives from visiting to
avoid "unsettling the patient."

In truth, it was Ginger who appeared most unsettled. She had
no desire to visit him. Somewhere in the mix of Peder's alcoholism,
womanizing, delusions, and attempts to kill his family, her enthusiasm for seeing him had dissipated.

For the first six months after his father was hospitalized,
Jason and his mother couldn't look each other in the eyes without
erupting into a flood of tears. They stayed with Grandma Libby,
and Ginger spent much of her time in bed. Then one day, she just
bolted out of the house, saying she had to get a job. Jason almost
never saw her cry again; perhaps she had used up her lifetime sup-
ply of tears.

In fact, Jason may have drained his own tear ducts as well.
Even later in life, he found it nearly impossible to cry, no matter
what happened. He often worried that people might question his
compassion. There were times when tears seemed to be the only

appropriate response, yet he couldn't squeeze any out. It was a constant concern.

Once she set out to find a job, Ginger returned triumphant with news of her sales position in the boys' clothing department at the Montgomery Ward department store. The job came with a nice discount on clothes.

A woman working outside the home was an unusual thing. It was a time when women, even single mothers with children to support, were not welcome in the workplace. The fear was that they would take jobs away from men.

It hadn't always been that way, though. During World War II, almost every woman in America went to work because there weren't enough men to fill the factories. When the war ended, however, they were exiled back home to do "women's work"—cook, wash clothes, and tend children. Ginger had loved her job making bullets at the tire factory, but the Korsen family had been ecstatic to have her back in the kitchen once the war was over.

This time around, Ginger had no choice but to get a job and work long hours. Ginger needed a good-paying job if her family was to survive.

Pretty much everyone suggested that what she really needed was a man to support her. "Find a good man" was definitely the wrong advice, unless the objective was to motivate Ginger even more to make it on her own.

Several of Peder's friends appeared at the door, offering to help. Jason thought that was awfully nice of them. He was just a naïve kid. Little did he know that the type of "help" they offered had more to do with his mother's social life than the family's welfare.

Ginger was not yet forty and tall and slim with long, flowing auburn hair. She was blessed with a very attractive face, and she displayed subtle humor, even in the worst of times—or perhaps because of them. She was exceptionally quick-witted, highly intelligent, and always flashing a disarming smile. Being the focus of men's attention may have been somewhat flattering, but most of the guys she didn't care to have around, and some were already married. A social life was not in the cards for her.

Okey, the radio-television repairman who sold the big television set to Peder, was especially persistent. Jason found Okey to be a bit weird, but kids are always fascinated by weird characters. A middle-aged, single guy who lived with his mother, Okey was a lumpy little fellow about five feet tall on a good day and more than a little portly. He didn't walk as much as waddle. His dirt-brown strings of hair were few and far between. He grew them as long as possible, waxed them stiff, and combed them forward into a flap door that flipped up in a breeze. Okey's eyes weren't blue or brown, just two large black dots floating in bloodshot white pools. When he talked, it was a nasally squeak, as if he had just sucked helium from a balloon.

Definitely Porky Pig's cousin.

In a benevolent act, little Okey volunteered to satisfy Ginger's sexual desires. She got all the satisfaction she wanted by grabbing a broom and chasing him out the door, across the yard, and into his dirty Chevy panel truck. The truck was emblazoned with a giant yellow lightning bolt that probably symbolized how fast he could escape from his female customers. He never came back, not even to fix the new Stromberg Carlson television set.

After the Okey incident, Ginger made it crystal clear to all the "boys" that she neither wanted nor needed their help. They stopped coming around. She never showed the slightest interest in a man again until many years later, and that was with her lifelong friend Arnie after his wife died.

Ginger found a better paying job with Shedd-Brown, where she spray-painted colors over giant stencils to make calendars. The factory was just a long walk from home, essential because they didn't own a car. It was tedious work with often twelve-hour days, occasionally six or seven days a week, but it kept her family going.

Ginger and Jason moved back to the Korsen house, and Sidney stayed with Grandma Libby. They all got together on weekends. At thirteen, Jason became a latchkey kid before anyone knew what that meant. He inherited the household chores of dusting, vacuuming, and washing clothes. He probably didn't do the jobs all that well, but it was his mother's method for keeping him occupied and away from trouble.

Trouble seemed to follow him around, though. Just getting home from school was no easy task. Two older kids—Jason never even knew their names—took particular joy in using him for their punching bag. There was a time when he couldn't make it home without getting punched, poked, and made the object of laughter.

"Hey, retard—when ya gonna go live with your crazy dad in the nuthouse?"

Realizing the bullies couldn't hurt him if they couldn't find him, Jason mapped out several circuitous routes from school to home. His favorite route was through McDonough Park, next to Dells Pond, and into the cemetery. Every giant headstone provided a perfect hiding place. The pièce de résistance was the storage shed hidden at the back of the cemetery, overlooking the pond. When the ground froze solid, making it impossible for the cemetery maintenance crew to dig new gravesites, they stacked coffins in the shed until spring. It was a bit creepy thinking frozen dead people were in that shed. The bullies wanted no part of his secret hiding place.

Shameful as it may seem, Ginger and her children moved on and mostly forgot about Peder. On rare occasion, an unintelligible letter would arrive in an envelope decorated on the outside with rhyming gibberish and meaningless symbols. Sometimes the state would make a feeble attempt to charge Ginger for his care. Jason and Sidney generally never knew of those occurrences unless they happened to be present when the mail arrived. Even then, the envelopes quickly vanished, never to be seen again.

One day, the mail delivered a new surprise:

Dear Mrs. Korsen,

The State of Wisconsin wishes to inform you that your husband, Peder James Korsen, has been transferred from Trempealeau County Asylum to the Eau Claire County Asylum. It is felt that patients are best served when they reside in their home communities and are closer to relatives. Please contact the Eau Claire County Asylum to obtain family visiting hours and regulations.

"What about us being unsettling to the patient?" she barked into the air, remembering how visits had been discouraged at the Trempealeau facility. "And what if we don't want him that close to home? What about him being dangerous?" She had developed an overwhelming fear of her husband. Having him back in town was terrifying.

She grabbed her purse and hustled off to meet with attorney John Kaiser. Kaiser had handled the legal considerations for Peder's initial commitment. He knew Ginger had little or no money to pay for legal services, but he never let that get in the way of doing what was right. Ginger was not about to ask for free advice, so she paid a small amount every month on a bill that appeared to be far less than normal, but still more than she could pay.

"I'll check with the court, Mrs. Korsen," Kaiser said, "but the reality is that he's already here in Eau Claire, and it's highly unlikely he'll be moved. I did call the administrator. He says Peder is adjusting well. They feel he is no threat, but they'll keep a close eye on his movements."

Nobody said it, but Ginger figured that money—taxpayer money, specifically—had more to do with him being moved to his hometown than anything else. Those Trempealeau County taxpayers did not want to foot the bill for an Eau Claire guy.

Even with Peder only miles away, life in the Korsen family went on just the same. The only noticeable change: Ginger started locking the back door for the first time.

Eventually, the family did make a trip to the asylum. The visit came after a new drug treatment showed limited albeit positive effects on Peder.

In 1954, every newspaper, magazine, and television station in America screamed the good news of the "wonder drug" chlorpromazine, marketed by Smith, Kline & French in the United States as Thorazine. There was a new glimmer of hope for those suffering from mental illness. Thorazine and other medications were popping up almost daily as the drug industry discovered gold in the mammoth, lucrative mental health market. Thorazine generated billions in sales and gave psychiatrists the belief that, at last, they were real doctors able to treat patients at mental hospitals rather than merely serving as insane asylum wardens.

Drugs such as Thorazine failed to free Peder from his prison of the mind, but they did seem to calm him immeasurably. They became a pharmaceutical leash that induced a sort of chemical lobotomy, making him extremely compliant.

"These people are all crazy," he told Jason during the family's visit. "It's difficult to deal with such lunatics."

Jason wasn't certain if his father was referring to the patients, the staff, or all the above.

Ginger clearly wanted to be anywhere else but visiting the man she had once shared her life with. She stared out the window, avoiding eye contact.

Even Jason, who had pushed for the visit, didn't know how to respond to his father. The seconds felt like minutes as he struggled to talk.

What do you say to someone with a sick brain? I don't want to upset him. Where did that guy who built our house disappear to? Is he still in there somewhere? Will he ever return?

Jason realized he really didn't know his dad anymore. He wasn't even certain his dad recognized them until a broad smile spread across Peder's placid face. He pointed into the cavernous white marble lobby that seemed more suited to a London bank or New York train station.

With the uncharacteristic enthusiasm of a carnival barker, he announced, "It's almost time! In a few minutes, Miss Magnuson will come down that big, circular stairway and sit down at that piano. You will like this."

On cue at precisely 4:00 p.m., a fragile but very proper elderly woman floated down the staircase despite the fact that she trembled violently. She was dressed in a severely faded black evening gown contrasted by her long veil of perfectly combed snow-white hair; a sparkling, ornate gold necklace; and bright red lips. She slid onto the bench behind the impeccably polished black onyx Steinway grand piano. The cold, white marble lobby was suddenly packed with people seemingly emerging through the walls.

Miss Magnuson seemed to freeze. She sat straight and as rigid as the marble pillars watching over her. She adjusted her dress, placed her bony digits on the keyboard, and proceeded to fill the chamber with heavenly music that reverberated off the hard stone walls. It was a concert beyond belief. After fifteen minutes, she rose, totally expressionless. She gave a slight, mechanical bow and floated up the stairway.

"That's all she ever does," Peder said. "She never speaks a word, never helps with anything around here, and never does anything but play that piano for fifteen minutes every single day. A nurse told me she once played with the Boston Philharmonic."

Miss Magnuson may have earned her keep entertaining staff and residents, but almost everyone else had a job. The facility was a virtually self-sufficient, bucolic 446-acre community. Most of the women worked in the kitchen or the sewing department, where they made clothing worn by residents. Many of the men came from farm communities, so they were comfortable working the fields and gardens or tending the cattle, sheep, and hogs.

The asylum's farm provided nearly all the food for 150 staffers and 350 patients, plus additional fresh produce and meat to generate significant income. Their cattle operation was so successful that it was named the best cattle farm in Wisconsin five years running. And the dairy farm was beyond compare. The asylum supplied a major share of dairy products sold in western Wisconsin.

The men who weren't farmers maintained the roads and grounds and provided janitorial services. A few men worked in the kitchen and dining hall. Peder wasn't overly fond of farming, yardwork, or janitorial service, so he managed to acquire a couple of books about baking. Peder was a quick study—the one good habit he had passed along to his children was for them to pick up a book anytime they wanted to learn anything. With a little book knowledge, he convinced the head chef to give him a chance as assistant baker. It probably helped that no one else wanted the job.

Within days, the man who had never entered the kitchen at home other than to grab a fork and knife was baking cakes, dinner rolls, and pies. He especially loved making pies with fresh apples and berries from the hospital orchards and fields. Soon everyone at the hospital was clamoring for Peder's tasty treats, and the staff sold his pies at the hospital's farmers market.

When Jason told Grandmother Libby about his dad's amazing baking skills, she reacted with uncustomary irritation.

"He never warmed a cup of coffee around here, but suddenly he's a champion pie maker," she harrumphed.

Without another word, she spun about and darted out the back door into her garden. Jason couldn't help but smile as he spotted a tiny hummingbird buzzing about the garden, seemingly mimicking Grandma Libby's every move.

He wondered what his dad was doing. Perhaps getting some pies ready for the evening meal. Jason was glad they went to see him, but he realized this was not the man he remembered holding hands with on the way to church the Easter day when they wore matching jackets and hats. This was a stranger.

CHAPTER 8

1954

Ginger struggled immensely to provide something resembling a normal life for her children, but money was always a problem. At thirteen, Jason wanted more than his dollar-a-week allowance. He decided to haul empty pop bottles to Stange's Corner Market for the penny-a-piece deposit.

Supermarkets mostly didn't exist, other than the A&P way across town. But in every neighborhood, a small, independent grocery store was within walking distance. The neighborhood grocery near the Korsen home was Stange's Corner Market, located in the middle of a block on Starr Avenue—nowhere near a corner.

Like all grocers, Mr. Stange greeted everyone by name. Stange's was something of a neighborhood communications center, where everyone visited and spilled their neighbors' secrets—a 1950s version of Facebook. Mr. Stange had no choice but to absorb every minute detail revealed by the neighborhood ladies, who seemingly knew everything about everyone.

Knowing the Korsen family tale, Mr. Stange took pity on Jason. He gave him odd jobs around the store—sweeping, taking out the garbage, and unloading deliveries.

The store was jammed with barrels of fresh flour, fruits, vegetables, crackers, cookies, and every staple imaginable. Mostly, there were no brand names to confuse shoppers. Everything was bulk. When Mr. Stange scooped your desires onto a sheet of extra-thick waxed paper atop his big white scale, rarely did he miss filling the scoop with exactly the amount requested. His meat counter was so popular that it pulled in people from other neighborhoods.

The building was no bigger than the nearby houses. It was one story tall with just one large room and a much smaller storage area in the back—essentially a receiving area and a very tiny bathroom with nothing but a toilet and a handwashing sink. The store's walls were hidden behind floor-to-ceiling shelves filled with essential foods. The floor was wavy and well-worn, constantly in need of Jason's broom.

In the center of the big room, Mr. Stange had carved out a checkout station from four-foot-tall display cabinets. They surrounded a small space where customers piled their purchases while he quickly calculated their day's debt on his manual cash register that barked every time he pushed the keys. At the end of the sale, he turned the crank on the right side of the register, and the cash drawer slapped him in his ample belly, igniting a boisterous roar of laughter.

Mr. Stange wore a full-length white apron proudly emblazoned with blotches of burgundy from the meat counter. Atop his head was a new square hat he folded every morning from a fresh slice of heavy waxed paper ripped across the extra-wide cutting blade from the giant paper roll.

There was no such thing as credit cards, and checks were few. When customers couldn't pay with cash, Stange would take out a little black tin recipe box filled with three-by-five-inch cards. Each card bore the name of a customer, and they were filed in alphabetical order. Stange would record the purchase amount on the cards and bill the customers later.

"Jason, please grab Mrs. Simon's card and jot down her purchases. Be sure to include today's date," he said one day as he was busy piling slices of beef and ham on his scale for Mrs. Stygar.

Dutifully, Jason surveyed Mrs. Simon's pile of groceries and scribbled the description of each item on her card.

After the customers cleared the store, Jason turned to Mr. Stange. "How will Mrs. Simon pay for all that food?" he asked, knowing she had lost her husband in the war and struggled mightily to care for her three children.

"I don't know. Maybe she won't, but she'll try. What I do know for sure is that she's too proud to come in if we don't mark her purchases on the cards."

Mrs. Simon wasn't the only person who received free food from the neighborhood grocer. They all stopped by from time to time to pay something on the bill. It was never much, but they felt good about it. So did Mr. Stange.

With Peder in the insane asylum, Mr. Stange seemed to recognize the role he could play in Jason's life. He became a guiding figure, full of warmth, humor, and wisdom.

Jason needed all the help he could get. Given his family's situation, playmates were becoming hard to find. Roy Pettit was the only other single-parent kid in class. That's all Jason had in common with him. He was a very good student; Roy was at the bottom of the barrel. Teachers probably kept passing him just to avoid dealing with him another year.

Roy always appeared to be malnourished and in need of a damp wash cloth. He wore the same grimy blue flannel shirt and frayed sandy-brown corduroy pants every day. He lived on the poor side of town, literally the other side of the railroad tracks. His dad was in prison for murder, and his older brother, Batshit Bart, was doing his best to follow in Dad's footsteps.

Roy and his mother resided in a little box smaller than a single-car garage. The tar paper roof leaked profusely during every rainstorm and when snow melted in the springtime. They strategically placed red Hills Brothers coffee cans throughout the tiny house. It was Roy's assignment to dump the cans before they overflowed and place each one back in its designated spot.

Jason didn't particularly care for Roy. But with no other takers for friends, Jason seemed to have little choice but to pal with him. One day after school, Roy enticed Jason into smoking cigarettes under the railroad viaduct. Jason turned green. Apparently, sampling cigarettes during the great chicken coop disaster wasn't lesson enough.

Roy had only two cigarettes, which he had stolen from his mother's purse. Now he had to have more "weeds."

"Jason, old man Stange likes you. Let's go there and grab some weeds. All ya gotta do is keep him busy in the back room, and I'll get 'em."

Jason recoiled. "What? I can't do that."

"Sure ya can. I'll do the dirty work. You just talk to him. It's no big deal. He ain't gonna miss a pack."

Roy grabbed Jason's collar and jerked him to his feet. Roy was tiny, but nothing and nobody scared him. He had kicked ass with just about every big kid in school.

Reluctantly, Jason strolled into the store and found Mr. Stange already in the back room unloading crates of bananas and oranges—far more tempting than cigarettes.

"Hi." It came out only as a weak mumble.

Mr. Stange looked up, realizing something was amiss.

"What's up, Jason?"

"Nothing. Just wondering if you need any help today."

At that moment, they both heard the distinctive rustle of cellophane as Roy grabbed a couple of packs of Lucky Strikes. That was followed immediately by the sounds of creaking floorboards and the front screen door slamming as he escaped. Cat burglary was not in Roy's future.

"Did you hear that?" Mr. Stange inquired.

"I *thinnnnk* it might be the wind."

Without as much as a good-bye, Jason darted out the back door. He caught up with Roy under the bridge. As Jason choked on nicotine once again, he wondered what would strangle him first—the smoke or his smoldering sense of guilt.

Two days later, Jason showed up to sweep the store as usual.

"Hear any wind today?" Mr. Stange asked.

Jason could barely meet his eyes.

"Jason, that boy is no good for you. You have a bright future, but it won't happen if you listen to him."

It was one of the few times Jason nearly cried.

Mr. Stange just patted his head, handed him two bucks, and said, "Don't worry. It'll be okay."

"Here," Jason said, offering the money back, "I'll pay for them."

"No. That's not necessary. But just do me this favor: always remember how you feel right now."

Mr. Stange gave him a big smile as his words burned into Jason's long-term memory.

"You know," Mr. Stange continued, "why don't you try to influence that boy? Rather than let him take you down the wrong path, why don't you take him down the right path?"

"What do you mean?"

"Show him how you have fun. You're in Boy Scouts, right?"

Jason nodded. He recalled how his mother had encouraged him to try Boy Scouts: "Just try it one time. If you don't like it, that's fine," she had said, almost pushing him out the door. As it turned out, he loved it.

"Take him with you to one of your Boy Scout meetings. He's just a lost little soul looking for somebody to push him in the right direction. You can help him be a better person."

"He ain't gonna like what I do."

"Try. If it doesn't work, at least you tried. But I bet you can do a lot of good for that kid."

The next day after school, Jason saw Roy a block ahead walking home on Birch Street. He ran and caught up with him.

"Hey, Roy, you want to come to Scouts with me tonight?"

"Naw, dat's for sissies."

"I'm no sissy. Tom and Geno are Scouts, and they sure as heck aren't sissies. Come on. Give it a try. We meet at Saint Luke Lutheran Church. It's really a lot of fun."

"I dunno. Maybe I come. Maybe I don't."

Two hours later, Roy was sitting outside the church when Jason arrived for the Scout meeting.

"Okay," Roy said. "I'll give it one night. But they better not try to make me do any sissy stuff."

Within a month, Roy was hooked and already talking about going to summer camp.

Geez, maybe Mr. Stange was right. I'm a good influence, Jason thought.

Joining Boy Scouts was the best decision Jason ever made—well, the best decision his mother ever made for him. He was learning so many things about nature, camping, life skills, and business. Twice he won the opportunity to be president for a day at a local business. And suddenly he was finding a few more friends—maybe not buddies yet, but at least guys who talked with him at Scout meetings.

Best of all, scoutmaster Bob McMillan had become almost a

father—so much that Bob Jr. occasionally appeared annoyed. The assistant scoutmaster, Lloyd Harris, also tried to befriend Jason. But the way Lloyd patted him on the head sent a chill up Jason's back. He remembered Anne, the triplet who liked to run her fingers through his hair when he had visited the bar with his dad. He avoided Lloyd and absorbed every word Mr. McMillan said.

Jason and Roy spent two great weeks at Boy Scout Camp Phillips in northern Wisconsin. As parents drove up and waited in the nearby parking area, all the campers and leaders assembled under the flagpole for one last ceremony. The flag slid slowly down the pole, and the camp director gave the standard farewell speech.

Waiting in the parking lot for Jason and Roy, Grandma Libby sipped her coffee—from an old brown whiskey bottle she decided was the perfect flask for transporting her beloved coffee on road trips. It had probably been tossed aside by a hobo who jumped off a passing freight train and slept under the railroad warehouse at the end of the alley behind her house.

While all the Boy Scouts stood at attention during the closing ceremony, several guys began to snicker. One whispered, "Wow, look at the old lady hitting the bottle."

To Jason's astonishment, the old lady was his grandmother, who deplored alcohol, downing a shot of coffee from her whiskey bottle.

When the ceremony ended, everyone lingered with eyes fixed on the shiny black Plymouth Belvedere with embarrassingly brilliant turquoise interior. They were dying to know who that old lady was picking up. Jason had no other option but to climb in.

Jason hoped no one would remember the moment by the time school started a few weeks later. He was now an eighth grader in junior high school. But memories of the hard-drinking grandma were still fresh. Jason endured some serious crap, but Grandma Libby acquired legendary status in ways she never would have approved. Even Roy was very impressed.

Jason quickly forgot the flack about Grandma Libby once he discovered the Paulson kids were targeting his little sister Sidney.

The Paulson family had lived down the street for more than five years, yet Grandma Libby still referred to them as "the new neighbors." Pa Paulson was testimony to sloth behavior. All he ever did was flop in a lawn chair in his two-car garage, drink beer, smoke cigarettes, and listen to ball games on his little transistor radio. For exercise, he would occasionally drag his chair into the driveway, where his beer belches echoed through the block, drawing loud clucks from Grandma Libby and the other neighborhood women.

Ma Paulson spent most of her time pregnant, cooking for her growing swarm, hanging clothes on the lines, cutting grass, shoveling snow, and eating. Her chubby fist was constantly filled with calories searching for her open mouth.

Everyone referred to the two oldest Paulson children, Arno and Adele, as the Katzenjammer Kids, based on a mischievous pair of newspaper cartoon characters. Arno was eleven, and Adele eight. They were particularly unpleasant little monsters, obviously infused with dominant fraternal genetics. Jason didn't remember, if he ever knew, the names of the next three kids or the one Ma Paulson had brewing in the basket.

There was nothing resembling discipline—Ma and Pa didn't believe in it. And it showed. The Paulson mob disrupted life in the quiet neighborhood with mindless acts of vandalism and theft. Piled by Pa's lawn chair drinking station were stacks of items stolen from neighbors, school, and stores. Apparently, he didn't notice the fruits of his kleptomaniac clan.

Living at home and going to junior high school, Jason was mostly oblivious to the rants and ravages of the Paulson clan. But Sidney lived with Grandma Libby. Arno and Adele tormented her every day she walked home from school. To make matters worse, she was in the same third-grade class as Adele.

"Sidney's old man's in prison!" Adele once shouted on the playground during recess.

Through the ravages of dealing with a dad in a mental hospital, Sidney had become permanently silent and isolated. She wanted to scream, "Liar! He's not in prison. He's in the hospital."

But she didn't get a chance to say or do anything before Adele's merry band of warriors pounced on her, knocked her to the ground, and proceeded to kick and punch her.

Teacher George Kramer interrupted the melee, tossing Sid's attackers to the side with his one good arm. Kramer's left arm was nothing but a shirt sleeve tucked under his belt. Rumor was, his missing arm was buried amid the rubble of some faraway German battlefield, but nobody knew for certain.

Kramer pulled Sidney off the ground and carried her to the second-floor first-aid room, where he tenderly cleaned and dressed the wounds with more care than most mothers might provide. Her most severe injury was a deep laceration on her knee. It bled through the bandage for nearly half an hour.

Throughout treatment, Sidney pleaded, "Mr. Kramer, tell her he's not in prison. Dad's in the hospital."

He didn't say a word, but once her injuries were treated, he clutched her tightly with his arm. She knew he understood.

Sidney never really recovered from the attack. From that time forward, whenever anyone inquired about her dad, she said her parents were separated and that she didn't know much about his life. That was her coping mechanism. In a sense, it was true.

Upon hearing of Adele's attack on Sidney, Jason never said a word to anyone, including Sidney and especially his grandmother. Rather, he took up position in the driveway behind the Paulsons' garage and waited for the evil Katzenjammer Kids to appear. The alley was a virtual tunnel lined with garages on both sides, providing a very private scene for a meeting. After hiding and running from his own bullies for years, Jason was more than ready to face the monsters that terrorized his sister.

"What the hell do you want?" Arno flashed his demonic stare that apparently worked with his parents and others.

Jason grabbed Arno's throat, jerked him off the ground, smashed him against the garage, and drove a fist practically through his stomach. Arno's eyes flared with momentary fear, then he retched and threw up. Even Adele recoiled in fear. It may have been the first time anyone had ever challenged that pair of junior devils.

"This is nothing compared to what will happen if either of you ever touch my sister again. Don't you talk to her or about her. Don't even look in her direction." Jason stuck his lips in Arno's face and spit his words. "Do you understand?"

"Screw you," Arno murmured, though with diminished enthusiasm.

Jason drove two more powerful blasts into the kid's body and tossed him in a heap on the sharp alley cinders. Then he turned and grabbed Adele.

"Don't think I won't do the same to you."

"Okay, okay." She burst into tears.

"And for the record—not that we owe you any explanation—our father is in a hospital, not prison. He has a severe head injury, and that's what you two will have if I ever have to deal with you again."

He pushed Adele aside like a rag doll. He didn't think he could actually punch a girl, but all he needed to do was convince her that he could.

Jason was greatly relieved that the Paulsons never bothered Sidney again. It felt good to stand up to those monsters.

But not all monsters can be stopped. Jason learned that a few days later, but he wouldn't breathe a word of it to anyone.

CHAPTER 9

1955–1956

As much as Ginger tried, there was never enough money. Life began to weigh her down until she no longer could make the house payment. Somehow her dream house had morphed into her nightmare.

Ginger was crushed. It wasn't that she even wanted to stay in that haunted house. It was just that her only other option was to move back to her mother's place at age forty. That tested her severely, but she had little choice. She sold the house in early 1955, and the whole family moved in with Grandma Libby.

Existing in a household with three women was an education unto itself for Jason. Grandma Libby's house, while stylish, boasted only two bedrooms. Jason, as lone male, inhabited the small bedroom in back. The ladies somehow divided up the master bedroom. The house was relatively large but never big enough. Having two alpha dogs in such a confined space assured that trouble was never far away.

Grandma Libby unquestionably was head of the house as well as baker, chef, gardener, and housekeeper. She was a force to be reckoned with. Although she had an eighth-grade education and almost never stepped foot in a church, Libby Hunter was recognized as one of the most intelligent, highly principled, spiritual people anyone knew. Decades later, Jason often found himself quoting advice she had offered so freely. Undoubtedly, he appreciated her words far more as an adult than he had as a teenager.

She scrutinized three newspapers daily along with anything else she could find. She measured all literary and journalistic quality against the *Chicago Tribune*, having lived in Chicago for nearly twenty years. Every day, she randomly harvested a new word from her tattered blue Webster's dictionary. Once she had the word, it was hers for life. The only words she never uttered were profanity—well, except *damn* and *hell*. "Those are in the Bible," she said, "so they must be okay." She was so proficient at crossword puzzles that the *St. Paul Pioneer Press* banned her from playing their weekly contest because she kept grabbing the prize money.

Living with such a strong-willed woman posed enormous challenge for Jason's equally strong-willed mother. But the two powerful ladies set their boundaries and kept differences under control. Mostly.

Ginger had no interest in housework. She found a new job at Davis Photo Art, a downtown photography studio close to their new home. She worked long hours at low pay, but she fell in love with photography.

Unlike her mother, a self-proclaimed morning person, Ginger had to force herself out of bed daily to make it to work by nine. But at night, she came to life. As the rest of the world disappeared under the cloak of darkness, she sat at her typewriter. Alone in the quiet shadows, she hammered out one story after another—writer's block was never a challenge. Pounding the keys of the old manual typewriter let her unload the day's tension. To Jason, the familiar tap, tap, tapping melody was more comforting than a lullaby.

Ginger sold stories to the *Milwaukee Journal* and got hired as part-time correspondent for the *St. Paul Pioneer Press*. Her new-found photography skill with the Argus C3 35mm camera added five bucks for every photograph she included with her stories.

But even with Ginger's regular job and freelancing, money was always scarce. The family learned to enjoy the good things in life, which are always free. Rather than take music lessons or join organized sports, Jason and Sidney spent much of their free time buried in books.

"The library is all you need," she always told them. "And it's free."

Reading sounded pretty good to Jason. Books provided the perfect portal of escape. He quickly discovered that reading inspired him to write. Even more than books, his pen gave him the key to do anything, go anywhere, be anybody. It was the perfect escape from people who tried to blame the son for the father—his newest monster.

When Jason wasn't reading, he ventured down to the rivers to "hunt" fish. Grandpa Ernie used to tell him, "You gotta be a fish hunter. Anybody can toss a line on the water. But a true hunter"—here he'd wink at the play on the family name Hunter—"stalks his prey. You need to read the water, know what they like and how they think."

Jason was never sure about wanting to think like a fish, but his grandfather's tips paid huge dividends as metaphors for life.

Jason often went to Grandpa Ernie's special fishing spot, near a lumber mill at the eastern edge of town. It was nearly a mile upriver from where the Chippewa River devoured the Eau Claire River. Jason always thought it was fitting that Grandpa Ernie's funeral was at the Stokes Funeral Home on the west shore of the

Chippewa. That day, the mighty river rose up and roared a relent-less symphony, slapping rhythmically against the building as if to honor the old fisherman who knew it so well.

One thing was for sure, living on the other side of town defi-nitely shattered Jason's opportunity to work at Stange's market. Jason missed Mr. Stange's valuable life lessons. He understood now more than ever what a good person Mr. Stange really was. Not everyone was like that, he knew.

Jobs were few and far between for a fourteen-year-old. Jason negotiated a deal with Grandma Libby to keep her yard neatly trimmed in exchange for free use of her hand mower, trimming shears, broom, and rake. With this equipment secured, he launched Jason's Yard Service. All the neighbors on the block signed up—except the Paulsons. But Jason didn't want their business anyway.

Two weeks into his booming business, Jason decided to invest some of his profits in a couple of candy bars. He strolled two blocks up Galloway Street to Lehman's Drug Store, next to what used to be Great-Grandpa Hunter's harness shop. As Jason pondered his choices, owner and pharmacist Carl Lehman said the Bit-O-Honey was his favorite. Jason preferred a Baby Ruth. He grabbed one of each.

Not unlike Mr. Stange, Mr. Lehman dispensed ample doses of concern and neighborly advice. The rotund, jovial guy was a virtual Santa Claus sans the white beard. Almost as wide as he was tall, he was a giant beach ball equipped with arms and legs and topped by a volleyball for a head.

As a pharmacist, Mr. Lehman knew everything about every-body in his little slice of the world. He kept the medical secrets and plenty of other personal information about everyone in the neigh-borhood. Jason was never quite certain what was the best medi-cine: the colorful pills Mr. Lehman dispensed or his disarming style and fatherly understanding. Either way, he did more healing than a team of doctors.

As Jason dropped two nickels on the counter, Mr. Lehman said, "I understand you have a new business."

"Yes, sir. Cutting lawns so I can buy candy bars."

Mr. Lehman chuckled. "That's great. You know, I can use some help at home. I live on Grand Avenue over by the junior high. You interested?"

"Interested? You bet."

"Come over Saturday about nine. I'll show you what we need."

The job started with just scooping up sticks and sweeping sidewalks, but it quickly launched into a full-blown lawn care assignment. It was a huge, hilly yard that was much more work than the other yards Jason tended.

But the sweat and aching muscles disappeared when Mr. Lehman slapped a ten-dollar bill in Jason's grubby, little paw. It was an enormous payday for anyone in 1955, a time when most adults only dreamed of earning $10,000 a year.

The ten-dollar bill smoldered in the secret compartment of Jason's billfold when the family went to the Carmel Corn Shop downtown that Friday night for ice cream. For the first time in his life, he had more money than he knew what to do with—he was rich.

Thinking only about the money, he mindlessly stabbed his spoon into a giant banana split. Just then, his mother stepped right into his dreams.

"How much do you plan to save?"

"Huh?" he said, snapping to. "Save?"

My god, he thought, *what an awful concept.*

"Absolutely. Now that you're earning money, you need a plan. Rather than just spend that money, you should decide how much you want to save for something really important and how much you want to share with someone in need."

"Share?" His ice cream turned sour.

Why would I share my money with someone in need? Let them get a job. There are so many things I want to buy for myself.

Ginger pressed on. "When you're finished eating, we'll walk across to First Federal Savings and Loan and open your savings account," she said. "Fortunately, they stay open late on Fridays."

Fortunately?

Somehow his banana split didn't taste so good. It began to melt, along with his dreams for spending his new wealth.

"You think about how you want to divide it up," Ginger said. "But you might want to keep half to spend, put a fourth in savings, and share a fourth with someone in need, perhaps at church."

As they crossed the street to the bank, Jason still thought it was a horrible idea. But then the banker handed him that little blue savings book with his name stamped in gold foil on the cover. It was like a hot coal in his hand, igniting a passion to watch it grow. His new dreams involved saving, not spending.

As lawn-cutting season came to an end, Jason needed a new job. He asked Mr. Lehman if there was anything he could do at the drug store.

"Sure," Mr. Lehman said. "I need someone to put prices on things with a red grease pencil. I can't have you in the store, but you can work in the basement. It pays fifty cents an hour. Does that work?"

"It's great," Jason replied. "When can I start?"

For six months, Jason wrote prices on everything and kept the basement storage area spotless. Then Mr. Lehman said it was time to climb out of the basement to work behind the counter. Now fifteen, Jason dove into a career stocking shelves and selling vitamins, cigarettes, candy, and all manner of sundries at the front counter, which was at the opposite end of the store from the pharmacy counter.

It was fantastic—until the whisperer showed up. A strange little guy stepped forward to the front counter and whispered so quietly, Jason could only guess what he was saying.

It sounded like, "I need peanuts."

Jason handed him a bag of Planter's salted peanuts.

"No, no. *Peeeeenuts.*" He stretched out the word, but it was still in a hushed voice, so Jason wasn't sure.

"Peanuts?"

"No. *P-E-A-C-O-C-K-S,*" he spelled it out slowly, emphasizing each letter.

"Oh, peacocks," Jason said, though it didn't make sense. "I don't think we have that."

"Yes, you do. They're right there behind the counter." The man pointed behind Jason, then glanced over his shoulder toward a woman who pretended to be shopping but clearly was locked in on the conversation.

"Just a minute. Mr. Lehman!" Jason shouted across the store. "Do we have any peacocks?"

Mr. Lehman's eyes lit up. He dropped what he was doing and bolted to the counter, shoving Jason out of the way. The woman covered her mouth in an unsuccessful attempt to conceal her laughter.

Jason returned to marking prices in the basement for a few weeks. When he came back to the front counter, he had a clear understanding that condoms were sometimes called by their trade names, such as Peacocks.

Life for the Korsens progressed with little thought about Peder. That is, until the mailman dumped a new dilemma in Ginger's lap: a massive bill for Peder's hospital and medical expenses. The six-digit demand was probably more than she could earn in a lifetime. It was laughable—except for the part about garnishing her meager wages.

Holding back tears—probably more out of anger than agony—she marched off to attorney John Kaiser's office. He assured her it was safe to laugh.

"Those pencil pushers are relentless if they smell blood or dollar bills in the water," he said with a smile. "We won't give them that pleasure. They'll have to move on to an easier target."

Kaiser took exceptional delight in taking on the government. But to his surprise, the state did not crumble or move on. The ridiculous battle carried on until, in a final desperate move, Kaiser orchestrated a divorce, an act that did little more than legalize the fact of Ginger and Peder's eternal separation. At last, that ended the state's fruitless treasure hunt for money where none existed.

Ginger considered not even mentioning the divorce to Jason, but she felt obligated. When they sat down at the kitchen table, she emphasized it was strictly a legal maneuver.

"It really doesn't change anything," she said. "I mean, your dad is still gone."

"So what does it mean for us?" Jason inquired.

"No change, other than the state will stop trying to charge me for his care. And I can focus on being your mother. That's my calling. It gives me purpose. Maybe that's the difference between men and women."

She looked out the window, and a smile nearly crossed her face.

"Before you were born, we had a wonderful marriage. I'm so sorry you never knew that man. We were so incredibly happy. Our friends were jealous. We started finishing each other's sentences a week after we met. It took my parents and other couples many years to find what Peder and I had. We had such good times. Until he got sick."

The near-smile faded.

"He had big dreams," she continued. "Then it was like he woke up one day, and his dreams were gone. He couldn't handle that. We weren't enough. I don't know if he inherited some brain virus. Maybe it was working full-time at the factory and building our house. Or his battle with scarlet fever. Or smashing his head in the car accident. Or just the weight of it all."

She looked down at her hands. Jason's eyes followed hers.

"I do know he left us a long time ago," she said. "Long before he was gone physically. He left and tried to hide in a bottle of beer. Maybe it was the beer that caused this all. Or maybe that was just his medicine of choice. Whatever the reason, I don't know that guy up at the hospital. He looks like your dad. But he's not."

With that, Ginger got up from the table and walked away.

Jason was left to wonder how his parents' marriage could have been so happy and turned so sour. It had to be that sick brain.

At least Grandma Libby had good memories about Grandpa Ernie, even though he was gone too now.

Not long before Grandpa Ernie passed away, he told Jason about the day Libby Oldhurst first rode into his view, sitting bareback atop a dapple-gray horse with a pistol strapped to her side. He had been fishing with his buddy Joey Stroud, but he was instantly smitten by the exotic, confident young woman. She was like no girl he had ever encountered with her bold spirit, hypnotizing sly smile, tantalizing freckled cheeks, and flashing dark eyes. She rode the horse as though they were one.

For a guy who never had trouble talking to the ladies, young Ernie suddenly was nearly tongue-tied. He managed to stammer, "Hey, I'm Ernie. What's your name?"

"I don't talk to strangers," she snapped and rode off without a glance in his direction.

Joey's dad was a cop, so he knew a lot about the people in town. He especially knew a lot about the Oldhurst family. She had three very big brothers and three beautiful older sisters. Joey himself was sweet on one sister, Emily. Their father was a little guy, but tough as granite—a rugged, hardworking farmer. He had been in the circus as an acrobatic clown. Her mother, who had recently passed away, had been Adrienne the Great, a famous bareback rider with the Ringling Brothers Circus.

Joey said Libby was a regular Annie Oakley. She carried the gun for protection as she rode through the woods from their farm up by the insane asylum down to Bellinger School.

"I hear she does target practice up at the gravel pit off Cameron Street on Saturday mornings," Joey told Ernie. "You might find her there. You might get shot too."

Undeterred, Ernie was sitting atop a giant boulder at the gravel pit early Saturday morning when Libby arrived on her sturdy brown steed. This part of the story Jason had heard from Grandma Libby too, who often told it with a twinkle in her eye.

"You didn't tell me your name," Ernie said.

"I said I don't talk to strangers."

"Yeah, well, we met before, so I'm not a stranger anymore. I'm Ernie. So, you gonna tell me your name or just shoot me?"

"It's very tempting. You're a bit of a pest. Maybe I could say I was just up here shooting varmints." She smirked. "I'm Libby, though I'm sure Joey already told you that."

"Yeah, he did. But it sounds a whole lot better coming from you."

"Oh, you're impossible." She shook her head and turned her horse around. "Nice meeting you, Ernie. I gotta get home now."

"What? You haven't even practiced shooting."

"Well, I guess the varmints here today are too cute to shoot."

She flashed an impish smile and rode away. Ernie almost forgot to breathe. His chest surged with that burst you feel turning up four aces at the poker table.

However, disappointment mushroomed as Ernie spent the

next three Saturdays alone at the gravel pit with no sign of Libby. Then she appeared.

"You still here?" she asked. "You must live here."

"Naw, I just been waiting for ya," he said.

"So I heard. Your buddy Joey told my sister Emily you were looking for me. Since my mother died last year, my sisters and I are busy cooking and cleaning the house while Dad and the boys work the farm."

"Joey told me about your mom. Sorry."

"It's rough, but we have each other. As for you, you're too old for me," she said flat out. "My brother Benny says you're twenty. I'm only sixteen. Dad would shoot you."

"Wow. You guys sure like shooting people. But really, we're not that far apart in age. I bet your dad was older than your mother."

"Maybe, but that's not going to matter to him."

Ernie and Libby continued their clandestine flirtation through the summer, and it blossomed into a love affair. Convinced no one would approve of their plans, they boarded a bus and fled to Texas one night.

Under pressure from their father, Emily revealed the elopement plot. The Oldhurst and Hunter fathers pushed aside the intense animosity that separated Baptists and Catholics and joined forces to chase down the young lovers and drag them home.

A year later, the couple took flight to Texas once more. This time, they married. Unable to find work in Texas, they migrated to Chicago. Even after moving home many years later to Eau Claire, Ernie and Libby always had a special place in their hearts for Texas. They escaped to the Lone Star State just about every winter.

Grandma Libby once showed Jason a letter she wrote about a side trip from Texas to Mexico in 1946.

By far the most incredible sight was on our stop in Chincua, Mexico, where our eyes feasted on clouds of monarch butterflies—millions of butterflies blanking out the sun and enshrouding every tree. It was breathtaking. We were told that these little fellows often fly up to three thousand miles, and it takes two or three months to make the trip.

Of course, Ernie wanted nothing to do with my "creepy crawler" friends and wouldn't get out of the car. But I was in a trance. As I walked toward the nearest orange cloud in the shape of a tree, a couple dozen of my little friends came out to greet me. I wondered if they were some of the butterflies I talked to in my garden last summer. I suspect they were Wisconsin natives glad to see a friendly face.

One by one, they landed so lightly on me and walked across my arm so gently that the tingle of movement raised goose bumps on my arms, even in the warm Mexican sunshine. Then two butterflies landed briefly on my cheek, and I'm certain they kissed me. I still get those goose bumps every time I think about it. It was one of the most sensual experiences of my life—don't tell Ernie that.

Jason reflected on how much life had changed in the ten years since Grandma Libby's experience with the butterflies. Grandpa Ernie had passed away. Peder had been hospitalized, released, then hospitalized again after the fire. Ginger went back to work. She and Peder were legally divorced. And all the while, Jason was just trying to survive adolescence.

Those left in the family now lived together under one small roof. Love was almost never expressed physically. There was no hugging or any thought of kisses. That was unnecessary, though. Love permeated the air. They all could feel it.

Jason certainly could.

CHAPTER 10

1958–1959

By fall of 1958, the house fire was a distant memory. Senior year got off to a good start for Jason. Life was good. Well, as good as it gets without a father and with a mother who endured more crap than any human should endure just to feed her kids.

Boy Scouts continued to be Jason's passion, but school, his job at a pizza restaurant, and the discovery of girls—especially the discovery of girls—made it more and more difficult to find time for scouting. That is, until word arrived that he was to receive the highest honor ever presented to a local Boy Scout.

scoutmaster Bob McQuillan grinned so wide Jason thought the guy's ears might pop off. "One of the head honchos from the Boy Scout headquarters in Philadelphia will be coming this spring to give you a huge national award for saving your sister's life during the fire!" he revealed. "We're going to hold a special ceremony that night. Your family and everyone in town will be invited. We'll even see if we can get your picture in the paper."

Awkward wouldn't begin to describe Jason's reaction. He felt he hadn't done anything special other than pull Sidney from her bed and drag her out the door.

What's the big deal? I don't want all that attention. And I certainly don't deserve it. Well, he thought, *maybe it's better than being ridiculed for my dad being stuck away in the nuthouse.*

"The only thing better would be if you could also finish off your Eagle award," scoutmaster McQuillan added. "You have to finish before you turn eighteen. You're only four merit badges short of the twenty-one you need."

"I don't know," Jason said. "My birthday is in December. That's not much time." School, his job, and of course girls came to mind.

"Don't blow this opportunity to do something important," the scoutmaster said with a knowing look. "If you don't do it, this would be a big, big mistake you'd regret for the rest of your life. I know, because I made that mistake. And now I can't go back and change it. I can never be an Eagle Scout."

Jason took that advice to heart. In two months, he knocked off a woodworking merit badge and met with Grandpa Ernie's old fishing buddy, Detective Joe Stroud, to study the fine art of fingerprinting.

Stroud seemed to take particular joy in hauling his young friend around the police station, introducing him to every cop in sight as "Libby Oldhurst's grandson." Jason was surprised to hear his grandmother called by her maiden name. But then he recalled his grandparents' stories, about how Detective "Joey" Stroud had helped bring Grandpa Ernie and Grandma Libby together. Jason also remembered that Libby's sister Emily was Detective Stroud's sweetheart back then.

As Grandma Libby told Jason later that night, "Everyone said Emily was the most beautiful girl in town, and he was totally smitten. She was only twenty when she died from influenza. That dropped Joey into a funk, a lonely black pit where he cowered until World War II called his name and jerked him back to life. Maybe that was the only good thing that came from Hitler's miserable war."

After making their way around the station for introductions, eventually Stroud settled down to teach Jason about fingerprinting. He pulled out six white sheets of heavy cardstock. Each sheet displayed ten convenient little squares across the front, one for each of a person's ten digits. He locked one sheet into a custom-designed metal frame on his desk, then spread a thin coating of black tar across a heavily stained four-by-eight-inch slab of glass that was one inch thick.

Detective Stroud next wrapped his massive but warm hand around Jason's left wrist. Jason was paralyzed in discomfort as the detective manipulated his hand and made Jason's index finger stick out. He rolled Jason's finger in the black tar, pressed it firmly on the white card, then rolled it inside the first square. On he went for all ten digits. It was more than uncomfortable having this big guy holding his hand and moving it around, pulling and bending fingers.

At least he seemed to sense Jason's discomfort. "Relax your wrist. Let me turn it. Don't pull, or the print is gonna smear."

Once all ten fingers were stained black and rolled across the sheet, Detective Stroud smiled. "Okay, now it's your turn to do me."

Stroud might as well have punched him in the face. Jason had heard those exact words before—although for something far different. Jason hesitated for a long, very uncomfortable moment as he considered spilling his guts to Stroud about that other guy. Just as quickly, though, he shook it off. He decided no good could come of it.

"Come on, Jason. We haven't got all day. This is pretty easy stuff."

Jason stashed unpleasant memories back in that remote corner of his mind and reached for Stroud's hand. When Jason completed taking Stroud's prints, a finger bath in alcohol swept away most of their black stains, but only time would erase the rest.

"Want to do some real detective work?" Stroud asked.

Stroud handed him a large handheld magnifying glass similar to the one Grams used to scour her dictionary. He also pulled out two tall stacks of fingerprint cards.

"These are prints from a string of actual, active burglary investigations," he explained, pointing to one stack. He then pointed to the other. "And these are prints from known suspects."

Without a word, he went off to attend other duties.

For Jason, taking the fingerprints proved to be fairly simple compared to examining the prints. His eyes began to blur after two hours of tracking whorls, loops, and lines on dozens of ink-stained cards.

He was so cross-eyed that he doubted himself when he noticed an apparent match between one of the suspects' prints and the print pulled off a broken window in the burglary at Kohlepp's Hardware Store. Unsure, he reluctantly flagged down Stroud to point it out.

Stroud grabbed the suspect's card and the print pulled from the store. "By George, you may be on to something."

Two days later, the suspected burglar was getting free meals in the county jail. Jason never got full credit for the collar, but Stroud did sign off on his merit badge.

Jason was only two merit badges away when he learned the final step toward attaining his Eagle Scout award was to attend a Scoutmaster Conference and an Eagle Scout Board of Review with assistant scoutmaster Lloyd. Earning merit badges was one thing. Putting himself through those meetings would be another. Jason knew he was so close, and he knew he might regret the decision, as scoutmaster McQuillan warned. But he let his eighteenth birthday come and go, ending his chance of ever becoming an Eagle Scout.

Before he knew it, spring arrived, and so did Jason's big night on May 5. Assistant scoutmaster Lloyd Harris and his merry band of Indian dancers took the stage. Calling it a "stage" probably was an exaggeration. It was an eight-by-ten-foot platform rising less than four inches above the church basement floor. It couldn't be any higher because the seven-foot-tall ceiling severely limited overhead space.

Standing center stage was Jason's buddy Roy Pettit with a massive Indian chief's headdress. Even with that giant headdress, he had plenty of room to spare. Sometime around fifth grade, Roy just stopped growing at a sliver over five feet tall. He was convinced God had cursed him. Adults often confused him for a younger child, and bullies took to chiding him as "runt" or whistling and calling him "Daddy's little girl." Jason wondered if it were true what folks said about cigarettes stunting growth. Or maybe it was Roy's pathetic diet. And then there was the fact that Roy's mother, brother, and father all were vertically challenged.

The church basement was overflowing when scoutmaster McQuillan called Jason forward so the national Boy Scout official could present the Certificate of Merit from the National Court of Honor. Fortunately, the Philadelphia guy wasn't terribly tall either. He fit comfortably on the stage. But at six feet one, Jason felt like he would be better off kneeling as he stepped on stage.

At first, Jason lingered somewhere between embarrassment and honor as the official said the Certificate of Merit was the first one ever presented in the Chippewa Valley Boy Scout Council. It bore the signatures of President Dwight D. Eisenhower, Admiral Richard E. Byrd, FBI Director J. Edgar Hoover, newscaster Lowell Thomas, World War I ace Eddie Rickenbacker, and other prominent folks.

But as Jason gazed out into the crowd, his embarrassment turned to pride. He looked into his mother's and grandmother's eyes. At that moment, he could not have been prouder if he had been elected president. There was Mr. Lehman from the drugstore. Mr. Stange the grocer. The barber. All his neighbors. Every relative he had ever met. All the Scouts' parents. Two reporters and a photographer from the *Leader* and *Telegram* daily newspapers. Plus a boatload of folks he didn't recognize.

Then the biggest shock nearly blew him off the stage. There, way at the back, in the shadows behind everyone, stood his father. Peder gave a broad smile, a slight nod, then vanished up the back stairway like a puff of smoke escaping up the chimney.

Jason blinked and searched for him again, but his father—or whoever it was—was gone.

That has to be my imagination playing tricks, he thought. *It can't be him. He's locked up in the asylum.*

Applause snapped him back to the ceremony.

Within thirty minutes, Sergeant Paul Middleton spotted a man walking briskly along Highway 12 just north of Truax Boulevard. He was heading west, less than a mile from Eau Claire County Asylum. The station had received a call from the night nurse at the asylum to report a missing patient. They had also received a call from a nervous neighbor who spotted a suspicious person and feared it could be related to the series of recent burglaries.

Middleton slowed down alongside the man. He knew him from high school—as well as from that ugly night ten years earlier when he had been one of the four monsters who ripped the man out of his home.

"Hey, Peder. Where you going?" inquired Middleton.

"I gotta get back to the hospital before they lock the doors at ten."

"How about I give you a ride?"

"Sure, that would be great," Peder replied. He opened the door and slid into the back seat.

"First, I need you to come to the station," Middleton explained. "We had some complaints in the area, and I need to clear that up. I'll call the hospital and tell them you're with me. We'll get you home in the morning."

Peder sat back. He hadn't ridden in a car for a long time. He and Middleton had never been what one might call friends, but there was some comfort in just being with a guy from high school—a piece from Peder's better life.

"Where have you been tonight?" Middleton asked.

Middleton was no stranger to hauling drunks, criminals, and all sorts of dangerous characters—they never bothered him. But Peder was different. Peder had been a star athlete, a big, powerful guy. And now he was legally insane. Middleton wasn't sure what to think or say. It was troubling.

"I walked up to Saint Luke to see my son get his Boy Scout award. They invited me. See—here's my invitation." He pulled an envelope out of his jacket pocket.

Truth was, nobody sent Peder an invitation. One of the asylum nurses had a son in Jason's troop. She had brought the announcement about Jason's award to work for Peder to see, then left it lying on his nightstand.

"You got to go to something like that," Peder continued. "I haven't been a great dad, so there was no way I would miss this."

"Yeah, that's pretty great. I heard about it from Detective Stroud. I understand why you wanted to be there. But aren't you supposed to stay at the hospital? Did they say you could go?"

"I didn't ask. I just left for a little while. I thought I could get back before ten, and nobody would care. I work in the kitchen, and they always let me go out for a smoke or to pick some fresh apples for my pies. I figured nobody would notice if I just kept going and didn't come back for a little while. I finished baking all my pies for tomorrow before I left."

"Do ya walk away often, Peder?"

"Naw, never before. This was the first time I had something that important."

Back at the station, Middleton filled out the necessary report, notified the hospital, and checked Peder into a twelve-by-fifteen-foot concrete suite at the Eau Claire PD Hotel. There was nothing but a single bed and stainless steel toilet. Middleton handed him a couple of blankets and said someone would get him back to the hospital in the morning.

Peder spotted the Faribault Woolen Mill Company label. His mind drifted back to the time he had spent living in the basement of his new dream house, where he had hung similar blankets as temporary doors. Clutching the blanket, Peder disappeared into dreamland about those good times, days when he had plans for a future.

By morning, Roy Pettit's young body was discovered, and everything changed.

PART 3

CHAPTER 11

MAY 6, 1959

Peder was still asleep when the heavy steel jail cell door screeched open and Detective Joe Stroud entered at 6:33 a.m.

It took Peder a moment to realize he wasn't in his room at the asylum. He was in a new cage. The bed was a simple steel frame with wire springs. The mattress was not much thicker than the woolen army-surplus blanket. It provided almost no protection from the springs in the frame.

While Peder noticed how uncomfortable the bed was, the drunks who paraded into jail every weekend didn't. With the dubious honor of having the highest per capita number of bars for any city in the country, Eau Claire had plenty of drunks. Jailers had to drag in extra beds and jam three or four prisoners into each cell. Repeat offenders usually got a ride out to the drug treatment center at the county asylum—ironically, where Peder should have been.

By Monday, the cells would be empty again, either because angry wives had bailed out their sheepish mates or because the drunks had gone to visit Judge Forester. Although the cells got hosed down, the drunks never were truly gone, thanks to the lingering stench of sweat, vomit, and stale beer that could never be completely flushed down the drain.

There was no cell for women, but there was almost never a need for one. Every weekend, the jailers were left to wonder what stirred up violence and stupid behavior in the brains of men while women were left to clean up and be caretakers.

Stroud stepped into the cell. "Good morning, Peder. I'm Joe Stroud. I'd like to talk with you about what you did last night."

"Yeah, I know ya," Peder replied. "You were Ernie's fishing buddy, right?"

Stroud nodded. He hoped the personal connection would make Peder comfortable enough to open up to him.

"Sorry about last night," Peder continued, seeming to relax at the sight of a familiar face. "I shouldn't have left the hospital, but I had to see Jason get his award. I knew they wouldn't let me go if I asked, so I just left. I woulda gotten back in plenty of time if Middleton hadn't grabbed me off the street. Ya know, Middleton and I never hit it off too well in school. I guess he was just having some fun with me."

"So where did you go last night?"

"Just walked up to the church, saw the ceremony, and tried to hustle back."

"Where else did you go?"

"Nowhere. That was it."

"Did you take a walk through the park by Dells Pond?"

"What? No. Why would I go there?"

Stroud stepped forward and placed a hand gently on Peder's shoulder. Looking into Peder's eyes, Stroud couldn't escape seeing the family resemblance with Peder's son, Jason. It rekindled memories of a day long ago when Stroud and Jason's grandfather Ernie took an innocent five-year-old Jason to Tainter Lake in Menominee for the boy's first fishing trip. The little guy almost capsized them all as he bounced about in near hysteria after jerking a puny five-inch crappie into the boat. Stroud and Ernie compounded the chaos by rocking the boat with uncontrolled laughter.

There was no laughter today.

"Are you sure you didn't go anywhere else? Think hard."

Stroud felt the tension melt from the big guy's body. As if Peder were reading Stroud's thoughts, he spoke calmly with a sudden, subtle smile.

"Positive. Nothing to think about. I didn't have time to go anywhere else. I needed to get back to the hospital. In fact, they must be wondering where I am. I better get back now, or I'll be in trouble. They don't have anyone to bake the rolls and pies for tomorrow."

Before Stroud could respond, Sergeant Olberdorf appeared outside Peder's cell with a tin plate and a smile. "Breakfast is served, my good fellow."

Contrary to popular belief, meals in the jail were not bread and water. The tin plate displayed a pile of gray scrambled eggs, limp bacon embedded in cold white grease, and a slice of burnt toast. Peder debated asking for the bread and water option. But at least breakfast came with a large cup of lukewarm coffee that tasted fairly good.

As he stared at his meal, Peder suddenly longed for his tiny room at the asylum. He had always thought of that place as a jail cell. But it was a palace compared to this. He had his own television and radio as well as books, magazines, and newspapers. His door remained unlocked into the ward. Most meals rivaled that of the finest restaurants.

He vowed never to complain again about his life at the hospital. He began to believe that old adage that no matter how bad your situation might be, it could always be worse.

Peder thought of Richard, a man he knew at the asylum. Richard was as blind as a bat, but he was the happiest guy on the ward, always staying positive.

"I don't have to see all the bad stuff that happens," Richard once said. "And I can do things you can't do. I can read in the dark. I can smell, hear, and feel things you will never notice."

Peder also thought of Marvin, the guy in the room next to his at the asylum. A paratrooper with the Eighty-Second Airborne Division, Marv lost his left leg jumping into Normandy on D-Day. Marv's roommate at Walter Reed Army Medical Center had lost both legs in battle. He referred to Marv's injury as a "paper cut"—a bit of callous but much-needed humor in the midst of a building filled with severely injured soldiers.

Marv always said he was lucky because his amputation was below the knee, enabling him to walk with a simple prosthesis. Even Marv's double-amputee roommate felt lucky—a nineteen-year-old soldier down the hall had lost both legs and both arms in comparison.

Peder sat back and smiled. Having to stay overnight in jail was bad, but it had taught him that his life at the hospital was pretty good. Life at the asylum was maybe better than his life before, back home. As he saw it, he didn't have to work all hours of the day and night at that rotten tire factory. He had no worries about money. His biggest challenge on any given day was whether to make blueberry or apple pies.

I probably should miss my wife and kids, he thought. *But that was so long ago. I barely think about them now. I probably should be ashamed of myself. But I'm not.*

Well, hell—I went to Jason's Boy Scout ceremony. I'm proud that he and Sidney are doing so well. But I don't really feel a part of it. Was I ever a part of their lives?

My life is at the hospital. That's all that matters. Doctor Mentzil doesn't let in those people trying to kill me. They do still manage to talk to me through the radio and television sometimes, but nothing like before. And Jessie, that cute college gal, and Madeline, my favorite nurse, treat me great. Just about everyone at the hospital is okay. It's peaceful and pleasant.

Still smiling, Peder looked at Stroud. "Please take me home now."

"We'll see, Peder," Stroud said. "But I think you'll have to stay here a little while longer."

For three days, police scoured the park in search of any clue. They knocked on every door within blocks of the murder scene.

One of Stroud's first stops was to meet with Roy Pettit's mother and brother. It was never easy questioning a grieving family, but the Pettits were perhaps more familiar than most families when it came to police visits. With Roy's father in Waupun State Prison and his brother, Batshit Bart, recently home from the same prison, the Pettits were always high on police radar for any crime.

If possible, Roy's mother appeared more malnourished than her sons. She was just a bag of bones concealed by ashen skin topped off by a somber, prune-like face featuring permanently puckered lips with a graying bird's nest for hair. She wore no makeup—probably chose not to spend the money. The only color other than gray was from her vibrant red eyes that dripped with tears cutting through the grime on her cheeks.

Bart showed no sign of distress. Perhaps he was just hardened to life.

Bart said the night Roy died, he was out drinking at the Wigwam Tavern with three friends. Stroud collected the names to check Bart's alibi, and his gut told him the alibis would check out.

As troubled as Batshit was, Stroud didn't believe he had raped and killed his own brother. But troubled people know other troubled people. Perhaps Bart had some enemies, and Roy had just been collateral damage.

"Bart," Stroud said, "you hang around with people who've done some bad stuff. And I assume you got to know some pretty bad guys in prison as well. Is there anybody upset enough with you to harm your brother?"

"Yeah, I know some crazy characters, but nobody who'd do this. Most of the nasty guys at Waupun are all still there. Nobody's around here other than the guys I was with at the bar. I got nuthin' to do with it." For a moment, a hint of a frown appeared, then disappeared. "And I got no ideas about who did it."

Stroud made a note to have Sergeant Gordon Richardson check with the warden at Waupun to see if anyone associated with Bart or his old man had been recently released. He doubted, however, it would produce any leads. Everything in Stroud said Bart was telling the truth.

They interviewed people who had attended the Boy Scout meeting at Saint Luke, plus anyone who attended choir practice upstairs that same night. scoutmaster McQuillan and assistant scoutmaster Lloyd Harris, both quite upset, explained how Roy had been the star of the Indian dance troupe performance.

Stroud himself went to Libby's home to interview the Korsen family.

"Good morning, Libby," Stroud spoke softly as he approached her working in her garden. "Wow, those tomato plants are huge for so early in the year."

"Hello to you too, old-timer. Yes, I start them in the basement so we can get going fast. Are you looking for Jason?"

"Yes. Just trying to talk with everyone who was at the church that night. Is he here?"

"He's here. Whether he's awake is another matter. That boy can sleep half the day if somebody doesn't rouse him, and then he'll run right to the refrigerator for a whole bottle of milk and anything else he can get his hands on. It's amazing how much that boy consumes. Come on—I'll get him."

Stroud had to stifle a laugh as they entered the kitchen to find Jason sitting at the kitchen table in his pajamas, tipping back a quart bottle of milk.

"Hey, Jason, have you got a few minutes to talk with me?" Stroud asked.

Jason slowly lowered the bottle, brushed his right forearm across his face to sweep away any lingering milk, and cast a wary look toward Stroud. "I suppose. Don't know what I can say that you don't already know."

Libby turned to head back outside. "Jason, get Officer Stroud some coffee."

Jason complied, then they both settled at the table with their respective drinks—steaming coffee for Stroud and the bottle of milk for Jason.

"We're talking to everyone who was at the church the night Roy died," Stroud continued. "I still think it all started there. Is there anyone at all who might have wanted to hurt Roy? Do you have any idea who might have done this?"

Jason hesitated as he slowly sucked another drink of milk. He did have one thought, but it was just that—a thought.

Better not start something you can't finish.

"No, I can't think of anyone who would do such an awful thing."

They talked about fishing with Grandpa Ernie, the finger-printing merit badge, school, and everything but Roy's murder for another fifteen minutes before Stroud headed out the back door, leaving Jason wondering if he should have said more.

CHAPTER 12

MAY 9, 1959

As Stroud entered his office, the desk sergeant, Olaf "Ole" Olberdorf, shouted across the room, "Stroud, the city council president wants to see you in his office right now."

Stroud knew where this was going. Milbrandt was a political opportunist embroiled in an election campaign he was in danger of losing. Solving this murder would be his grand distraction from real issues. He was gearing up to take full credit.

Percy Milbrandt jumped from his oversized mahogany desk as Stroud entered. "What have you got on the Boy Scout murder?"

"The investigation is just underway, sir. We collected evidence at the scene, and we're interviewing everyone in the neighborhood, any kids and teachers who knew him at school, and all those at the church Tuesday night."

Milbrandt spun about, barking like a mad dog ready to attack. "Stop wasting my time. I know you've already got the killer in jail—the nut who escaped the asylum. We need to set up a press conference. I want you there with Chief Schmidt."

"Your honor," Stroud said, "I want to wrap this up as quickly as you do. But we do need to follow the evidence and make a solid case. We have every available officer talking to anyone who was at the church and all of Roy's friends and family. We're following up on every lead, no matter how small it is. We're making good progress, but I can tell you that the more we look, the more I'm not convinced we have the right guy."

"Bullshit. He's the right guy. Stop wasting my time. The press conference is at three on Monday. I need you or the chief to tell the public that we have our guy in jail and that charges have been filed. Do whatever you want until then, but you will be there and you will charge this crazy guy with murder, unless you have another suspect. Is that clear enough for you?"

"Sir, that would be a mistake. I need evidence that will hold up in court."

Milbrandt was in no mood for discussion. Clearly, he had no time for ideas that were not his own. Practically sticking his index finger in Stroud's left eye, he shouted, "Stroud, if it looks like a duck, walks like a duck, and quacks like a duck, you can pretty damn well assume it's a gawddamn duck."

"Sir, we don't know if Peder had enough time to do this or what his motive would have been," Stroud said.

"He doesn't need a motive. He's a certified nutcase. They do things like this all the time. He's your guy. Do your job."

Struggling to contain the volcano of rage building in his gut, Stroud bit down on his tongue before he said something he might regret. He managed to utter, "Yes, sir. I will do my job. Thank you for your input."

As Stroud left the ostentatious office, he was half tempted to slap the idiot council president for his trite clichés. Unlike Milbrandt, Stroud was not convinced that crazy people "do things like this all the time." In fact, he wasn't aware of it ever happening. He needed to learn more, and he had a good idea where to look for answers.

Stroud climbed into his unmarked squad car and headed off to the county asylum to meet with Dr. Cecil Mentzil, asylum superintendent. The antique rust bucket displayed 203,144 miles on its odometer. It coughed and trembled like an old man at every stop sign. Given all the mayhem Stroud had seen dumped on good people in Europe and at home, Stroud wasn't sure what he thought about God—but at that moment, he uttered a silent prayer that the old police car would survive another month to his retirement.

Dr. Mentzil was a small man with a graying mustache, immaculately trimmed goatee, and thinning hair. He always wore a dark woolen suit with a buttoned vest, a perfectly pressed brilliant white shirt, and a dark-blue bow tie, even in the summer months. He bore a striking resemblance to Sigmund Freud. In fact, with their similarity in vocations, his nickname was Dr. Freud—to the point where he seemed to believe it himself. He too was brilliant, and his innovations at the asylum had greatly benefitted many patients. If he had a weakness, it may have been an excess of kindness. No matter what the offense, he always looked for the good in everyone and sought a solution that inflicted as little pain as possible.

The superintendent greeted Stroud upon his arrival. "Good morning, Detective. How may I be of assistance?"

"I need to know everything you can tell me about Peder Korsen."

Dr. Mentzil greeted Stroud with restrained pleasantness and more than a little apprehension. "I understand you arrested him and suspect he murdered and sexually molested a young man. That's very difficult to believe."

"Yes, sir. He's being held at the jail while we investigate, but he hasn't been officially charged with anything at this time—other than escaping from your hospital. I'm hoping to get a few more answers."

Dr. Mentzil nodded. "Peder suffers from dementia praecox, also known as schizophrenia. But through extensive counseling and new medications, he has made tremendous strides. If you were to talk with him, you would not find him different than any other so-called normal person, except that he may be a tad smarter than most, especially considering he never attended college. He reads voraciously and is current on everything in the newspaper. He can quote chapter and verse from the Bible better than our chaplains, and he serves as our interpreter for our Norwegian-speaking residents. I know him well, and I just don't believe he did what you say."

"I know," Stroud agreed. "I spoke with him this morning, and he did seem pretty normal. The jailer said Peder was mostly just upset that he didn't get his newspaper today. I had them grab one for him. So, tell me, then—if he's doing so well, why is he still confined to this place?"

"Well, that's an excellent question, Detective Stroud. You should probably ask the state assembly that one. He was brought here ten years ago by court order when he endangered his family and assaulted his supervisor at the US Rubber plant. Once someone is declared a threat to society, it becomes extremely difficult to get them released, no matter how well they do or what we say."

Stroud nodded in affirmation. The two men stared across the desk in prolonged silence as if weighing the impact of Dr. Mentzil's thoughts.

Finally, Stroud broke the silence. "Do you think Peder is capable of murder?"

"Anyone is capable of murder, but Peder has become very calm. I can't imagine him getting angry enough to commit murder. He's probably less likely to murder than you or me. And this suggestion that he sexually attacked a young man is totally out of character. Peder has never shown the slightest homosexual tendencies whatsoever. In the past, he may have been more than a bit obsessed with chasing skirts, but never men or boys. Detective, I think you're barking up the wrong tree and picking on the most convenient target."

Stroud couldn't disagree. But regardless of what he thought about Peder Korsen or what Dr. Mentzil said, everyone in town was ready to execute Peder. And without another suspect, the investigation was rapidly becoming a runaway train heading for disaster.

"Okay. Then tell me another thing, doctor. This is a security hospital—how did he escape?"

"First, this is not a prison. It is a medium-security medical facility. We give our trusted patients great freedom to roam about the grounds. Occasionally one will wander off the farm, but they always come back. We have never lost anyone until now, and we've never had any serious incident involving the public." Dr. Mentzil gave a knowing look. "By the way, I understand that Peder was picked up just a short distance away, heading this direction."

"So you're saying Peder is a trusted patient?"

"Absolutely. He had some very difficult times in the early years, but he's been a model patient the past seven years or so."

Stroud drove back to police headquarters with more questions than answers. The likelihood that Peder Korsen killed Roy Pettit was shrinking with every passing minute. But if not Peder, who? There was no one else on the radar. Not a clue.

CHAPTER 13

Stroud was coming out of the breakroom after returning from the asylum, but he stopped in his tracks when he overheard someone say, "My son found a body!" He struggled unsuccessfully to avoid splashing hot coffee on the already dark-brown carpet.

The detective quickly headed over to a man and his son standing in front of Desk Sergeant Fred MacDonald.

"What's this all about?" Stroud asked.

"We were fishing at Half Moon, and we saw a hand and arm," the boy said. "My buddy Doug hooked it. When we saw it, we got the hell out of there."

The boy winced as he realized he had just sworn, but neither his dad nor the police officers appeared to notice.

"Oh shit." Like the boy, Stroud winced as he swore. "Sorry. It's just that the last thing we need today is another body," he said. "Tell us everything."

McDonald began jotting down the slim details as the boy rattled them off.

Pud Jones, a carefree fourteen-year-old, loved fishing more than anything, except maybe banana cream pie. Earlier that morning, he had skipped happily along the muddy dirt road, vaulting gaily over tiny puddles lingering from a shower. The air was still saturated with a pleasing aroma of freshness.

Pud was a man on a mission, slip-sliding across the north

face of Carson Park with pole in hand. Worms wriggled in the left pocket of his dad's old army jacket. Spike, his wire-haired mongrel dog, trailed behind, darting from tree to tree, straining to squirt a drop of urine on every one.

Early-morning sunrays exploded like the petals on a giant blooming tiger lily. Pud cast furtive glances in all directions of the lazy landscape—no good angler would reveal his secret fishing hole. Convinced no one was in sight, he disappeared into the woods. A faint path wound through towering white pines like a snake silently slithering down the secluded, steep bank to taste the cool water of Half Moon Lake.

"Hey, Fatso!" Pud called out, startling his best friend.

Doug Smet was a roly-poly lad whose severely bent gold wire-rim glasses kept sliding down his stubby pink nose.

"How they bitin'?" Pud asked.

"Dey ain't," replied Doug.

Thirty minutes later, Pud agreed. He was ready to concede this was nothing like that monster day the previous summer, when the sunfish and crappies were so hungry the savage little buggers grabbed onto anything the boys dropped in the water. That day, they even experimented with an empty line. It trembled as little fish struck it repeatedly.

They filled a giant washtub to the rim with fish—but lost track of time. When they failed to return home by dark, their worried mothers summoned the cops. The boys were severely reprimanded for terrifying their families, not to mention for violating state fishing limits. Their parents coughed up healthy fines. Pud and Doug spent almost a year working odd jobs to cover the costs. Today was the first time their parents had granted them permission to return to the lake.

"Man, this is a total waste," Pud said.

"Wait a sec. I got sumpn'. Wow, it must weigh a hunnert pounds."

Doug struggled to breathe as he strained and wrestled to reel in what he was certain must be a muskie or a giant catfish.

"Yeah, sure. I suppose it's a 'pine fish' or maybe an 'oak bass,'" Pud said with a laugh, convinced his friend had merely snagged an old log.

"No, I ain't kiddin'. I really got sumpn'. And it's huge."

Horror spread across the boys' faces as a hand and an arm suddenly broke the placid surface, grabbing for the sky, thirty feet from shore.

"Oh crap! What's that?" Pud cried.

"I'm outta here," Doug spit.

His fishing pole plopped into the lake. He raced into the woods faster than his short-keg legs normally moved.

"Wait!" Pud yelled after him. "Let's see if we can pull it to shore."

"Is ya nuts?" was all he heard as Doug disappeared.

Pud reached into the water, searching for Doug's pole. But in early May, Half Moon Lake still held the icy chill of winter. He quickly abandoned the idea, gathered his equipment, whistled for Spike, and raced home.

His dad, Duane, was relaxing in his well-worn La-Z-Boy recliner, hidden behind the *Telegram*.

"Dad! Dad! Doug and I found a body at the lake!"

"What kind of body?" Duane mumbled with faint interest.

"A human body! Fatso hooked it when we were fishing."

Pud was prone to fantasy. But as Duane peeked over the newspaper at his son, he was struck by the electricity igniting Pud's blue-green eyes. His son's choppy speech told him this was no tall tale. They took the short ride up the Grand Avenue hill to the police station tucked behind city hall.

Stroud could also tell Pud's story was no fiction. First Roy Pettit. Now this. He opened his mouth to ask more questions. But just then, Jeremy Drake stepped into the station with a new dilemma.

"I need—to report—a missing person," Drake spoke in stuttering bursts like a robot. His face revealed the symptom of shock that besets most humans in the face of extreme tragedy.

Owner of a Ford dealership, Drake was a prominent local businessman well known for his support of numerous foundations and for donating vehicles to the Eau Claire police and fire departments. He was also City Council President Percy Milbrandt's major financial backer.

"Who's missing?" MacDonald inquired.

"My only child, Sonja. She never came home from choir practice at Saint Luke last night."

Stroud had just raised his coffee to his lips. Now he nearly choked. He plunked it down a bit too firmly on the nearest desk he could find, sending bronze splashes across piles of paper.

"I'll take this, Fred. You finish up with the Joneses." Stroud gestured to Drake. "Please come on back to my office, Mr. Drake."

Drake sat down at Stroud's desk. He failed to show emotion until he pulled from his billfold a photo taken for Sonja's impending high school graduation. A muffled sob escaped as his trembling hand pushed the picture across the desk to Stroud.

"Mr. Drake, what was Sonja wearing last night?"

"I don't know. I was working when she left. I'll get my wife to call you with that."

"What time did she leave home, and when did you first realize she was missing?"

"Sonja had choir practice at seven and should have been home by nine or nine thirty."

"Why did you wait all night to report her missing?"

Drake seemingly froze, as if realizing for the first time that his failure to track his daughter's actions could be seen as negligent. He quickly rejected the idea. "She frequently stays overnight with her friend Sharon Nelson. We didn't worry too much until we called the Nelsons this morning and found out she was never there."

"Can you give me a list of all of Sonja's friends? I'll contact the church to find out who was at choir practice last night," Stroud said. "We'll get on this right now. We want to be certain we get to everyone who may have some information."

Stroud knew this would dump gallons of fuel onto the fires of discontent already flaring up after the murder of Roy Pettit. A girl goes missing on the same night from the same church. This was too much coincidence.

Could that body in the lake be Sonja? Stroud wondered. *Or do we have multiple murders?*

Stroud weighed the decision to reveal his concerns to the bereaved father. "Mr. Drake, I don't want to alarm you, but I feel obligated to tell you we have received a report of a possible body being spotted at Half Moon Lake. The details are very sketchy at this time, and it's probably nothing. But again, I feel obligated to inform you because I don't want you to get blindsided by somebody else asking you about it. We have a diver heading down there to search. I'll immediately let you know what he finds."

Two hours later, Rick Otteson donned his gear. A volunteer firefighter with a passion for deep-sea diving, he prepared to dive into Half Moon Lake. This dive promised none of the brilliant colors nor the fascinating marine life he explored every winter in the warm blue-green Atlantic waters of John Pennenkamp Coral Reef State Park in the Florida Keys.

Rather, he would be searching for a body—perhaps that of Sonja Drake. Just the thought of finding a young girl's body gave him pause on the edge of the boat. But the lingering image of Jeremy and Sandra Drake's pleading eyes pushed him into the water.

His powerful underwater spotlight struggled to penetrate fields of minute particles suspended in the calm lake water. Otteson quickly discovered that the slightest motion stirred up massive clouds of particulates. Every time he startled a school of fish, his vision was shut down for five minutes. Searching the big lake would be like a virtual braille adventure. Further complicating his movement were nests of snagged fishing lines weaving through every bed of logs. Fish seemingly laughed at the colorful lost lures decorating their lake-bottom sanctuaries.

In addition to the body in Half Moon Lake, Otteson heard about the Boy Scout near Dells Pond. He knew, however, that more than just two bodies linked Dells Pond and Half Moon Lake. He was getting a close-up look at the city's lumber history.

At one time, nine sawmills dotted the shores of Half Moon Lake, the most notable being Daniel Shaw Lumber Company. For their mutual benefit, the lumbermen joined forces to construct the dam on the Chippewa River that created Dells Pond. The plan was to divert logs into Dells Pond, then release them back into the river to float three miles downriver to the sawmills on Half Moon Lake.

That plan nearly collapsed, though, when workers realized that, for most of the year, Half Moon was as much as eight feet higher than the Chippewa. The lumber companies could float logs only during times of high water, unless they wanted to attempt the laborious task of pulling logs up the steep riverbank with horses.

Undaunted, Shaw built a 1,200-foot-long gated canal to guide the logs from the Chippewa River to Half Moon Lake. The canal measured eighteen feet wide at the bottom and eight feet wide at ground level with a depth of twelve feet. It was a public works project that would be a major undertaking today. The city capitalized on Shaw's aqueduct by turning it into a major tourist attraction, allowing residents and visitors to swim when the flume wasn't in use transporting logs.

The flume and sawmills were long gone, but a hundred years later, Otteson found himself amongst tons of bark and mountains of sawdust beneath huge piles of waterlogged timbers on the murky bed of the lake. Like a vast manmade beaver dam, it may have been perfect for nurturing colonies of sunfish, bass, crappies, and wall-eyes. But trying to find a human body hiding in the ancient debris field was clearly a fool's errand.

Good God. What am I doing? Otteson thought. He struggled to convince himself the search was a good idea. *Those parents need an answer, but does it have to be me? Geez, rutting through this slime is bad enough. How would I ever sleep again if I looked into that dead girl's tortured eyes?*

Otteson had found bodies underwater in the Atlantic. But those were nothing but anonymous piles of bones deposited at the bottom of the sea in centuries-old shipwrecks. That was nothing more than a spectacular underwater museum. This was more like a horror film.

This is Sonja Drake, he told himself. *A healthy, beautiful young girl I know.*

After four hours of searching the area where the boys said they had hooked an arm, Otteson had enough. He couldn't bear the thought of digging through one more pile of slimy logs, let alone finding Sonja's body. He knew there would be plenty of logs in his dreams tonight.

Hopefully, no young bodies.

CHAPTER 14

MAY 11, 1959

"What the hell? Who are all these guys?"

City Council President Milbrandt had started his march through the door to the Eau Claire City Council chamber. But once he looked out into the jam-packed room, he nearly stumbled as his feet stuck to the floor.

Instantly, his pretentious attitude was nowhere to be seen. Rather, his richly tanned complexion turned to chalk dotted with glistening drops of perspiration. His roaring voice stuttered in choppy, childlike chirps.

"You said you wanted a press conference, sir," Ronald Atkinson, Milbrandt's suddenly anxious assistant, whispered. "I put out the call through Associated Press, and they dumped it on the national newswire. Now we've got newspaper reporters from St. Paul, Minneapolis, Milwaukee, Madison, and Chicago. Plus all the locals. And more radio guys than I've ever seen."

Milbrandt couldn't help but think of the old song about being careful what you wish for.

"No shit," he said. "I've never seen anything like it. I don't understand."

"Sir, we've got a Boy Scout viciously murdered, a choir girl missing from the same church, and an escaped mental patient as a suspect all on the same night. Plus reports of a dead body in a lake. That's big news anywhere," Atkinson suggested.

"Where's Chief Schmidt?" Milbrandt snapped back to his usual self. "We better get our facts straight right now. This isn't just the local yokels from the *Leader*, *Telegram*, and WEAU. Now I don't know what to say. Damn it—where the hell is Chief Schmidt? Close that door!"

Atkinson was tempted to point out, *But you had plenty to say a few minutes ago.* Rather, he said, "The chief is right behind you, sir."

"Why isn't Stroud here?" Milbrandt barked next. "Get his ass in here immediately. This is a nightmare." He pointed at Chief Schmidt. "You need to tell them we got the killer in jail and there's nothing to worry about—before this gets totally out of control."

"Council President Milbrandt," Atkinson said, "Detective Stroud is on his way, but he said he's got nothing new for the press."

"We don't need anything *new*. We just need to wrap this thing up. We got that nut locked up."

When Stroud appeared, reluctance smeared his normally confident face. He looked ready to tap dance as he glanced into the city council chambers.

Without greeting or negotiation, Milbrandt spit words at Stroud. "I need you to back me up on this arrest, Detective. Let's go. We're already twenty minutes late."

The roar of meaningless chatter evaporated instantly as Council President Milbrandt, Chief Schmidt, and Detective Stroud entered the chamber and slid into high-backed black leather chairs behind the perfectly polished white oak city council desk emblazoned with a four-foot circular City of Eau Claire seal. The herd of fifty-three chirping journalists froze midsentence. One hundred six eyeballs snapped forward.

"Wow, we don't even get this many people for a city council meeting," Milbrandt muttered.

With pursed lips, he then leaned into the microphone.

"Good afternoon. Thank you for coming. As you know, our city experienced a child murder this week. Crimes such as this are foreign to our community. In fact, outside of domestic disputes, there has not been a murder in Eau Claire for nearly thirty years. As horrific as this crime is, I am extremely pleased to report that our outstanding police department had captured the perpetrator before the murder was even reported. Now, before we take any questions, Chief Orville Schmidt will recap what we know so far."

Schmidt paused in realization that he had little to add beyond what everyone already knew. He busied himself scribbling meaningless circles and boxes on the notebook in front of him, stalling for time and trying to come up with something relatively coherent to say.

"Gentlemen," he eventually began, addressing the all-male crowd of police reporters, "as you know, a seventeen-year-old male victim, Roy Allen Pettit, was found deceased in McDonough Park at Dells Pond on the evening of Tuesday, May 5. The body was discovered by a citizen who made an anonymous call to our office. We would like to talk with that person. We ask that you do whatever you can to encourage her to call my office as soon as possible.

"Earlier that evening, the victim attended a Boy Scout program at Saint Luke Lutheran Church six blocks from the park. He was wearing his Boy Scout uniform when he died. The medical examiner has confirmed death by asphyxiation—strangulation— and that the boy was molested prior to his death. We have a suspect in jail on a minor charge of escape from the county mental asylum. He is pending further investigation."

Out of the corner of his eye, Schmidt saw Milbrandt's face turn red. He looked out at the reporters, and their faces frowned with confusion. Milbrandt had just said the asylum patient was the "perpetrator," whereas the police chief had merely called him a suspect pending investigation. Schmidt suddenly needed to sit down.

"At this time, this is still an active investigation, so that is about the extent of what I can say."

All fifty-three reporters leaped to their feet with military precision and began firing questions.

"Detective Joseph Stroud is our lead investigator," Milbrandt barked into the microphone over the deafening roar. He pointed a trembling hand at Stroud. "If you can ask your questions one at a time, he will attempt to respond."

The council president turned and dumped his mess squarely in Stroud's court.

Glancing across the sea of overly eager reporters standing with sharpened pencils aimed at him like swords, Stroud fought off an overwhelming urge to smile, even to laugh. How would that play in the midst of describing a dastardly murder? But looking down on the teeming school of reporters flapping their lips with inane questions, all he could think of was tossing bread crumbs on the water beneath the railroad bridge on the Chippewa River and watching ravenous carp snapping at the surface.

The questions flew.

"Detective, is it true you have a girl missing from the same church? What can you tell us about her?"

"Why haven't you charged the crazy guy with murder yet? Is he the perpetrator, as Milbrandt claims?"

"Do you have any other suspects?"

"Okay, okay. Listen up," Stroud quieted the crowd. At least

he had the microphone on his side. "As Chief Schmidt said, this remains an active investigation, so I cannot divulge some of the facts. What I can tell you is that we are questioning a suspect who is in custody. However, other than the report that he left the asylum without authorization and was at the church, we do not have any evidence that connects him to the murder scene.

"As for the missing girl, finding her is our first priority. We received a report that two boys fishing at Half Moon Lake spotted what they thought was a body. The fire department is dragging the lake as we speak, but that lake is littered with waterlogged snags left over from long ago, when lumber mills lined the shores. They put a diver down there, but they tell me it's slow going. We'll let you know as soon as we learn anything."

"Archie Kemp, Associated Press," one of the reporters shouted. "Do you know if the boy and girl were together? Maybe they were in the park and were attacked."

"The parents of both youngsters tell us the boy and girl did know each other from school and church but they were not friends. It is unlikely they were together."

Left unsaid was the fact that Sonja's wealthy parents were positive she would never associate with a guy like Roy Pettit.

"It wouldn't be the first time parents didn't know what their kids were doing and who they were with," Kemp persisted.

"We appreciate that," Stroud said, "and we are pursuing every angle. But at the moment, we have one murder, one missing child, and one report of a potential body in a lake. We don't know whether the incidents are connected, but the coincidences of time and place are impossible to ignore. We will follow every lead, no matter how remote it might be."

Another reporter chimed in. "Steve Sorenson, *Saint Paul Dispatch*. If you're telling us you really don't know much at all, then why are we here?"

Stroud was tempted to say it was because they were invited by a council president who needed to enhance his election campaign.

"We're not used to major crimes like you have in the Twin Cities," he said instead. "We want to err on the side of openness with the press. Everyone is asking questions. People are worried. We don't want to be seen as uncooperative. More important, we need your help. We're hopeful that any attention you can focus on these crimes will encourage the public to contact us with anything that may be relevant. It doesn't matter how minor it may seem. Did you see Roy Pettit on Tuesday? Were you near Dells Pond Tuesday night? Did you see any suspicious characters or vehicles in the area? Anything at all may be the clue that will lead us to solving the boy's murder. And we really need to talk with that young woman who called in about finding his body."

"Gentlemen, that's it for now," Milbrandt said, abruptly ending the meeting. "We'll contact you as soon as we have more information."

Nobody was happy. Reporters grumbled and shouted after Milbrandt as he slipped out the door, leaving Chief Schmidt to fend off the reporters. Schmidt sat there like a good soldier more to block access to Milbrandt than anything else.

"I'm really sorry, but that's all we got," he said. "I promise we will get back to you as soon as we learn anything."

"Yeah, right," exhaled a very unhappy reporter. "Please don't waste our time again unless it's something we don't already know."

Stroud used the distraction to slip out the door. He fled across the alley to the police station—where Bobby Lauder, reporter for the *Eau Claire Telegram*, was lying in ambush.

"Okay, Joe," he said. "That was a joke. I'm assuming Milbrandt dragged you in there against your will. But all that aside, what the hell is going on? I get the sense he wants to hang the asylum escapee but you're not totally convinced he's your guy."

"Bobby, you know I can't comment on that. But I will say that we are not closing our minds to anything at this point. I need solid facts to charge someone with murder. And right now, we just don't have enough information."

"Fair enough. I understand the missing girl is Sonja Drake."

"What makes you say that?" Stroud dug for his best poker face. He considered whether Lauder was playing some reporter's game, implying he knew more than he did.

Lauder pushed ahead. "Her parents were at the back of the council chambers during that so-called press conference. Jeremy Drake told me himself."

"As I said in there," Stroud explained, "we don't know what happened to her. A boy came forward claiming that he and his buddy hooked what they said was an arm while fishing, but they panicked and let it drop back into the lake. Until we have more information, the only real facts are that Roy Pettit was murdered and Sonja Drake is missing. We need to be careful not to get too far ahead of the facts."

With a dismissive wave, Lauder moved onto another topic. "Yeah, yeah. I get it. One last question: How does Milbrandt stay in office the way he beats down everybody at city hall?"

"You're the news expert—you tell me."

"It seems he just tells every group what they want to hear," Lauder said. "I saw him speaking to a women's club at the Catholic church recently, and he was spouting Bible verses and doing his Prince Charming act. The gals ate it up. At the Chamber of Commerce, he's all business. And down at the Rubber Workers Union Hall, he's all for the people—damn near a socialist. But I was most amazed at how he treats you and other city employees like crap when the public isn't watching."

"Milbrandt confuses intimidation for motivation," Stroud said. "He thinks aggression is a synonym for leadership. Unfortunately, he's pretty symbolic of what we have for government and business leaders today. Quite a few so-called leaders were officers in the war, but they forget that they're not in the army anymore. They don't know how to get out front, set an example. They prefer to push. Nobody works harder because of Milbrandt; it's more in spite of him. Thankfully, we have a lot of people at the city who care deeply about what they do, and they want to do it right."

"Okay, I get that," Lauder said. "But unlike in some states, Wisconsin cities have police and fire commissions that are supposedly nonpolitical, independent bodies that pick the police chief and officiate over promotions, compensation, and complaints. That means Milbrandt has no authority over you. So why would the chief and the rest of you take orders from him?"

"You put your finger on part of the answer," Stroud replied. "You said 'supposedly nonpolitical.' And Milbrandt is a true political animal. His breed never lets anything like rules, regulations, laws, or commissions get in the way of a grandstanding political performance. And keep in mind, that no matter what the police and fire commission says or does, the city council still controls the budget."

Stroud direly wished he could just head home, flop in his easy chair, and thumb through retirement magazines, but he headed into his office, where the chair was anything but comfortable. Time was running out to find answers. He pulled out his crumpled notebook, thumbed through his notes, and started making a list of people he needed to push for answers.

Milbrandt was dead wrong about city council meetings never attracting as many people as his press conference. Wednesday night, the council chamber was filled to overflowing. Nobody was there to talk about sewer pipes or zoning code variances. The topic was murder.

"Ladies and gentlemen, I understand you all want to know who killed that boy," Milbrandt began. "We are very close to wrapping it up. But please be patient. This meeting is to conduct the city's business and not—"

"This *is* the city's business!" shouted an irate man. "We have crazy people running around killing children, and you aren't doing anything to stop it."

"You work for us, Milbrandt," another angry voice screamed. "We want answers and we want action and we want it right now!"

Milbrandt saw that the outraged crowd was in no mood for compromise. He leaned back and instructed the council secretary to summon Chief Schmidt and some officers. "Okay, okay. Folks, the case is progressing. I am confident no one is in danger. We have the perpetrator in custody."

"Apparently, the cops don't share your confidence," Otto Jensen, a burly rubber company worker shouted. "Some people wonder how your 'perpetrator' could have committed the murders and had enough time to get from the church back to the hospital."

Otto knew Peder from high school and had worked alongside him for a decade. They never became close friends, but they did slip out to the Hilltop Bar occasionally after a long shift. Otto knew Peder had issues, serious issues, but he also seriously doubted Peder would sexually assault a child.

"First off, we don't know there have been two murders—" Milbrandt began, but was cut off.

"How about the possibility that he had help?" the factory worker persisted. "Let's come right out with it—we all know this is Peder Korsen we're talking about here. His kid was at the church too that night, and he has a car. Face it—it looks like it runs in the family. Now the kid is probably nuts just like his old man."

"Council President, this guy just walked away from the insane asylum and started killing our kids," a new voice spoke. "We need to shut that place down or, at the very least, make certain that people can't just walk out of there. Nobody's safe!"

While their neighbors raged in city hall, Ginger and Jason stayed home. They wanted nothing to do with being the center of attention at the city council meeting. Little did they know how this bad situation was threatening to get far worse.

CHAPTER 15

MAY 16, 1959

Scoutmaster McQuillan feared for his boys. They hadn't had a troop meeting since Roy was found dead nearly two weeks earlier. McQuillan knew the boys were trapped in the eye of the storm that had overtaken the city. Especially Jason. He needed to change that.

At a loss and unable to put the right words together on his own, he asked Detective Stroud to attend a special meeting for the Scouts and their parents. McQuillan requested it be at Longfellow Elementary School rather than Saint Luke. Just the thought of going into that church basement, where they last saw Roy, was difficult. McQuillan then personally visited every Scout's house and invited the boys and parents to the special troop meeting on Saturday, May 16.

That night, every Scout came along with his parents—and so did a massive crowd of uninvited neighbors. They filled the gym beyond capacity before 7:00 p.m. It was well beyond standing room only, and an overflow crowd jammed the hallway, pushing and shoving to gain entrance.

Amidst the din, the normally rambunctious Scouts were deadly quiet, eerily quiet. Even assistant scoutmaster Lloyd Harris looked uneasy as he sat motionless staring into space in uncharacteristic silence.

Jason found it impossible to ignore the accusing glares fixed on him.

"We gotta get out of here," he whispered to his mother.

"No. That would only suggest we have something to hide. We need to show them otherwise. You didn't do anything wrong." Ginger shifted in her chair, turned to look deeply into Jason's eyes, and struggled to wish away his pain. "And despite his troubles, your dad would never do what they said."

Scoutmaster McQuillan gaped at the crowd. "Excuse me, folks," he called out, trying to gain some control. "This is a private meeting. If you're not part of this Scout troop, I would ask that you please leave at this time."

"Why is that kid here?" one of the nosy neighbors barked, aiming a finger at Jason.

"Because he's one of us," McQuillan shot back. "I know him well and I trust him absolutely."

"Well, I don't trust him one bit."

"Yeah, did you hear that Jason kills animals?" a new voice interrupted. "Everybody in town heard about him slicing a cat in half with a butcher knife the other night. That's how Ed Gein started, you know."

Jason tried to melt into his chair. While the accuser had several points wrong (for starters, there was never any report that Gein, the infamous butcher of Plainfield, Wisconsin, killed animals), Jason couldn't deflect the entire statement. In truth, Jason had killed a *rat*, not a cat, a few nights earlier. And yes, he had sliced it in half with a butcher knife.

Jason hadn't attended school since Roy's death and his father's arrest. Unable to focus amid the incessant, worried chatter at home, he often escaped to work. He was night manager at Ralph Heckel's Crispy Chick, one of Eau Claire's first pizza places. He cooked up deep-fried chicken and fish in boiling vegetable oil as well as baked the "world's finest pizza" in Ralph's giant oven. Scars from burning the back of his hand scooping hot pies from the 450-degree blast furnace served as permanent reminders.

The night in question, Jason had no more than tied his chef's apron when Patrick, one of the delivery guys, burst through the front door screaming that a giant rat was patrolling the curb, flashing vicious white incisors, and driving away customers. Patrick dove for cover behind the front counter.

As manager, Jason took action. He grabbed the meat cleaver he used to quarter chickens, and he walked to the front door still wearing his blood-stained apron, reminiscent of Mr. Stange. The rest of the crew cowered a few paces behind.

Sure enough, right outside the door stood a defiant rat swelling to the size of a rabid Doberman pinscher. Without thinking, Jason flung the cleaver at the beast, hoping to scare it away. Rather, the flying steel blade sliced the rat in two. Jason spun around and marched triumphantly into the restaurant, pleased with the unexpected solution to the problem.

Every eye fixed on Jason. Mouths hung open in momentary paralysis.

"Patrick, clean up that mess and sterilize my cleaver!" he ordered.

The next day, the story was all over town, swelling with exaggeration in each retelling. At first, Jason basked in the sunburst of his fame as the rat slayer. He was happy that something positive was blowing away the constant haze of darkness surrounding his dad's arrest. But now it seemed the darkness had enshrouded Jason again, turning the rat incident into seemingly damning evidence.

Just then, Detective Stroud, two uniformed police officers, and a young woman wove their way through the crowd. McMillan looked as relieved as Jason did to see them.

Stroud moved to the front of the room. "Good evening. Thank you for coming. But as scoutmaster McMillan said, this is a private meeting for the boys and their parents. Everyone else must leave at this time."

Grumbling and hollow threats rumbled through the room as the outsiders slowly departed.

McQuillan stepped forward with renewed confidence. "I have nothing new to tell you about Roy's death. Or Sonja's disappearance, for that matter. I just called this meeting because we're all suffering, and our boys need to know we care deeply about them. Before we hear from the police, does anyone have a question?"

Feet shuffled and heads turned back and forth, but there was barely a sound for at least a minute. Finally, a woman's voice almost whispered from the back of the room.

"What are we to do? Roy was murdered and that choir girl has disappeared. And the police don't seem to know what happened. How do we protect our kids from this invisible monster?"

McQuillan's face suddenly glistened with sweat as he searched for an answer. "You are right. It's terrifying. That's why we're here—to support one another. It's important that everyone think really hard about what they saw that night and what they know about Roy and Sonja and all the people who were at the church. There is an answer and we can find it. I asked Detective Stroud to come tonight to answer your questions, but please do not hesitate to call me any time you want to talk. I am available to meet with you or your sons. We are in this together. That's how we'll solve it."

He paused, waiting for another question, but the parents and

Scouts sat motionless. McQuillan turned to Stroud.

"I am so sorry you have to deal with this horrible situation," Stroud said, addressing the crowd. "I wish I could say we've wrapped up the investigation. But the more I learn, the less convinced I am that we have the right man in jail. In fact, after talking extensively with Mr. Korsen, meeting with his doctors and nurses, and trying to work out the timeline for him that night, I doubt very much that he was involved with the murder of your friend Roy."

Jason snapped his head forward, ready to applaud. It was the first positive sentence to enter his ears since Roy died. Maybe there was hope. As he looked around the room, it felt as though a chain had been removed from his neck. The nasty, penetrating stares suddenly turned to surprise.

"What are you saying? If it's not him, is the killer still running around?" a startled mother shouted.

"The investigation is continuing, but yes—unfortunately, that may be the case. It's highly probable that the person who killed Roy Pettit has not been identified or arrested."

This revelation was not the calming comment anyone sought. Now there was plenty of noise as restless parents struck up conversations throughout the room. What started as a din rippled back and forth, growing into a roar.

Stroud spoke up in a loud voice imploring parents to listen. "Ladies and gentlemen—please give me your attention. As scoutmaster McQuillan said, we are in this together, and that is how we will solve it. You were all present at the meeting on May 5. Someone in this room may have even a small bit of information that could lead us to the perpetrator. These two officers and I will be available following this meeting, or you can take one of my cards and call me anytime, day or night. Your name can be on the record or anonymous.

"Right now, we just need information. Something to go on. Anything. If you saw Roy after the meeting, was he with anyone? Do you know why he went to the park that night? On your way home that night, did you pass the park and notice anything—a car, somebody walking, anything at all? Even the most seemingly inane observation may prove pivotal to our investigation. Don't worry about 'wasting' our time. What you saw may be a small piece in the bigger puzzle, and every piece helps build a complete picture of what happened."

He then turned to the woman seated next to him. She rose to her feet. Her disarming pixie appearance—with blemish-free skin framed by jet-black hair trimmed to a perfect bob—belied the strength and determination just under the surface. She was far too attractive to be labeled tough, but everyone simply knew she was. No one in her presence—not even powerful, well-educated men—could avoid being engulfed in the aura of strength she radiated.

"I'd like to introduce Mrs. Jessie Simonson. She is a nationally recognized expert in mental health care. She has been a nurse at the Eau Claire County Asylum and a psychiatric assistant. She now teaches psychiatric nursing at the college while completing her doctorate. She'll be available to answer your questions and to assist anyone in dealing with the pain."

With that, Stroud brought the meeting to an end. He was more than a little disappointed when many people flocked to Jessie but no one came up to him. No one, that is, except *Telegram* reporter Bobby Lauder, who had somehow managed to sit in on this private Scouts-only meeting.

"So, you still don't think Korsen is your guy?"

"At this point," Stroud said, "I don't know what to think. We don't have a lot to go on if nobody comes forward with a tip. I sure wish that girl who found the body would call me back."

Unlike the police, Jessie Simonson drew a crowd of anxious mothers asking what to tell their children, how to keep them safe. After more than an hour, the crowd finally filtered out the doors with more questions than answers.

"Let's get going," Ginger said, glancing at her watch. "Your grandmother and Sidney are waiting for us in the car."

Jason followed his mother to the doorway, then hesitated.

"Go ahead, Mom. I'm gonna talk to Mr. McQuillan. I'll walk home or get a ride with him."

White lies are sometimes necessary, he thought as his mother headed for the car. It wasn't the scoutmaster he wanted to talk with; it was the psychologist.

When Jessie appeared at the door, heading to the parking lot, Jason spoke up. "Mrs. Simonson? Excuse me. I'm wondering if you know my father at the asylum."

She smiled. "Absolutely. He's one of my favorite patients. I've known him for many years."

Jason hesitated. "Do you think he did this?"

"No. I'm quite certain he did not."

"Well," Jason said with a sigh, "then you're about the only person in town who thinks that other than me and maybe Detective Stroud. Nobody seems interested in finding out who really killed Roy. But what can I do? I'm just a high school kid—son of the crazy killer. Could you help me?"

She pointed to the park bench on the lawn outside the now-dark school. Jessie and Jason sat as scoutmaster McQuillan and his son Bob Jr. exited the school and headed to their car. They waved and smiled in passing.

As they waited for everyone to clear the area, Jason was unsure how to proceed. He glanced left, toward the playground where he had spent so many hours in recess and playing sports after school. There at the far end, he spotted the jungle gym, where he had learned one of life's bitter lessons.

It was a chilly sub-zero December day during third grade. After school, he and Rhonda Lewis were at the jungle gym. She told him his tongue would stick if he licked one of the metal bars. He didn't believe it. What did she know?

As she spurred him on, Jason proudly grabbed the horizontal steel bar and showed his arm strength with five quick chin-ups. With each curl, he stuck out his tongue and teased it near the bar. Then on the sixth chin-up, he pulled himself up six inches off the ground. And just to prove how stupid Rhonda was, he tasted the bar with the tip of his tongue.

She was right. Try as he might, there was no way to pull his tongue free—until his arms grew weary and he tumbled to the ground, leaving the tip still attached. He stuck what was left of his tongue in a snowball to quell the bleeding. The snow turned crimson.

But that pain was minimal compared to what happened the next day. As Jason entered Mrs. Kopp's third grade room, late as usual, Rhonda led the class in sticking out their tongues and roaring in a chorus of laughter. Mrs. Kopp demanded silence and order even as she turned her head to avoid revealing a smile.

At the time, Jason thought his world was coming to an end. Life couldn't get any worse. Little did he know that a year later, his father would disappear in the mental asylum. And now the murder of his friend Roy and his dad being a prime suspect ratcheted his misery scale even higher.

What next? If he had learned anything, he knew better than to ever think life can't get any worse.

Seeing Jason staring out at the playground, Jessie brought him back with a gentle hand on his shoulder. As she looked into his eyes she said, "I do have some thoughts on what kind of person killed your friend," Jessie offered. "Your dad just doesn't fit the profile. The police should be looking closely at everyone who was at the church that night, especially those who work with kids. It's highly unlikely this is just someone out of the blue, like your dad. Roy didn't know him. Rather, it's probably someone Roy trusted."

Jason slowly nodded. He had been thinking the same thing all along—with one specific person in mind.

"Then again," Jessie added, "while we highly doubt your dad is the one, we both need to keep an open mind to that possibility. If we're going to find the right killer, we can't be like everyone else and start with any preconceived ideas. We need to be open to all possibilities."

"We?" Jason repeated, leaping to his feet. "So you're going to help?"

Jessie stood in affirmation. Tall for a woman, she looked him in the eyes and said with conviction, "You bet. I don't know what I can do, but I'll try."

"Well, you're a big wheel and people will listen to you, especially the police. I saw that newspaper guy talking to Detective Stroud. Would you be willing to tell him what you told me about the kind of person they should be looking for? And could you tell him you know my dad and that he doesn't fit the profile? Maybe we can at least get people thinking there might be another suspect."

"Sure. I can do that."

"And one more thing," Jason said quickly, then paused. "Will you tell me about my dad and what it's like there at the asylum?"

"What do you want to know?"

"Everything."

CHAPTER 16

Jason and Jessie settled back onto the bench while Jessie revealed details of a life Jason had never known—his father's life.

"Your dad is definitely my favorite resident," Jessie revealed. "He almost never causes a problem. He's a voracious reader to the point that we have difficulty finding enough books for him. At breakfast, he regales staff by retelling every story from yesterday's newspaper almost verbatim. Everybody calls him the Professor."

As Jessie explained, that nickname came from his intellect as well as his habit of smoking a pipe. Almost every night, the college aides and some of the staff played cards, drank coffee or pop, and smoked cigarettes with the residents. Smoke was so thick that a blue cloud covered the lounge.

"I'm amazed everyone doesn't have lung cancer," Jessie added.

Peder had to give up his Chesterfields when he came to the hospital. Cigarettes had to be hand-rolled with fragile papers and with tobacco scooped from large red Prince Albert cans. Peder bypassed the cigarette assembly line and stuffed tobacco into his hand-carved basswood pipe instead. Pipe tobacco was free.

When he wasn't reading or working in the bakery, the Professor watched television in his room or walked in the fields smoking his pipe, wearing a frayed light-gray Perry Como sweater unbuttoned. He always stuffed his left hand in the pocket, permanently stretching that side of the sweater out of shape.

"He's not very social," she said. "At least not with the other patients. He mostly only talks with staff. He sees himself as one of us, having to deal with 'the crazies in this prison.'"

Jason smiled, remembering his father making a similar comment the time the family visited him in the asylum. But then his smile faded.

"Do you think my dad is dangerous?" Jason asked.

According to Jessie, Peder was never a threat except on rare occasions when he decided he no longer required medication for his schizophrenia.

"He has those bright blue eyes that are almost hypnotic," she said. "I can see it in his eyes whenever he begins to show symptoms of agitation."

She detailed how he would become more antisocial than normal with the other patients and how he'd walk about in circles, mumbling incoherently. Left unchecked, his behavior would take a sudden turn and manifest in shouting, tossing books, and warning of impending invasion by demons that would inhabit vulnerable people's minds.

"What's it like working at the asylum?" Jason inquired, moving the discussion in a new direction. "How did you ever decide to do that?"

Jessie grew up on a 100-acre farm just west of town, right below the hill where the asylum overlooked everything. As she described it, Jason realized it was the farm where Grandma Libby grew up.

"I think we may be some kind of distant cousins," Jason said, remembering stories about who had taken over the Oldhurst farm. "Or as Grams says, 'shirttail relatives.'"

Before most kids got out of bed each morning, Jessie fed a large herd of cattle as well as pigs, goats, sheep, chickens, and her horses, Albert and Starr. Her brothers drew the tasks of keeping the barns clean and doing the twice-daily milking. She thought nothing of tossing around fifty-pound bales of feed hay as if they were bed pillows.

She spent more time playing ball games with the boys than playing with dolls or anything normally associated with young ladies. By sixth grade, she popped up to five-feet-nine and was by far the best hitter and pitcher on the Eau Claire Junior Bears Little League baseball team.

Unfortunately, no girls were allowed by Little League rules, so the coaches called her James and passed her off as a boy. Most of the boys on the other teams didn't realize she was a girl—or they were afraid to admit it.

Jessie "James" was the star player until hormones started organizing during eighth grade. That was when her body decided she was no boy. It suddenly displayed all the right parts in all the right places.

One guy who had no trouble identifying gender was her teammate Skeeter Davies. He was a couple of inches shorter than her, but he decided it was time to get friendly with his pitcher.

"Hey, *James*," he said with a chuckle. "I'm your second baseman. So how 'bout you let me get to second?"

"Stay away from me, you sick little dweeb, or I'll give you a good look at my fastball."

The speedy little infielder grabbed Jessie's left breast with all the flash and finesse he normally saved for turning a double play. He was looking for a reaction, but he got a violent left hook to the face instead. A volcano erupted under his nose, quickly turning his clean white shirt to crimson. An unsympathetic chorus of laughter roared from his teammates.

In high school, Jessie reluctantly joined the girls' softball team, where she dominated every game. She even tried powder puff football but dropped out when the other girls complained she was too rough. Mostly, she continued to be infuriated that she couldn't play baseball and "real" football with the boys.

Jessie was a college sophomore at Eau Claire State Teachers College in 1949 when she spotted a poster describing job opportunities at the asylum. She didn't bother tearing off a phone number dangling from the bottom of the sheet like a row of teeth. She just ripped down the entire poster and stuffed it into her book bag.

Most people, including her parents, were terrified when she applied for a job at the "nuthouse" as a mental health nursing aide. The mere thought of working there was unsettling enough to discourage most students, but not Jessie.

Jessie remembered heading to the asylum to interview with Assistant Administrator Thelma Livingston. She walked rapidly up a winding road obscured from the sky beneath a long dark-green canopy of majestic white oaks. The road led to a foreboding dark castle planted high atop a tall hill. She couldn't keep her eyes off the farm fields, where zombielike inhabitants strolled about.

Most students never made it up the driveway to the asylum. Of the few who did, hardly any ventured through the mammoth porch that threatened to digest trespassers. Jessie was undeterred, however—more energized with every step.

Livingston leaped to attention as Jessie appeared in her office doorway. The office was sterile white with a blond wooden desk that may have dated back to the previous century. There was no art on the walls, but there were three photos of grandchildren on the desk and a ten-by-twelve-inch dish to display a miniature garden she tended daily with a tiny rake and watering tin.

Livingston never left home without being impeccably dressed, and she visited Rona's Beauty Salon every Thursday. More than slightly overweight, she seemed to bring her battle with calories into every discussion, even while munching on one of the sweet treats she kept in the lower left drawer.

"Come right in," Livingston said, working to mask her

enthusiasm. She was desperate to hire nursing aides.

Jessie settled into one of two straight-back wooden guest chairs and smiled at the matronly administrator.

But before the interview even started, a ruckus erupted in the hallway right outside the office. A shrill alarm blared down from the ceiling, summoning immediate assistance.

Bolting to the door, Livingston confronted two elderly men yelling, wrestling on the floor, and throwing wild punches in the air. Four large staff members materialized, seemingly from nowhere, and quickly separated the pugilists.

"Norman, what's this all about?" Livingston demanded, looking at one of the elderly men.

"He looked at me."

"Now, Norman, that's no good reason to punch somebody. I thought Joe was your friend."

"Yeah. I guess. But he shouldn't be lookin' at me."

"Oh, Norman—stop it. Right now. These gentlemen will take both of you back to your rooms. They'll give you something to calm your nerves and help you sleep."

Without skipping a beat, Livingston slipped behind her desk as though she had only stepped outside to check the weather. She assumed a business-as-usual attitude.

"Well, let's talk about you, Jessie."

"I saw a poster about job opportunities here, and it seems perfect for me. I'm a psych major." She paused. "So, what was all the commotion out in the hallway?"

"Nothing serious. Those boys really are harmless. You just can't let them push things too far. I hope that isn't a problem for you."

"Naw. I've got four older brothers, and I go toe to toe with them just about every day. Plus, I've got cows and bulls a lot bigger and tougher than your guys."

Looking at Jessie's application, Livingston wanted to shout for joy. "Jessie, your application looks very, very good. When can you start?"

Jessie was thrilled. If all worked out with this job, she would have steady income and invaluable on-the-job experience for the next five years while she finished her bachelor's and master's degrees in psychiatric health. Maybe even a doctorate. The perfect plan.

By the end of her first week, Jessie was convinced she had accrued enough education in mental illness to already qualify for her bachelor's degree. Her second night on duty got interesting when the charge nurse handed the nineteen-year-old student aide a flashlight and told her to go up to the third floor to count the patients.

"Keep the lights off. Just get a head count," the nurse instructed.

Okay. No problem, Jessie thought. *I can do this. It's no different than walking into the barn with all the animals at night.*

The third floor was very dark, illuminated only by two forty-watt side lamps and slivers of muted moonlight peeking through the windows. A long hallway spanned the front of the building, interrupted every few feet by one of several doorways opening into a gigantic room. There, thirty stark white-steel beds sat side by side with just enough room for staff to tend to patients. The cavernous room was ghostly silent with the exception of an occasional grunt or snore.

Some of the big blobs concealed under bedsheets didn't appear to move, so Jessie decided it would be wise to make certain everyone was breathing. She played her flashlight on each bed until she detected movement.

Suddenly, heavy footfalls slapping down the hallway in a rhythmic pattern shattered the calm stillness. Jessie spun around just as the most mammoth human creature she had ever encountered stepped up to her.

"You!" he roared. "Will get a pot of gold at the end of the rainbow!"

Then he slowly turned and walked away.

When Jessie started breathing again, she hastily finished checking off the remaining beds. She then shot downstairs, where she reported to the charge nurse.

"Twenty-seven living souls. All breathing and sound asleep— except for the giant."

"Oh, sorry. I forgot to tell you about Harold. He wanders around talking about rainbows every night. He's a bit scary but totally harmless. For some reason, his sleeping pills don't always work."

Through her years on the job, Jessie always thought calling the asylum a "hospital" was a misnomer. In her mind, hospitals were places where sick and injured people were sent. Once they got well, they went home. With exception of a few patients who responded well to treatments, most people who arrived at the asylum took up permanent residence there—they joined the family.

Of course, Jessie realized the word *asylum* had its own issues. An asylum, by definition, was a calming place of refuge and protection from a noisy world. But with most people fearing mental illness, the word *asylum* seemed to incite horror.

It didn't help that psychiatrists throughout the region saw the county asylums as their personal laboratories. Eau Claire had three resident psychiatrists, plus a herd of visiting psychiatrists who regularly ventured eighty miles down Highway 12 from Minneapolis and Saint Paul. For them, the asylum was a place to experiment with insulin shock therapy, hydrotherapy, electroshock, and lobotomy as well as every manner of new pharmaceutical potion. A few treatments worked miracles, but the calming effect—especially of the medications—was generally more beneficial to the hospital staff than to the patients.

The bulk of the more than 350 residents just adapted to life in the small bubble that had become their entire world. Most residents tended to be reticent, some catatonic. A few unique personalities made daily life entertaining, and a couple could be threatening.

Viola was a petite middle-aged woman who occasionally suffered severe manic episodes. Most of the time, she appeared absolutely normal. So normal that while she was home with her family on a weekend pass in preparation for possible release, she responded to a nearby nursing home's help-wanted ad for a cook. She had the wherewithal to assemble a respectable résumé, and she impressed the nursing home director sufficiently to get hired. But when the first meal was burnt to a crisp, Viola broke into tears and confessed she was no cook.

Back at the asylum after this emotional experience, she immediately donned her favorite leopard-print pajamas and began pacing briskly back and forth in the hallway.

"Quick—call for assistance," Livingston told Jessie. "Viola's about to go ballistic."

Before the orderlies arrived, Viola was screaming profanities at the walls. Within seconds, six big orderlies arrived, and it took all their energy to subdue Viola as they tumbled to the floor.

A diminutive nurse raised her arm high with a hypodermic syringe full of sedative. She slammed it down toward Viola. But the human pile jerked left, and the nurse punctured her own thigh with 250 milligrams of a potent sedative. As the orderlies carried Viola to a "seclusion room," Jessie managed to drag the nurse to a nearby couch, where she was left to sleep it off.

There was one seclusion room on each ward. It was considered a necessary evil to confine "overly excited" patients until they calmed down. It was essentially a small, sterile space with padded walls, windows covered with stout wire mesh, and nothing but a mattress on the floor. Generally, a strong sedative and a night of rest were sufficient.

A week after the Viola incident, another commotion caught Jessie's attention. Inside one of the rooms, she came face to face with Agnes, who had busted out a window and was violently slicing through the air with a large, jagged piece of glass. Agnes wasn't attacking Jessie as much as she was attacking some invisible creature.

Jessie grabbed Agnes's arm to prevent her from injuring herself or Jessie. Just then, an orderly appeared and slapped Agnes from behind with a wicked blow, causing her to drop the glass.

"Watch out! She's going to bite you," the orderly barked. "You can't let that happen. Human bites are the worst."

Jessie did her best to avoid Agnes's gnashing teeth until more orderlies magically materialized. They wrestled Agnes into a straight-jacket and secured her to a gurney.

Jessie had already witnessed how even a tiny patient such as Viola could somehow morph into a powerful combatant during a manic episode. But Agnes was not tiny. She was nearly six feet tall, young, stocky, extremely strong, and known for violence. One other night, she got behind a large male orderly, wrapped her arms around him in a powerful bear hug, and smashed him face first into a wall. She busted his nose, spray-painting the dingy white wall in burgundy, and broke three of his ribs before help arrived.

This night, they made certain to get her under control. Agnes lurched so ferociously on the gurney, they feared she would topple it. A nurse administered three shots of Haldol, but it only seemed to infuriate the increasingly distressed patient. The team held her to avoid injury to anyone, especially herself. A nurse kept talking calmly.

And then, without warning, it was over. Agnes just fell asleep. When she awoke the next day, it was as though nothing had happened. She didn't recall the incident at all. She would be calm and agreeable for days, but her capricious nature and physical strength demanded that staff always stay vigilant around her.

The most acute and dangerous residents lived in the Two-North ward, where Jessie worked in the Active Treatment Unit. At one time, the administration and nursing offices were isolated on the first floor. But one of Dr. Mentzil's first actions as superintendent had been to move his staff right into the Active Treatment Unit, a move not universally applauded by staff and fought vigorously by the union president.

"We need to be part of the residents' lives all the time, not just for medical treatments and emergencies," Mentzil told his staff. "Get to know them as people and treat them with respect. We can't just lock them away like zoo animals. People tend to do what you expect of them. If you lock them up like animals and don't talk with them, then they will act like animals. On the other hand, if you engage in casual conversation and treat them just as you would your friends and neighbors, they will grow to trust you and will be far less likely to cause problems. If we hope to adjust their behavior, help them recover, we need to adjust our own thinking and actions. We need to gain their trust."

He was right. There were exceptions, to be sure, but most residents became like family. They freely shared their thoughts and dreams with staff—sometimes more than desired, especially for Livingston, who had a constant parade of residents dropping into her office. Staff compared notes at the beginning of every shift and got to know every resident thoroughly. They knew who to trust, whose buttons they could push, and who they couldn't mess with.

Oscar—a silent, stern-faced mountain of a man—was one of the special residents who demanded constant attention. With his square jaw, always stern expression, and blank stare, the big man was an earthquake lying dormant just below the surface. And sometimes a sudden tectonic shift would throw his mind into high gear. Without warning, he'd erupt into a violent, dangerous beast, yet a beast that could be controlled with the right approach.

Livingston was sitting in her office one day when she heard Oscar yelling and the echo of shattering glass. Rushing down the hallway, she discovered he had tossed a metal chair through the window.

"Oscar! What in the world did you do?" she shouted.

He froze in his tracks.

"Go to your room, Oscar," she ordered with authority.

And he did.

Jessie arrived on the scene and followed Livingston back into her office. "Are you okay? Wow. I guess we're gonna need some heavier screens on the windows."

"Oh, my God," Livingston replied. "He could have snapped me like a matchstick."

She collapsed into her desk chair, reached into the bottom drawer of her desk, and grabbed two Hostess Twinkies.

"God, I love these stupid things," she said as she stuffed one in her mouth and handed the other to Jessie.

Jessie wasn't a Twinkie fan, but she felt compelled to accept it and choke down a couple of bites.

The orderlies found Oscar resting peacefully in his bed. They locked him safely in the room after ensuring he felt fine—he just wanted to sleep.

The only truly egregious event at the asylum started under the watch of Gary Simonson—Jessie's now-husband. Like Jessie, Gary was a student aide from Eau Claire State Teachers College. After years of working together, Gary eventually asked Jessie out. Romance caught fire instantly. Within a week, they were spending every available minute together. Two weeks after graduating from college, they married.

Two years before they married, however, Gary was charged with the task of repainting the asylum's 130-foot-high water tower one warm summer afternoon. Two trusted patients, Jake and Raymond from the maintenance crew, were assigned to help. Gary had frequently worked with them on painting, cleaning, and repairing tasks throughout the facility. Both guys worked hard, and neither had ever posed a discipline problem. They seemed to love maintenance work and were good at it.

Less than an hour into the job, unexpectedly Jake decided he didn't want to paint anymore. He just sat down on the top of the giant pot of water.

"How come he don't work?" Raymond demanded.

"Don't worry about it, Ray—I'll talk to him," Gary said.

But before Gary could move, Raymond stomped across the top of the tower, right through the wet baby-blue paint. He grabbed Jake and tossed him over the side. Gary stared at the open space where Jake had been. He was engulfed in shock, imagining himself locked inside the scene of a movie. *That didn't just happen.* He almost didn't notice Raymond quietly stroll past and descend the metal ladder as though nothing had happened.

Jake died on impact. With no known family, he was buried in the hospital cemetery, where indigent patients and those who were unwanted by their families were laid to rest.

Raymond was immediately retrieved from his room and taken to Dr. Mentzil's office, where Livingston and Gary were asked to assist. Gary couldn't clear his mind of the graphic vision of Jake flying off the water tower—it kept replaying over and over in an endless nightmare from which he could not awaken. He was barely aware of the procedure as he was instructed to secure Raymond to a narrow operating bed with leather straps and to place a red rubber guard in his mouth.

Dr. Mentzil completed a lobotomy in less than ten minutes.

Raymond was semiconscious as Gary wheeled him back to his room. Gary or an orderly took shifts sitting by Raymond's bed through the night to watch for complications. Other than two black eyes and a severe headache the next morning, the previously violent offender said he felt no pain. He became calm and cooperative. It would take three weeks for the headache to subside, but Raymond was no longer a discipline problem. He sat motionless, staring off into space most of the time. He spoke only when asked simple questions, and then he responded with yes or no or just nodded his head.

Three days after the lobotomy, Jessie was in Livingston's office when resident psychiatrist Dr. Nigel Rigby stormed past them without as much as a nod or a hello. He burst into Mentzil's office.

"My God, Cecil. What in the hell were you thinking? You can't be performing lobotomies in your office like some goddamn dentist pulling a tooth. Are you completely out of your mind?"

"Don't say another word, Rigby. I know exactly what I am doing. If you bothered to examine Raymond, you would know he is much improved."

"*Improved?* He's a vegetable. You call that improved?"

"Absolutely. He is no longer violent. He is beginning to participate in some activities, and he communicates calmly with the staff. He may have some ways to go for full recovery, but he is much improved."

"You're no surgeon—what possessed you to perform this procedure?"

Mentzil slowly rose to his feet, tugged downward with both hands on his vest, and paused to gather his thoughts. "I have had surgical training. I studied and practiced on cadavers with Walter Freeman, who has done hundreds. As you may know, he developed the transorbital lobotomy."

"Are you talking about Freeman's infamous ice pick lobotomy?" Rigby asked.

His face contorted in a mixture of shock and anger at his associate's casual acceptance of what many deemed an unacceptable, horrific procedure.

"Yes," Mentzil replied somewhat distastefully. "The press may like to sensationalize the procedure, but it's far less dangerous and much more successful than previous methods."

Rigby shook his head. "If you insist on continuing with such procedures, I'm not sure I can continue to work here."

"That's your choice, Nigel." Mentzil flipped his hand toward the other doctor as if dismissing him. "I can say the procedure is not something we will do often, but in extreme cases, I will keep it as an option. Freeman has done hundreds of them all over the country. Is it better to just leave people locked away forever, or do we take a slight risk to give them the potential to have a life back? Walter said forty to fifty percent recover sufficiently to be released, and even those who remain hospitalized are far better emotionally and safer for our staff and other patients."

"Cecil, this has the making of some Hollywood horror film. You are feeding into the worst image people have of mental hospitals. Hell, it borders on thoughts of Frankenstein or Josef Mengele. And all this time, I've supported your decision to integrate the staff into the residents' lives and not treat them as wild animals caged in a zoo. But this—this I will not tolerate." He spun about and departed, leaving his words to dangle about Mentzil's head.

For whatever reason, Mentzil never performed another lobotomy. He claimed no other patient met his criteria for the procedure. But Jessie just figured that Rigby had made his point.

There on the bench in front of the school, Jessie let out a long breath, then gave Jason a small smile.

"As with everything in life, the strange and exceptional events at the asylum stand out. But most of the time, I really enjoy working there. I see it as ninety-nine percent routine and one percent absolute panic. The residents are like my adopted family. I've grown to love most of them very much. It's truly only a handful that cause problems. Not unlike society in general," she added.

Jessie described how she and Gary often loaded up the hospital bus and hauled patients to parks, theaters, and the Chippewa Falls Zoo. But activities and entertainment mostly happened at the hospital in a large ballroom and a canteen area that offered a variety of snacks and nonalcoholic beverages.

There was also a leather workshop, a woodworking area, and a photography studio with complete film-developing facilities. Residents had many opportunities to learn new skills. Many studied painting with a visiting artist.

Movies were shown several nights a week in the grand hall. Gary often brought in giant bags of popcorn he purchased from the Cameo Theater. Perhaps the biggest event of the month was dance night. Live bands filled the hall with lively tunes, and there was dancing until 11:00 p.m. Not everyone danced, but just about everyone enjoyed the music.

"Wow," Jason said.

He tried to absorb everything Jessie had revealed about his dad, the asylum, and her own life.

"It's like my dad lives in something of an alternate universe," he finally said. "Thank you for sharing all this."

"That's a good way to look at it—it is something of an alternate universe," Jessie said. "I find myself often thinking of the two worlds in which I live, and sometimes I'm not certain which is the 'sane' one. Speaking of my worlds," she said, getting to her feet, "I better head home. Your mother probably is wondering where you are as well. I'll go see Bobby Lauder at the newspaper tomorrow morning. I promise. Do you need a ride home?"

"No, but thanks. The walk home will give me time to think. I can't tell you how much I appreciate talking with you. Thank you. Thank you."

Jessie smiled and headed for her car. Jason began retracing the steps he had taken every school day from kindergarten to sixth grade—right past the church, McDonough Park, and the cemetery. As he walked, he replayed Jessie's comments like a recording in his mind.

For the first time, it struck him that mentally ill people might be calm, happy, and talkative one second and burst into violent, dangerous animals the next—like two different people in one body. With that in mind, he couldn't entirely cast aside the thought that perhaps his dad had just snapped and killed Roy. But the more he considered that option, the more he believed his dad didn't do it.

And the more he believed he knew who did.

CHAPTER 17

MAY 18, 1959

**POLICE NOT CONVINCED OF KORSEN GUILT,
RESUME SEARCH FOR MURDER SUSPECT**
By Bobby Lauder, *Eau Claire Telegram*

EAU CLAIRE, Wis. (AP)—Eau Claire police detectives said yesterday they are not convinced that Peder James Korsen committed the sexual attack and violent murder of Roy Allen Pettit on May 5 in McDonough Park near Dells Pond. Lead Detective Lt. Joseph Stroud said they have been unable to find evidence connecting Korsen to the scene and that interviews with county hospital officials cast serious doubt on Korsen's involvement.

"We are exploring other potential suspects," Detective Stroud said. "But we really could use some help from the public, particularly from the young woman who called to report Roy Pettit's murder. Somebody out there saw something that will give us the answer. They need to contact our office immediately before we have to deal with another child being murdered."

Eau Claire County Asylum Superintendent Cecil Mentzil, MD, reinforced Stroud's view. "Peder has been my patient for the past nine years and has become a trustee at the hospital. Through extensive treatment and drug therapy, he has improved remarkably to the point where I would trust him in my home. The idea that he viciously attacked a youngster is not believable. He is a very gentle man and has definitely never shown the slightest inclination toward pedophilia. I am confident he is not involved in this situation."

Another staff member who has worked closely with Korsen for several years, Jessie Walker Simonson, a nursing aide at the hospital and instructor in psychiatric nursing at Wisconsin State College, concurred with Dr. Mentzil. "Extensive research tells us that those who suffer from mental illness actually are far more likely to be victims of crime than perpetrators. I have worked with Peder almost every day for several years. I can say without question that he is less likely to have committed that murder than is City Council President Milbrandt. It is the height of hypocrisy for someone in authority to use this horrific event for political gain and to deflect police attention from focusing on finding the real killer."

Mrs. Simonson added, "The information I have obtained through years of medical research pertaining to pedophiles leads me to believe that the real killer most likely is an unmarried man, age twenty to forty, who lives alone or with a demanding parent, may work in a school or somewhere else where he can be in regular contact with children, possibly at the church. He probably is something of a social outcast, although he works very hard to win the trust of parents, and he is adept at talking with young people. He's someone who knew Roy Pettit well and is still walking around among us."

Milbrandt vigorously disagreed with the medical officials. "I have no doubt we have the right person in jail. Our police are compiling evidence that will keep him there for a long, long time. The folks from the asylum are merely trying to put a good face on their embarrassing failure."

A major challenge for police in charging Peder Korsen with the murder is the timeline. The Boy Scout program ended at approximately 8:30 p.m. and Korsen was stopped by police four miles away from the crime scene walking toward the hospital less than an hour later. Police feel it would have been nearly impossible for him to have committed the crime at McDonough Park and have had sufficient time to walk more than four miles. The suggestion that Korsen's son, who owns a car, may have been an accomplice is refuted by the fact that the son was with his family and Boy Scout leaders at the church until well after 9 p.m.

Police are combing through evidence collected at the scene and will resume canvassing people who were at the church on Tuesday, May 5. They ask that anyone who saw Roy Pettit or Peder Korsen after 8:30 p.m. that night or any other person who witnessed activity in the area of McDonough Park on the evening of May 5 to call Eau Claire Police at TEmple 4-9999. They are particularly anxious to hear from the young woman who called in after finding the body.

Bobby Lauder's story in the *Telegram* was hot. So hot, in fact, that it was the front-page lead for the *Leader* as well.

Like most cities of the mid-twentieth century, Eau Claire boasted two daily newspapers—the morning *Leader* and the afternoon *Telegram*. City Council President Milbrandt often painted both sets of reporters as nothing more than "local yokels." Truth was, they were the primary filters for all the news folks in Eau Claire and its surrounding territories consumed. Newspapers were "real." Anything on radio or television tended to be nothing more than excerpts lifted directly from the papers.

The *Leader* and *Telegram* were owned by the same company, and their newsrooms were in the same building, yet they were totally separate, physically and ideologically. Competition could not have been fiercer. Getting scooped on a story by the other daily was a capital offense that would push an editor toward violence.

It was highly unusual, therefore, for the *Leader* to pick up Lauder's story verbatim. Standard practice said, if a story had to be picked up from the other paper, the scooped paper would never run the story verbatim. Rather, the copy editor would bang out a quick rewrite to embellish some new twist to claim a level of separation and originality.

Printing Lauder's article as is was a blow to the *Leader*—though it was softened slightly by the fact that the national Associated Press newswire had also picked up the story. Thus, the *Leader* could consider it an AP feed rather than a *Telegram* reprint. The distinction meant nothing to anyone outside the newsroom, but somehow it seemed important within the ink-smudged chambers where twenty manual typewriters clattered away constantly.

Newsroom politics aside, the article enraged Milbrandt and tossed the city into a mass of confusion. It ignited fear of a child murderer still roaming their streets.

Back in his jail cell, Peder Korsen just wanted to know what was going on.

Why am I here? Where's my newspaper?

With exception of that outburst at work that led to his hospitalization, he had always been a rather stoic, even-tempered man. Years of treatments and medications in the asylum had solidified him as someone who never wavered greatly in emotion. Thus, neither rage nor fear erupted as he sat in jail. But he was growing increasingly curious and annoyed.

"Where's my newspaper?" he inquired as Sergeant Olberdorf delivered lunch.

Olberdorf cringed slightly and hoped Peder didn't notice it. "Oh, I forgot it," he fibbed. "Let me see if I can find one."

Olberdorf made a beeline for Stroud's office.

"Detective, your prisoner wants his newspaper, but I didn't know if that was such a good idea, seeing as his name is splashed all over the front page. What do you want me to do?"

Stroud nodded. "I see what you mean. Tell you what—I'll be down there soon. Give me the paper, and I'll bring it to him. I need to talk with him anyway."

Olberdorf retreated after dropping a copy of the *Leader* on Stroud's desk.

A few minutes later, Stroud appeared at the cell with the newspaper tucked under his arm. "Hello, Peder." The heavy door let out a piercing squeak as he opened it. "Geez, gotta get Olberdorf to squirt some oil on the hinges."

"It's okay. Nobody can sneak in that way," Peder said with a slight smile.

"How you feeling today?" Stroud asked.

"I'm fine, but I'm getting pretty tired of being here—especially with this torture board you call a bed. Why am I here anyway?"

"Well, that's what I want to talk about. First, why don't you read this?" Stroud handed the newspaper to Peder.

Peder sat almost motionless as he read. He slowly went over Lauder's article at least two times before he looked up in apparent disorientation.

"Why is my name in there? I had nothing to do with this. I never met that kid. What's going on here?"

Stroud decided to level with the man. "Peder, I'm sorry we had to put you through this, but City Council President Milbrandt has made you the lead suspect in this case. You did leave the asylum without permission, and you did attend the Scout meeting where that boy disappeared. I'm doing everything I can to clear you, but people tend to be fearful of anyone from the asylum."

Peder sat down abruptly on the bed, rubbed his chin in thought, and popped his jaw, a habit that had always greatly annoyed Ginger.

"It's ridiculous. I had nothing to do with it. I would never do anything like that. See what Dr. Mentzil and Jessie said?" He pointed to the article. "They know me. They know I would never do anything like that."

Stroud pulled the chair over toward the bed and sat down facing Peder.

"I believe you, but Milbrandt won't let you go until we have another legitimate suspect. We're trying to shake up whatever leads we can." He gestured to the newspaper. "That article should hopefully do a lot to clear your name and convince people this isn't a closed case."

Stroud leaned in to give Peder a pat on the shoulder.

"We'll get you back to the asylum. I'm sure everyone is anxious to have you back baking pies and pastries. This will be over very soon, but until it is, I'll keep in touch. Is there anything you want?"

Peder glanced through the bars toward Sergeant Olberdorf, who was pretending not to be eavesdropping. "Yeah. Make sure

Olberdorf remembers to bring my newspaper. And the food is rotten. Can you have somebody grab me a good burger and a beer?"

Stroud smiled. "It'll have to be root beer, but I can probably work that out. I'll be back later."

After Stroud's departure, Peder remained seated, thinking about the boy who had been murdered. What did he even look like? He must have seen him at the meeting that night. But plenty of Boy Scouts were there, and the only one he cared about was Jason.

Peder was completely baffled as to why anyone would think he could do such a horrible thing—to sexually assault and murder a young boy.

Never mind that Peder had once tried to kill his own family in a fire that earned Jason an award the night in question.

That was an entirely different situation.

CHAPTER 18

May 20, 1959

He felt the urge again. It was a hunger he could not ignore. He headed to downtown La Crosse and his special place under the Interstate Bridge. There in the darkness, he spotted Toby Swartz, who was oblivious to his visitor and the rest of civilization as he cast a red-and-white Daredevle spinner into the Mississippi River, searching for a hungry northern pike or maybe a wayward muskie.

Life was mean at home for twelve-year-old Toby. The only peace came when his dad got so drunk he fell asleep and stopped beating on Toby, his mother, and three sisters. And from the cries and prolonged sobbing he heard seeping through the thin wall separating their bedrooms, Toby knew his sisters suffered far more pain than any beating he could imagine. Mom wasn't much help. She seemed to pretend it wasn't happening. Maybe she just didn't know what to do, or maybe she feared worse beatings.

Well, I can't pretend it isn't happening, Toby thought. No more than an hour earlier, he had confronted his dad, igniting a major battle. He had to get the hell out of there, grabbing his pole as he hightailed it out the door. Did he even dare go back home?

Suddenly Toby heard a voice behind him.

"Hey, fella. How they biting?"

A skinny stranger, kind of a short Ichabod Crane, invaded Toby's secret space.

"Well, nothin' yet," Toby replied. "But sometimes you just gotta be patient and hit the quiet spots. No fish in the quick water today."

"You fish here often?"

"Pretty much every time I can," Toby said. "It's my spot. You can fish down there if you want." Toby pointed downriver, clearly proclaiming the bridge as his personal place.

"I'm not much good at fishing. I just love the river. Is it okay if I sit here and watch awhile?"

"Free country. But stay outta my way so I don't catch you when I cast—treble hooks are nasty. They'll rip your eye out."

The creepy stranger edged back a few feet. "Do you live close by?"

"Yeah. Couple blocks up on Third Street."

"It's getting pretty late. Won't your parents get worried?"

"Naw, my old man's probably passed out drunk, and Mom's hiding in her bedroom. I pretty much come and go as I please. They don't pay me no mind."

Toby wasn't about to tell this guy he wasn't sure if he would ever go home.

"Wow, that sounds like my house when I was your age. My dad was a mean drunk, and my mom just looked the other way."

"Hey, exactly." Toby became a bit more interested in what the funny-looking little man had to say.

"What's your name, kid?" the stranger inquired.

"Toby. What's yours?"

"Well, most folks just call me Digger."

"That's a weird name. Why do they call you that?"

"I guess it's because I do a lot of digging in my job."

"Roadwork?"

"Yeah, something like that." Digger wasn't about to say he was a gravedigger. That usually seemed to bother people.

Toby tightened his grip on his pole—he had a hit. "Whoa. Whoa. I got one!"

Digger crept close behind the distracted young fisherman, wrapped his hands around the boy's neck, quickly located the carotid artery, and deftly squeezed with perfect *Shime-Waza* judo technique he had learned from martial arts instructor Keno Wyn at Camp Pendleton in California.

Digger was certain his expert use of judo to render Toby unconscious would make Mr. Wyn proud. How often did the instructor say that, if done properly, this move could render someone unconscious in ten to twenty seconds without the risk of death? Cops and prison guards everywhere were trained to use this choke hold technique.

Judo was about the only good thing Digger could recall from his years as a marine drill sergeant's son. With his jarhead haircut trimmed to perfection before dawn every day, the sergeant was known as the Beast, a name used by almost everyone outside of his hearing range. Truth be told, he knew of the name and was more than proud of it.

Digger's dad was one of the first drill instructors to haunt the recruit barracks at Camp Pendleton when it opened at Oceanside near San Diego in 1942. He was charged with molding eager, raw kids into hardened US Marines for service in World War II. He had no friends, and the other training instructors often cautioned recruits to tread lightly in the presence of the Beast. It was said that surviving six weeks training under him would make real war seem like a party. Digger was only fifteen at the time, but he envied those marines who escaped to war, away from the Beast. He was the meanest bastard on the base—and at home.

He once told Digger, "Boy, if you're gonna be a real man, people should tremble with fear when you walk in the door. Show 'em who's boss. Leave absolutely no doubt about it."

Digger had smiled to himself thinking, *Yeah, maybe they do tremble when the Beast appears. But no one respects him.*

In the two years the family stayed at Camp Pendleton, Digger focused on nothing but judo. Finally, he had something he could do well. Then the Beast did what he always did—crushed Digger's dream.

"I'm not wasting another damn dime sending that worthless slug to judo lessons!" he bellowed across the dining room into the kitchen, where his wife, Marjorie, was carefully pulling a tuna hot dish from the oven. "Boy, sit up straight and get your elbows off the table."

Meals were more punishment than pleasure. The Beast constantly harassed Digger for not holding his spoon correctly, for making sounds when he sipped his soup, or for any number of minor etiquette infractions. In some twisted way, he seemed to think his drill sergeant tactics would work on Digger.

In comparison, though, the Beast rarely noticed what Digger's older sister, Claire, did. Maybe he just didn't bother because he thought she was worthless—that was essentially his view of all women. A daughter was not as important to him as a son. Digger was the Beast's major disappointment in life.

"The kid's absolutely worthless," he again bellowed at Marjorie. "Hell, I have a really hard time believing he came from my seed—but who else would be with an ugly cow like you?"

"Leroy," Marjorie said. She knew her words would only inflame him, but the mother in her rose up out of embarrassment and fear for her children. "Stop it right now. Don't talk like that in front of the children. He's a good boy and very smart."

"I'll talk any way I damn please in my own house. But what the hell are you talking about woman? Smart?" He pointed at Digger. "He thinks Cs are good grades. They're not. Jesus H. Keeyrist, he's nothing but a waste of space. He's totally worthless. The little bastard is not only dumber than a rock, he's butt ugly, puny, has no friends, and has never in his life said a word worth hearing. He's an embarrassment. At least the girl is a decent student, even if she's uglier than a weathered fencepost."

Digger glanced quickly at Claire, who glared at her father. If a person could project lightning, she was about to blast away. Even as her brother, Digger knew most guys found her more than okay. She brought traffic to a halt when she strolled across Pendleton. Marine eyes always snapped in her direction.

"And I ain't gonna spend one damn dime sending her to college just to crawl into some guy's bed and trap him like her mother did. She may be book smart, but she's nothing but a damn woman. How did I end up with two women for kids?"

How does Mom stay with this animal? Digger wondered.

"Leroy! That's enough!" Marjorie exclaimed. "Why don't you take a nap, and things will look better? You've had too much to drink. You don't mean all those ugly things!"

Suddenly the Beast tossed his bowl of hot soup across the room and slapped her hard across the face. "Don't you ever tell me what I mean!"

The room went silent. Marjorie was stunned and too mentally damaged to cry. Claire and Digger watched a red handprint pop up almost immediately across their mother's cheek. This time, there would be no claiming she had "accidentally fallen." Bruises were the major reason why their mother rarely left the house.

After two years at Pendleton, the family moved to Eau Claire,

Marjorie's hometown. They moved following her parents' tragic deaths in a traffic accident on Highway 53 as they returned from the Northern Wisconsin District Fair in Chippewa Falls. As their only child, Marjorie inherited the house, their investments, and their worldly possessions. Initially, LeRoy balked at the idea of transplanting his family to the "sticks," but the lure of cash proved too much to resist.

Lucky for Claire, she didn't move with them. She was gone the second she grabbed her sheepskin and stepped off the stage at her high school graduation ceremony. She told her brother she hated their father and would be happy if she never saw him again.

Also lucky for her, she didn't need any of the Beast's money for college. She pulled down a full-ride scholarship to Stanford. She volunteered every summer, a few times with student-study projects in South America or Europe, and one time to help black girls from poverty-stricken areas in Oakland learn basic life skills and how to succeed in school.

Much to Marjorie's dismay, Claire never once came to the family home in Wisconsin. She sent the occasional letter and called every Wednesday at noon, when she knew the Beast would be at work.

Two months after graduating from Stanford with honors as a chemical engineer, she married a nuclear physicist from her class. They moved to Los Alamos, New Mexico, where they both went to work for the federal government. Contact with her mother continued with the occasional letter, though less occasional than before, and a phone call once a month.

With Claire gone from their lives, Marjorie virtually disappeared from Digger's life. Physically, she was there, but emotionally, she went dark. Digger, too, never realized how he had depended on Claire until she was gone. Now he felt abandoned, alone to face the Beast through daily torment. He withdrew from any social contact, pounded on his piano with vengeance, and struggled to hide sexual desires he feared would incite violence from the Beast.

Digger lifted Toby's limp body into the trunk of his car, hidden from view on the dirt utility road under the bridge.

I gotta be more careful, he thought. *I never should have gotten involved with somebody in the Scout troop. This kid is better. As much as I hated the Beast, the one good thing I learned from him was attention to detail—always have a plan and stick to it, no matter what. Easier said than done.*

Toby Swartz pried his eyes open, but his body was not ready to move. Consciousness slowly crept into his body. He was naked, and the room was cold. As he rubbed his arms in a wasted effort at trying to wipe away the goose bumps, he searched for a blanket or anything to fight off the chill. His brain began to clear, but that only spawned painful questions as he surveyed his bizarre surroundings.

Geez, what's wrong with me? Where am I? How'd I get here?

A tiny low-watt bulb illuminated a twelve-foot-square space with barely enough room to stand. It looked a lot like the jail cell where Toby's dad took up residence on many Saturday nights after more than enough booze. Those were good nights for everyone else in the family.

But this cell didn't have the luxury of a wall of bars to look through. It only had a small solid-metal door that didn't even wiggle against Toby's weight. A rust-stained toilet, a small table with two wooden chairs, and a single bed were the only items in the room.

Toby sat on the tattered blue-and-white-striped mattress, trying to make sense of it all. Trying to fight off nausea and sheer panic. He'd been beaten and locked in the basement more than once by his drunken father. This was different. He wasn't in the basement, and he wasn't bleeding or aching from getting punched. But his asshole hurt like hell, and it felt all slimy with some kind of grease.

Looking around, he struggled to control himself. A plain white T-shirt, Jockey shorts, and blue jeans lay folded neatly on the table. Toby quickly discovered they were his size and got dressed to keep warm in his cool cell.

"Help! Help!" he cried out. "Anybody there? Get me outta here!"

Absolute silence swallowed his screams in a tomb encased in concrete. The deadened sound meant no one was going to hear his frantic pleas. Pounding on the walls did nothing but punish his hands.

Toby tried to piece together what had happened. He remembered standing up to his old man, getting into the fight, then heading to the river. It went sort of black after that.

God, it was that goofy-looking creep at the river, he suddenly realized. *He did something to me. What's going on?*

Toby carefully examined his prison cell inch by inch. There wasn't much to search, but he was desperate. Behind the toilet, he spotted faint writing on the wall, apparently in crayon. One spot said, "Rod Smith 1956." A second mark appeared to be slightly different but with a similar message read, "Terry Fullmer here '58." Other areas of the room revealed faint remnants of messages, but somebody obviously had scrubbed them away. They must have missed the words etched in the dark spot behind the toilet.

Maybe this is some kind of play area. But then why am I locked in here?

Confined in the windowless room, there was no way to tell if it were night or day, let alone what time it might be. Hours passed, perhaps, before a muffled click sounded and the door slowly moved inward.

Digger's ugly head crawled into the room brandishing an unsettling, broad smile.

"You comfortable? I have a hot breakfast for you." He carried a meal on a tray. "What else can I bring you? Comic books? Checkers? Paper and pencil?"

"How about a ride home, sicko?"

Toby tried to put up a tough front, even if just to convince himself. He needed all the toughness he could muster. Whenever he'd been locked in the basement, all Toby had to do was wait for his old man to fall asleep upstairs, then his mother would unlock the door, greeting him with tears and a bear hug. But this guy wasn't drunk. He was some kind of monster. And it didn't appear that anyone was coming to the rescue.

"Oh, that's no way for a guest to talk. We're going to be great friends. I think you'll grow to like it here. But if you don't, that's okay too."

"Why are you doing this? Just let me go home."

"Toby, that's not going to happen. You might as well try to enjoy your new life. I'll give you everything I can, but this is where you live now. Eat your breakfast. I'll be back later, and we can talk about your future."

Digger crawled out the little door, pulled it behind him, and turned the lock.

Toby stared at the food on the tray. Normally, a fried egg, toast with strawberry jam, two slices of crisp bacon, and a tall glass of orange juice would have hit the spot. Not now. Toby's stomach was gripped with fear. He wondered if the breakfast foods meant it was morning, which in turn meant he had been here all night. No wonder he was incredibly hungry. But there was no way he would eat anything the slimy creep dragged in. It was probably poison.

He wants to talk about my "future." What does that mean?

A jail cell suddenly sounded very inviting to Toby, compared to this tomb. Strange thoughts began to ricochet through his head.

Will I suffocate in here? He remembered hearing about miners dying from bad air, and this windowless, damp place felt like some kind of hole in the ground.

This crazy guy could just lock me in here forever and let me starve. What if he decides to kill me? His mind began to spin with scenarios—none of them good.

This is really bad. If I don't find a way out of here, I'm gonna die.

Toby couldn't tell how much time passed before Digger reappeared.

"You didn't touch your breakfast." Digger looked genuinely concerned.

"I'm not hungry," Toby lied. "I'll eat when I get back home."

Digger frowned. "You don't seem to understand. *This* is your home. So, you better eat if you don't want to get sick. You gotta eat if you're going to stay healthy and strong. Oh, well. Your breakfast is too cold now anyway. I'll get you some root beer and a peanut butter sandwich to tide you over until lunch. Anything else you want?"

Hunger was beginning to speak up—shout, actually—but Toby would fight it as long as possible. On the other hand, maybe the creep was right about Toby's need to keep up his strength. He would need a strong body and mind if there was any hope of getting away.

Almost in desperation, Toby answered, "Yeah, there's something I want. I want you to let me out of here."

"Other than that. You ain't going anywhere. Like I said, we're going to be best friends."

In his young life, Toby had become something of a turtle, growing a hard shell to shield him from life's low blows. But none of the nastiness he experienced at home could compare to the terror filling his head at this moment. This monster had complete control over him and was probably going to kill him. Toby's dad was mean, but Toby had never feared for his own life. Until now.

Toby gave a convincing nod. "Okay. Sure. Gimme some paper and a pencil. I like to write."

Toby figured a pen or pencil could be a weapon. He could stab this creepy guy and make a run for it.

Digger was gone only minutes, then he returned with a Dixie cup filled to the brim with root beer and a white paper plate with a peanut butter sandwich and a handful of Old Dutch potato chips. Under the plate was some paper.

"Sorry, I couldn't find a pen or pencil," Digger said as he set everything down, then reached into his pocket. "But here are a couple crayons. Red and blue okay?"

Damn, Toby thought. *He knew exactly what I was thinking. I'm in serious shit here.*

With Digger standing there in front of him, Toby processed that the only possible way out was through that door. It was way too thick and strong to break, just like a bank vault door. Somehow, Toby would have to get past Digger while the door was still open. Or he'd have to talk Digger into letting him out for a while.

Maybe I can club him with a chair next time he sticks his ugly mug in here.

As soon as the thought came to his mind, however, Toby rejected it. He could clearly see the room was so confined, he would only hit the ceiling if he tried to swing a chair.

Maybe I can bust up a chair and whack him with one of the pieces. But what if it doesn't work? Then he's really gonna be pissed and things might get worse. Can things get any worse?

"Toby, have you ever had a girlfriend?" Digger asked, breaking Toby's train of thought.

Toby wasn't sure how to respond or if he even wanted to get

into a conversation. Then again, he realized this guy controlled his future, if there was any future. Maybe it would be better to talk with him. Gain his confidence. That might be the only way to get out.

He looked up at Digger and tried hard to sell his little-tough-guy act. "What's it to ya?"

"Just wondering."

Toby shrugged. "No, I've never had a girlfriend. Not really."

"Love is a wonderful thing, Toby. I loved you the moment we met. In time you will come to love me too." Digger inched closer with a broad smile that might seem warm and heartfelt under different circumstances. He reached across and put his hand on Toby's neck, pulling him forward. It took everything Toby had to avoid jerking away.

Digger looked in Toby's eyes as if pleading for understanding. "I got to go to work now, but I'll be back later, and we can talk more. Enjoy your lunch."

Toby tried to keep his face blank until Digger stepped out of the cell and shut the door with a thud.

Holy shit. What's this nut talking about? He's some kinda pervert. I heard about them. Oh, my God. What is he gonna do to me? What has he already done to me?

CHAPTER 19

MAY 22, 1959

Serious crime was rarely a major concern in La Crosse, Wisconsin, during the 1950s. Until now. Now there was enough skulduggery to keep even the most lethargic cop busy. But Randy Olson, the city's only full-time detective, was not among the lethargic. Far from it. Between a bungled armed robbery attempt at the Standard Oil station, the bloody disappearance of babysitter Evelyn Hartley, and three missing boys all presumed to have drowned while playing in the river, Olson hardly found a moment's peace.

Sometimes he just had to get away from the ugliness, escape to the solitude of the Mississippi River as it gurgled relentlessly under the Interstate Bridge early in its meandering 1,800-mile slide south through the middle of America into the Gulf of Mexico.

For his part, Olson especially loved sitting along the banks and imagining the ghosts of historic paddlewheel riverboats quietly churning up the mighty Mississippi, snuggling up against the river wall, and energizing the whole town with a burst of activity.

But darkness always found a way to invade even his most serene moments. Today as he stared across the dark shimmering river surface, he saw the heads of teenage boys bobbing along. These visions of lost boys usually vanished with a shake of his head, yet they continued to haunt him.

As unpleasant as it was, he could understand how college kids might stumble into the river after a night of heavy drinking. But how could he explain three younger boys vanishing in four years? Something just didn't smell right, and it wasn't just rotting fish.

Often when Olson stopped by the river, he shared the space with a boy fishing under the bridge. He wondered if one day that boy had been Toby Swartz, the lad who vanished two days earlier.

Where are you, Toby?

A veteran cop gets a gut ache that rumbles without end when something isn't right, and Olson's gut was roaring. Okay, maybe that extra shot of diablo sauce on his fourth taco for supper last night was a contributing factor. Tacos were "foreign" cuisine that rarely stung the tongues of the Norwegians and Swedes populating Wisconsin, but Olson couldn't get enough of them.

He had his grandfather, Captain George Olson—or Cappy, as everybody on and off the river came to call him—to thank for his love of the fiery food. Olson acquired his taste for tacos years ago during his annual holiday visits to Cappy's adobe hacienda in faraway New Mexico. But after twenty years of retirement life in the Painted Desert, the joints in Cappy's sea legs began to bark, and the old river captain reluctantly moved back to La Crosse. He now lived in a seniors' apartment eight blocks from his grandson.

At ninety-five, Cappy still snarled and chewed constantly on a long-stem pipe, just as he did as the gruff captain of the big riverboat *Capitol*. With Cappy roaming the decks, the *Capitol* hauled passengers, livestock, and supplies up and down the entire length of the mighty Mississippi before railroad trains spread across the country. The cantankerous old seadog still fumed about how the railroads sank his beloved riverboat business. Cappy took unnecessary delight when airplanes eventually became the preferred mode of freighting and nearly derailed "those gawddamn, smoke-belching steel contraptions" he despised.

Olson glanced at his watch, cast one last troubled gaze at the rushing waters, picked himself up from the riverbank, and made his way to Cappy's apartment.

"Hey, Gramps," Olson greeted the old river boat captain after a quick knock at the door. "How's it going? Got time for lunch?"

The old sailor rose, mechanically unfolding his trim, still-muscular frame. His old bones creaked and complained, but once he reached his full six-foot-two-inch extension, he beamed with great pride and puffed out his massive chest. Walking was another story. Mere mention of a walker always drew a loud demonstration of salty dialogue, but following three bruising tumbles, he had conceded to using a cane.

"Damn straight, boy. Anything to get outta this joint. I'm done listening to that pack of damn sodbusters chattering constantly about rain, no rain, hail, no hail, drought, too much rain. Holy shit, all that worthless chatter is enough to drive a man to drink."

Olson suggested a fine-dining restaurant, but as always, Cappy wanted nothing but two cheeseburgers, large fries, and a large Coke. After they settled into a booth at the Corner Café, Olson glanced up at his grandfather.

"Gramps, I got a strange question for ya. When you were piloting the *Capitol*, do you remember hearing about small boys drowning in the river . . . kids twelve to fourteen?"

Olson knew what he was getting into by posing this question. On one hand, he hoped Cappy might have some nugget of information that could help him with this Toby Swartz case. Plus, he couldn't explain it, but whenever he was with his grandfather, he somehow fell back in time to being a little boy reveling in Cappy's river tales.

But on the other hand, one of the dangers of engaging Cappy in talk about the river was that it was like pulling the plug on a dam. One little question was all it took. There would be a flood of words, with no way to control it. Once Cappy got started, no one else got in a word.

His eyes lit, showing a hint of what was once a hardy ship's commander. He bit down on his lower lip as he scoured fifty years of river history locked away in his memory bank.

"Uffda. Oh, Christ, no," Cappy began. "We had a lotta sad tales, but can't say that any kids ever drowned. Not that I know of. Ya know, it was a pretty different time. Life was tough and families sometimes couldn't feed all their kids. There was no help from the government or much of anything else outside of a few churches handing out bread and milk. Some of those kids became beggars, thieves, and pretty good pickpockets. And we'd get plenty of real young ones who ran away from home or got sent away. Most of them were damn good little workers 'cuz they were desperate, hungry. And if they didn't work hard, we just dumped them off at the next port. We even picked up a few little black ones down South."

Distant memories ignited a broad, toothy smile that pushed his cheeks into a mass of wrinkled leather surrounding his ageless blue eyes.

"I remember one—Jeremiah. Geesus, he was a funny little fella, always had everyone laughing. I still have to laugh when I think about that kid. He'd dance on the swing stage every time we made port, and folks would toss nickels at him. He bragged that he made more money than the captain, and I think he coulda been right."

Olson took a bite of his burger, chewing as patiently as

he could.

"I never had any little boys drown," Cappy continued, "but we had plenty of gamblers and drunks go overboard—some with a helping hand. Ha, I remember a funny one. Well, not so funny. Maybe just strange. It was a wedding aboard the *Capitol*. We were coming up the Mississippi on June 15, 1890. We picked the wedding party up at Lake City, and the ceremony was in the middle of Lake Pepin, which is a wide spot in the river below Red Wing.

"About an hour after the wedding, the groom just up and jumped overboard. Body popped up downriver three days later. Wedding folks said he was just showing off, but I wondered if he had just come to his senses when he got a good look at his ugly bride and her demanding mother. The really amazing part was there were these two women who seemed to be the least upset of all by the tragedy—a couple rich bitches. They were more concerned that the groom had spoiled their party."

This time, Olson took a long sip from his Coke.

Cappy massaged his chin and swung his head casually from side to side. "Oh boy, that was a really bad summer. The big *Sea Wing* disaster happened almost in that very spot near Red Wing about a month later. The *Sea Wing* came off the Wisconsin side at Diamond Bluff with the *Jim Grant*, a small barge, tied alongside. They had a bit more than 200 passengers for a Sunday excursion.

"Midstream, my old friend Captain Dave Wethern spotted a big black storm a-comin'. All he could do was point his bow into the twister and pray. I doubt God even recognized Wethern's voice, though, so that was little help. His top-heavy boat spun—some witnesses said it flipped three times. Most of the folks in the cabin died, but the *Jim Grant* that Wethern thought would give the *Sea Wing* some stability broke loose and miraculously stayed upright. Ninety-eight died in the boat. Most of the folks on the barge survived." With barely a half-second pause, Cappy pointed at Olson and asked, "Randy, ya know what was the worst maritime disaster in the US?"

"The *Sea Wing*?" Olson guessed, trying to sleuth out the old man's logic.

The old man gave a "gotcha" smile. "Naw, that was nothing compared to the *Sultana*. Ya heard about the *Sultana*, right?"

"Ah, I don't think so."

"Nope. Nobody's heard of it, except every guy who worked on the river. Bit before my time, but we talked about it on the *Capitol*. It was the country's worst sea disaster ever. Still is. Nearly 2,000 folks died on the Mississippi right there in sight of Memphis—more people than died on the *Titanic*.

"The *Sultana* was built to hold 376 passengers, but they jammed it with 2,400 Union soldiers just released from the Confederate prison camps at Andersonville and Cahaba. The boat departed from Vicksburg, struggling mightily to make headway upriver. Three days into the voyage, on April 27, 1865, the *Sultana* was passing Memphis when the boiler exploded. Those who didn't die in the explosion drowned. Only a handful survived.

"Nobody's ever heard about the *Sultana* disaster because the nation was totally distracted by what had happened thirteen days earlier—when President Lincoln decided to go to the Ford Theater. Betcha heard about that."

"Oh yeah. John Wilkes Booth and the assassination."

"All those bad things happened. But I gotta tell ya, Randy—in nearly sixty years running the river from Saint Paul to New Orleans and up the Ohio River, I never heard of any young boys drowning. Just some older boys."

"So, how's that burger, Gramps?" Olson quickly interrupted, hoping to get the old man eating his yet-untouched food.

Olson recoiled as he watched his grandfather's hamburger turn white under a blizzard of salt.

"Wow. You think ya got enough salt on it?"

Then Olson recoiled with even more alarm as Cappy slipped the saltshaker into his pocket.

"Gramps, you can't just steal the saltshaker!"

"Didn't steal nuttin', boy. I'm gonna leave 'em two bucks." He pulled two dollar bills from the same pocket and slapped them on the table where the saltshaker once sat. "Damn chow at the home is so bland, I can't taste nuttin'."

"Maybe it's just your taster."

"Could be. Doc Meister says that too. But I gotta get a little flavor somehow."

"Tell you what," Olson said. "I'll bring you some salt and a little special seasoning. But you need to be careful not to go too crazy. It's not good for you."

"Geesus, I'm ninety-five. Who gives a shit what's good for me?"

"Well, I care. I also need to get back to work. Let's eat, then get you home."

After a morning at the river and lunch with the old riverboat captain, Olson's head was crammed with thoughts of bygone days. But even the romance of history couldn't stop those familiar dark visions of young boys slipping under the surface. Why did three young boys vanish without a trace in four years?

Hoping to tame the fire in his gut, Olson went back to the office and started calling every police force he could find along the river from Saint Louis to Saint Paul. After two hours, he hung up the phone and rubbed his hands along his face.

"What are you up to, Olson?" asked Sergeant Gerald Miller, whose desk faced Olson's.

"Playing a hunch about Toby Swartz and those other boys who went missing. I just don't believe three boys drowned all by themselves. So, I'm checking other river towns to see how many other kids in that age group have disappeared and never been found."

"Yeah? What have you found?"

"Zero. Nothing. Not one drowning anywhere else. Apparently, it's only in La Crosse that kids fall in the river and vanish. It doesn't even happen downriver, where the current is far worse and the river is wider."

"Well, maybe that's because the nasty current scares 'em away from the river down there."

Olson shook his head. "No, I don't think that's it. Our kids aren't any dumber than theirs. But I'm running out of ideas."

Olson went back to his map. *Okay*, he thought, *if it is something with the current or the size of the river, let's take a look upriver.*

He dialed Joe Stroud. Eau Claire wasn't on the Mississippi, but the Chippewa was close enough. Plus, Olson needed an excuse to get a beer and some advice from a good detective. The two men had been close friends since they were classmates in a criminology seminar at the University of Wisconsin in Madison so many years ago.

"Hey, Joe. It's Randy Olson in La Crosse."

"Randy—man, it's good to hear your voice. Been way too long. Suppose you're looking for a six-pack of Leinenkugel's."

"You bet. That sounds great. We'll have to work that in soon. But at the moment, I'm on what might be a fool's errand. I'm checking up and down the Mississippi to see if anyone has had any ten-, eleven-, twelve-year-old boys go missing, possibly in the river, with no bodies left behind."

"Yeah," Stroud said, "I heard you had another boy drown down there."

"Well, that's the problem. Everybody is convinced he just dropped into the river and drowned, but I'm not so sure. He's the third kid to vanish here in four years under the same circumstances. That's just too much coincidence for my liking. So I'm checking with cops in every town on the river. I thought of you too with the Chippewa."

"Nope, we haven't had any young boys disappear in the river."

Just then, Stroud paused, and Olson could all but hear gears turning.

"But you know what? I am working a strange case—a seventeen-year-old boy was raped and murdered in a city park near Dells Pond, which is part of the Chippewa River flowage. He's older than your guys, but he's unusually small for his age. Seems like it might be an impromptu case of opportunity for the pervert—the kid was just at a Scout meeting a few minutes earlier. I dunno—maybe it's a stretch. But could be something worth taking a look at."

"At this point," Olson said, "I'm looking for anything, and that's more than what I've come up with anywhere else. If there's anything you need, I'll take care of it personally."

"As a matter of fact, could you send me everything you have on your three missing boys? I'll get our file on Roy Pettit down to you too."

Once again, Stroud paused.

"You know, I just thought of another case. Probably even a bigger stretch, but we had this kid, Danny White, who supposedly fell through the ice and drowned in Dells Pond a few years ago. But it bothered me 'cuz his body never came up. It usually takes three or four days before bodies start decomposing and pop to the surface. Folks here thought maybe his body got hung up on a log underwater, but I was never comfortable with that reasoning."

"I know it," Olson agreed. "The same thing's been haunting me about the three kids down here. Why don't the bodies show up? I suppose you could make a case that one got stuck on a snag underwater or got carried downriver under a big barge. But not all three."

"To make it even worse," Stroud added, "Danny went to the same church and was in the same Boy Scout troop as our new case.

I really don't like coincidences. Like I said, maybe it's nothing, but I'll pull Danny's file too."

"Tell ya what—I'll pull my files right now and be there in a couple hours. You got time to catch dinner and a couple Leinies and go over these cases? Let's get our heads together. I bet we spot something."

"Sounds great, Randy. Why don't you come by the house? Bette will be excited to see you. I'm gonna give her a call and have her cook up something special for dinner."

Olson set the phone down but left his hand on the receiver as he sat motionless, mulling over the conversation. Nothing really connected, yet it all felt like pieces from the same puzzle scattered across the state. That aging cop's gut was churning again.

Something's going on here, and Joe and I can figure it out.

CHAPTER 20

MAY 23, 1959

It was time. Time to say something. Only Jason didn't know what exactly to say and to whom he could say it.

Why aren't the cops talking to him? Jason thought as he sat in his bedroom. *If my dad is "crazy," then this guy is something beyond crazy. He's thirty and still lives with his mommy. I mean, he literally calls her Mommy. And that dingy old place where they live would be the perfect setting for something straight out of Alfred Hitchcock's twisted, dark mind.*

Why haven't the cops thought of him? How did they miss him? How come they're only looking at Dad? What kinda cops are they?

They really need to check him out. I guess no one will, though, unless I say something. But, man—who's gonna listen to me?

"Hey, Grams," Jason said as he came into the kitchen. As usual, it smelled warm and inviting.

Grandma Libby had her back to Jason as she donned a mitt and opened the oven door. "My goodness—isn't it interesting how you always manage to show up just when pie is coming out of the oven? Blueberry or apple?"

"Blueberry, of course." He watched as she pulled out first one then the other tasty treat. "Say, are you busy?"

"You're kidding, right? Got pies and bread to bake and a birthday cake for your mom. And soap to finish. Of course, I'm busy. What's up?"

Along with everything else, Grandma Libby made bars of hand soap. She began by collecting fragile white oak ashes from the wood-burning stove and then cautiously stirring them into a pot of boiled rainwater to make lye. This process played out over two weeks. Next she mixed the lye with fat drained from beef or chicken, added a dash of perfume, then poured the concoction into molds. She always saved some lye to sprinkle atop the mulch piles in her garden to hasten decomposition.

Once the soap firmed up, it was Jason's task to slice the hardened blocks into bars. He was convinced this soap was far better than Lava, a gritty skin scraper promoted for really dirty hands. Lava was maybe suitable after a day of digging in liquid rubber at the tire plant, but it was very unpleasant for anyone else.

Grandma Libby set a slice of blueberry pie in front of Jason. "When you're done, can you cut the soap and wrap the bars in waxed paper?"

"Sure. But I need to talk about something."

"Go ahead. I'm listening," she said as she headed back to the counter. She was a human hummingbird, always darting back and forth, buzzing around the kitchen without pause.

"Dad didn't kill Roy."

She flitted to the oven and slipped in two loaf pans on the top shelf, above where the birthday cake was nearing completion. She deftly slid a toothpick into the cake, pulled, and announced it needed another five minutes.

"Your dad had an awful lot of bad habits," she said as she closed the oven door, "but I have to agree he didn't kill that boy."

"Well, I know who did."

She backed away from the oven, untied her bright-yellow apron, and dropped into a kitchen chair. "What are you talking about?"

"I know who the killer is. But nobody is gonna believe me. They'll just think I'm trying to save my dad. They're already saying I'm nuts too."

"Wait a minute. How do you know who the killer is?" She was motionless, staring at her grandson.

Jason hesitated only a second. It was time.

"It's Lloyd Harris," he said.

"What? You mean that Boy Scout guy?"

"Yes. But nobody will believe me."

"Who have you told?"

"Just you."

"Well, of course nobody's going to believe you if you don't open your mouth. What makes you think it's him? Do you have any proof?"

"See, that's the problem. I just *know* it's him, but I can't prove a thing. Jessie, that nurse from the asylum, told me what kind of person would do something like that. Lloyd is that kind of person. He fits the description perfectly."

Libby stared through him and slid into deep thought. "You need to talk to Joey Stroud. He knows you, and he was almost your uncle. He's eager for any little clue. He'll listen."

The thought of talking to a cop, even a friendly one, caused Jason's heart to beat faster and tiny beads of sweat appeared on his forehead.

"I don't think so. Everybody thinks Lloyd is this great guy. Detective Stroud needs real proof, but I've got nothing but my gut."

"Jason, you've got to talk to Joey. At least give him something to think about. He's the best cop in town. If there's anything there, he'll find it."

"You don't understand . . ."

Jason struggled with what to say next. It was time to talk about Lloyd being the killer, but he wasn't sure it was time to say more than that.

"I mean, I know some stuff about Lloyd"—he glanced away just as Libby's mouth made the slightest frown—"but who would believe me? It's my word against his. If I talk, word will get out. Joan Killian's dad is a cop, and she's got the biggest mouth in school. She sits next to me in homeroom. The second she hears what I said, everybody in town will know. Lloyd will get away with murder because I don't have any real proof, but my life will be ruined."

"You have to trust Joey. He's a good man. A great detective. He'll get to the truth."

"I hope so, Grams. But now I sorta wish I'd just kept my big mouth shut and not even told you."

"Finish your pie. I'm going to call Joey and ask him to come over. You did the right thing," she added as she stood and walked straight to the phone.

God, how he wanted her to be right, but his head was about to explode with doubt.

Who's gonna believe the son of the guy everybody is ready to hang. What can I do?

An hour later, Stroud gave a quick knock, shouted "Libby!" and lumbered up the three steps into the kitchen from the back door. The giant man ducked his head as he came through the doorway.

"Libby, I'm glad to hear from you. Figure you called me over because you have more than just pie for me. But if this is about another Boy Scout merit badge, I'm sorry to say I just don't have a lot of time right now. You know, with the murder and a missing girl."

"The murder is what we want to talk about, Joey," she said.

"I know, but it's still under investigation, and I just can't talk about the case right now."

He gave her a polite but slightly dismissive smile, but Libby wiped it from his face.

"We're not looking for information *from* you. Jason has information *for* you."

With that, Stroud grabbed a kitchen chair. He parked in front of a giant piece of blueberry pie, but he was more interested in Jason. He thought back to the day he first interviewed Jason about Roy's death. Replaying it in his mind, he recalled how hesitant the boy had been with his brief answers. At the time, he chalked it up to Jason's anxiety about his father being the main suspect. Now Stroud realized it might have been because Jason had been withholding something.

"What's this all about, Jason? Did your dad say something?"

"It's nothing with Dad," Jason said, shaking his head. "I know who the killer is, but I ain't got any proof."

The silence was deafening. A mourning dove resting on the electric wire just outside the kitchen window added its sorrowful call to the somber mood hanging over the table.

"What's your theory? Maybe we're already on it."

"That nursing teacher you brought to our Scout meeting talked to me, and she said the killer is most likely somebody who knew Roy pretty well and is involved with kids. Well, there's this guy everybody thinks is wonderful." Jason's eyes dropped down to the pie. "But some of the guys say he does, you know, weird stuff. He's really careful to pick out guys who don't have dads around—like Roy," he quickly added. "But nobody is going to believe me.

Probably not even you."

"Try me, Jason," Stroud said, straight-faced. "What's his name?"

Jason dipped his head and said something almost inaudible into his chest, a name that ran together as a single word. "Lloydharris."

"The Boy Scout leader? What makes you think he would do something like that?"

Flipping his head up, Jason glared at Stroud and Libby. "See?" he spouted with a mix of anger and fear. "You don't believe me. Everybody will think I'm just trying to save my dad."

"Jason, stop it," Libby said. "Joey's here to listen."

"That's right," Stroud said. "Doesn't make any difference what I believe or don't believe. We're going to take every lead seriously until we know it's a dead end. And actually, Lloyd Harris makes some sense. He was there that night and he knew the victim."

"Oh yeah, he knew Roy, all right," Jason said, his voice growing stronger. "Roy was in Lloyd's Indian dancing group for our troop. They performed that night at my award ceremony. That giant Indian chief's headdress Roy was wearing is Lloyd's. It was a special thing to let him wear it."

"What headdress?" Stroud asked, leaning forward.

In all the interviews with people who attended the Scout ceremony the night of Roy's murder, everyone said Roy had performed with the Indian dance troupe, but no one had mentioned Roy wearing a special headdress. His mind flashed to the scene there in the park, under the picnic table, where feathers lay next to Roy's dead body.

"What do you mean it was a special thing?" Stroud asked.

"Because Lloyd took me to his house a couple years ago and gave it to me. It was a big deal to him." His eyes darted back to the pie again, and he shifted in his chair.

"Wait—is that when you suddenly quit the dance group?" Libby interrupted. "Your mother and I were really puzzled about that. You seemed to love it so much, but then you just quit, and that's not like you."

Jason tried to shrug. "Yeah, well, Lloyd is a bad guy and he does weird stuff."

"Did he do things to you?" Stroud asked. He lifted his coffee cup and took a long draw, more to relax tension than to taste the hot brew—although Libby's coffee was always good.

But it would take more than coffee to ease Jason's anxiety. He was beginning to regret having started the conversation. "I don't wanna talk about that."

"Jason, it'll be pretty difficult going after this guy unless you can give me something more specific."

Jason sat there for a second, then quickly rose. "See, Grams—I knew this was a bad idea." He went to his bedroom.

Stroud sighed and stood as well. "Libby, I'll start a file on Lloyd. I'll do some checking, and we'll keep an eye on him. But we need something that ties him to the murder scene or proof of past bad behavior. In the back of my mind, I've got a strong suspicion Jason may be on to something. It's good to have another suspect. That article in the paper sure as hell stirred the pot, but it was all a bunch of dead ends. I'm glad Jason spoke up this much, but he definitely knows more than he's saying. You need to talk with Jason and see if you can get him to open up."

"I'll do what I can, but he's just as stubborn as me when he sets his mind."

Libby's normally effusive confidence was shaken. She too was beginning to wonder if calling the police was the right thing to do. But she had faith in Stroud. Her fear now was how Jason could be hurt and embarrassed by coming forth with what he knew—though perhaps that wouldn't be as a bad as having your father convicted for murder.

"If his problem with Lloyd is what I think it is, he won't talk to me about it. When he's ready, he'll need a man. And right now, you're the only one available."

"Let me know when he's ready. But let's not wait too long. I don't want to look at any more dead kids."

"And you don't want to miss out on that retirement party either."

Stroud gave a weary smile. "You're right—I can't quit until we wrap this thing up. Then Bette and I are headed for a Florida beach, where I'll never have to think about monsters killing kids." He rubbed his forehead. "We gotta get a break on this thing soon. There just isn't much to go on, other than a fingerprint from the kid's belt buckle and a litter bag full of wastepaper and some feathers I now think came from a special headdress."

By the time Stroud made it back to his office, he had himself almost convinced that Lloyd Harris was Roy's killer. But then he found Sergeant MacDonald waiting with more news.

"Looks like you finally got a suspect," MacDonald said. "We just got a call from one of the mothers of a choir girl at Saint Luke. She said we should be looking at the choir director, Martin Goodrich. Thinks he fits the bill for what that asylum nurse described in the newspaper last week."

Stroud frowned. "Yeah, but thanks to that article, everybody in town thinks their neighbor is a crazed killer. It was good to get people thinking, but I went through a whole pile of phone messages, and none of them held a lick of water. So why is this lead any different? Why does she think this guy could be our murderer?"

"Apparently, he got fired from a teaching job in Stoughton, down by Madison, a few years ago. Rumor was that he got a bit too friendly with one of his students. There wasn't any evidence to charge him, so they just sent him out of town. He's teaching choir at the junior high here and is the volunteer choir director at Saint Luke. He was at the church the night Roy was killed, and Sonja was in his choir. This mom says she's heard he's a bit too friendly with the girls in the choir. It makes some of the mothers uncomfortable."

Stroud sat back and let out a long breath. "Well, I happen to have a new lead myself, but this one maybe has more teeth than mine. We better start a file and check this guy out as best we can."

CHAPTER 21

MAY 24, 1959

With nothing to do, not a sound to be heard, and only bare concrete walls to see, it was impossible for Toby to calculate time. Minutes were hours. For what was apparently three days, Digger appeared periodically with what he claimed was breakfast, lunch, and dinner. Nothing significant happened. Every time Digger appeared, Toby feared he might be raped again—and he'd be awake this time. But it didn't happen.

Did I imagine he did that stuff to me? No. It happened. So why it he trying to be Mr. Nice Guy now? Why hasn't he done it to me again?

Time crawled so slowly Toby began to anticipate Digger's brief visits just for the break from absolute boredom and maybe for the conversation with another human—assuming this sicko was human. Toby would then chastise himself for entertaining any positive thoughts toward his captor.

On what may have been the fourth day, Digger brought the

morning newspaper with breakfast.

"Hey, I thought you might enjoy knowing how famous you are. Here you are on the front page of the *La Crosse Tribune*." He held the paper high, turning it to capture the dim light. "I'll read it for you.

CHIEF BOYSTON SAYS MISSING BOY BELIEVED DROWNED
By Sherri Gustland, *La Crosse Tribune*

La CROSSE, WI—An intensive three-day land and water search along 20 miles of the Mississippi River from Interstate Bridge south turned up no sign of Toby Swartz, 12, who disappeared while fishing at the bridge Saturday evening.

According to La Crosse Police Chief Gerald Boyston, "It appears the boy may have fallen into the river or was swimming alone at night in the strong current. His fishing gear and clothing were found under the Interstate Bridge, where his parents state that he fished frequently. Divers from the La Crosse County Sheriff's Department worked nearly dawn to dusk for three days in the river but found nothing but abandoned cars, fish and garbage. We are asking anyone who has any information about Toby Swartz to contact us immediately."

Toby's mother, Mary Swartz, said her son went almost daily to his "special fishing hole" under the Interstate Bridge and that he was a very experienced swimmer, having swum across the river channel at that point many times. Chief Boyston noted, however, that even expert swimmers can get into trouble quickly in the rapid spring current. He added that Toby is the third young boy to disappear in the river in recent years. He urged parents to caution their children about the dangers of swimming alone, especially in the river, where invisible, powerful spring undercurrents can pull down even the best and strongest swimmers.

Three years ago, on June 15, 1956, Rodney Smith, 11, vanished from the same general area and has never been found. And on May 27, 1958, Terrence "Terry" Fullmer, 12, also disappeared while fishing near the downtown area. In each case, personal items were discovered near the river, but their bodies were never recovered.

Although the three boys are believed to have drowned, their cases remain open, Chief Boyston said, as does La Crosse's most famous missing child case, that of Evelyn Grace Hartley, 15, a straight-A student at Central High School.

Evelyn disappeared Oct. 24, 1953, from the home of La Crosse State College professor Viggo Rasmussen, where she was babysitting. When Evelyn failed to call home at 8:30 p.m. as promised, her parents attempted repeatedly to reach her by phone. Finally, at about 9:30 p.m., her father drove to the Rasmussen residence, where he discovered that a basement window appeared to have been removed. Inside the house, he found Evelyn's broken glasses, one of her shoes on the living room floor and one in the basement, and her five school books scattered around the living room. Investigators found two pools of blood in the yard and a bloody handprint about four feet off the ground on the wall of a nearby garage.

Two days after her disappearance, a local man, Ed Hofer, told police he had seen a two-tone green 1941 or 1942 Buick speeding westward about 7:15 p.m. with a male driver and a man and a girl in the back seat. He said the girl was slumped against the front seat. At the time, he assumed they were going to the homecoming game and had been drinking.

A few days later, police discovered a pair of blood-stained underpants and a brassiere alongside Highway 14 two miles south of La Crosse. Evelyn's parents confirmed the clothing items were consistent with what she had been wearing. A bloodstained size 11 B. F. Goodrich tennis shoe and a men's size 36 blue denim jacket with metallic buttons and bloodstains on the front, back and sleeves also were found a short time later near Coon Valley, south of La Crosse. The shoe soles appeared to match footprints at the crime scene, and the blood was the same type as Evelyn's. Her body was never found.

Chief Boyston said that although the formal search for Toby has concluded, the Swartz family has chosen to continue searching the riverfront and nearby areas with volunteers from Central High School, First Presbyterian Church and other community organizations before accepting the drowning verdict. He asked that anyone who was in the area of the Interstate Bridge Tuesday evening contact the La Crosse Police Department immediately.

"Even the slightest, seemingly innocent observation may help in the investigation. We're looking for anything that will help find Toby. This appears to be a horrible accident, but our detectives do have some concern about the similarities involving the three boys' disappearances. They were all about the same age and disappeared in the downtown area at the river under similar circumstances. We don't like coincidences."

"Lucky for you, I saved you from drowning." Digger emitted a false chuckle and dropped the newspaper on the small table.

Toby threw a glance back behind the toilet, where the names were scrawled on the wall. Rod and Terry. Those were the names the article mentioned. He fought back a shudder.

"Those other guys in the newspaper—you took them too, didn't you?"

"Ah, Rodney and Terry? Yes, as a matter of fact, they both spent some time here. They both had great fun. I still love them very much. And Danny White too."

"What about the girl?"

Digger shook his head and made a face of distaste. "No. Not her."

"So, what happened to the guys? Did you let them go? If you love me so much, why don't you just let me go?" Toby tried to smile but failed. "You can come fishing with me anytime. I won't tell anybody what happened. Nobody listens to me anyway."

"Well, that's not how it's going to work. That's not how it worked for the others." His faced clouded in a frown. "They all had to leave. I suspect someday you'll move on too. But not for a long, long time."

The conversation stirred fond memories of Rodney, Terry, and Danny in Digger's twisted brain. Digger couldn't resist having his way with each of his boys when they were unconscious after he kidnapped them. Once they awoke, however, he held his carnal desires in abeyance and instead served up every slice of charm to win their favor. Over time, a sour blend of fear, loneliness, and extreme depression weakened each boy's will to resist. Lloyd mistook their acquiescence as acceptance of his love. The boys bit their lips, shed tears, and swallowed screams.

God, how he loved those boys, but they all eventually betrayed him. When they were young and small, the boys couldn't hurt him.

But then they got bigger, stronger. And rebellious. They got strange ideas. Rodney was with Digger for nearly two years. Then one day he, like Toby, asked for a pencil, and he tried to stab Digger with it.

None of them realized how much I loved them, Digger thought.

Digger left the paper on the table as he made his way to the small door.

"Okay, Toby—enjoy reading about yourself. I'll be back with dinner. Maybe we can try a game or two tonight. It'll be great fun."

CHAPTER 22

MAY 25, 1959

Jason found Grandma Libby in the garden. Her garden was more than a hobby; it was a miniature farm shoe-horned into her small back yard, where she produced fruits and vegetables that lasted most of the year.

Her most prized accomplishment was nurturing a peach tree to life in the harsh Wisconsin climate. In the winter, she sheltered it beneath a soft blanket of snow. Throughout the growing season, she pampered it with more attention than would be given to a new-born child.

But in truth, this baby was the product of an accidental birth. The tiny fruit tree sprouted next to the garage, where she had dumped a bucket of peach pits during her annual fall canning adventure. Every year, she bought several lugs of Colorado peaches from the Farmers Store and baked peach pies that were so good Jason would often sit down and devour a whole pie smothered under a snowdrift of Dolly Madison vanilla ice cream. The rest of the peaches Libby canned for storage in her basement storehouse.

Sprouted from discarded pits, the little tree grew tall under her constant care and actually offered up a small batch of puny peaches that looked more like apricots. Though small, her Wisconsin peach harvest was featured in the *Saint Paul Pioneer Press*, thanks to her photojournalist daughter.

"Grams," Jason said as he walked up to her, "you know everybody. Do you know Lloyd's mother, Marjorie Harris?"

Libby looked up from her bed of healthy green beans, dropped a handful in her small fruit basket, and raised an eyebrow at the mention of Lloyd's name. "No, but my friend Victoria Cunningham lives in that neighborhood and might know her."

"Can you call Victoria? See if we can meet?" Jason didn't elaborate. He just glanced hopefully at his grandmother, who he knew would read between the lines.

She settled back and resumed ripping beans from the stalks. Jason wasn't certain if she were considering his request or dismissing him.

"I don't know if you want to start meddling in police work and scoping out the Harris place on your own," she eventually said. "If you're right about Lloyd, then you're messing with a murderer. That's dangerous."

"If I'm right," Jason countered, "then he already sees me as a problem—as someone who can report him to the police. That's already dangerous. Besides," he added, "when did *you* start worrying about taking risks? I heard you took on a big-time murderer in Chicago."

She let the basket of beans drop to her feet as she popped up, swiping black dirt from her hands across her blue jeans. "Who told you that? Well, makes no never mind. That was different."

The story Jason's mother had relayed went back to her childhood in Chicago. The Windy City was ground zero for prohibition and organized crime during the Roaring Twenties. The heart of the action was the Italian section on the west side, where Libby, Ernie, and young Ginger lived in a seven-story tenement building on Randolph Street.

One afternoon while Ginger and a group of children played in the alley behind the tenement building, a behemoth black sedan rumbled through, sending children diving for cover. Libby raced down the alley after the sedan, pounding on the side window until the car stopped at a cross street. The rear window slid down slowly, and a quizzical, pale-white, melon-shaped face emerged.

"Slow down when you see children!" she shouted.

"Sorry, ma'am," the chubby face replied. "I'll have my driver be more careful. I promise."

Returning to the growing crowd, Libby encountered a wide-eyed beat cop, who grabbed her arm.

"Libby, do you know who that was?"

"Everybody knows who he is. Doesn't matter. He was driving way too fast with all these children around."

"But—but—that was *Al Capone*," stammered the terrified cop.

"Well, I bet he slows down now," Libby replied, then returned to her apartment.

As the story goes, Capone's car did slow down after that. Capone was quite popular in the Italian neighborhood. The much-feared public enemy took special care to assist his neighbors, thereby creating a cocoon of loyalty.

Whenever stopping by the area, Capone's driver joked with Ernie about who wore the pants in the Hunter house. And after their surprise encounter, he always rolled down his window, smiled, and waved to Libby.

Grabbing the basket of beans, she headed for the house. "Jason, let me think about it. I'm not sure about this. Maybe I can just call Victoria and see what she knows."

"No. Don't say a word on that stupid party line. All the busy-bodies will be listening, ready to start a forest fire of gossip spreading across town faster than the *Telegram*."

As soon as the words left his mouth, Jason wanted to suck them back. Her glare scorched her grandson, but she didn't say a word. Mentioning the party line to Libby was risky territory.

In 1959, most residents didn't have a private phone line. Rather, they shared a party line with their neighbors. One line for many houses. It was almost impossible, then, to have a phone conversation without hearing a click that indicated another neighbor had picked up their receiver, attempting to make a call themselves. Protocol stated that the neighbor should promptly hang up, unless they needed to interrupt your conversation to make a call of greater importance. But more often than not, you'd hear a subtle click but no hang-up—which would betray the presence of a neighbor simply eavesdropping on your discussion.

As it turned out, the glare burning through Jason was due to the fact that as party line busybodies went, Libby Hunter was probably top of the list. Libby adamantly condemned the act of spreading rumors and gossip, yet somehow saw no harm in quietly eavesdropping on her neighbors' personal calls. In fact, it was her favorite pastime, one of the few times she actually sat still. When she thought no one was watching, she would slip into the virtual phone booth behind the kitchen door. She had become expert at cautiously lifting the receiver to avoid detection.

Or so she thought. In the midst of a juicy conversation, Mrs. Wagner would often say, "What do you think about that, Libby?" Usually Libby would quickly hang up and burn off energy buzzing around the kitchen.

Jason slipped back into the house and let his grandmother think about his idea—and calm down from the busybody reference. Reluctantly, Libby called Victoria Cunningham and arranged for a visit without divulging any details. She and Jason made the ten-minute drive to the Third Ward neighborhood. Victoria's house turned out to be right next to Lloyd's. Jason didn't know if that was good or bad news.

"Hi, Libby," Victoria said as she held open the door to her stately home. "Well, who's your handsome young friend?"

"Victoria, perhaps you remember my grandson, Jason."

"Oh, my goodness. It has been far too long, Libby. I cannot believe that cute little boy is this big young man. Come on in."

She escorted them into a library that may have boasted more books than the city library. It was definitely far more elegant, with three enormous Tiffany chandeliers and dark mahogany ladders on rollers attached to three walls filled floor to ceiling with books. The fourth wall was covered with classic oil paintings in gaudy gold frames.

"Check these out," she said with obvious pride as she pointed to a nearby stack of books. "These are all first editions from Ernest Hemmingway, F. Scott Fitzgerald, and John Steinbeck. And every one was autographed in this very room. They sat where you're sitting and drank from the very same china cups."

Her live-in maid—appropriately attired in a perfectly pressed brilliant-white dress with light-blue piping and a half apron—appeared in the doorway, waiting instruction.

"Jenny will bring us coffee and some fresh sugar cookies," Victoria said.

As the maid disappeared on her errand, Victoria gestured for Jason and Libby to make themselves comfortable in the large red velvet chairs surrounding a white maple reading table.

If Victoria and Harry Cunningham weren't the wealthiest couple in town, they were the top two or three. Their money came from Victoria's family, who had owned a couple of lumber mills on Half Moon Lake. The family smartly sold before the lumber industry died out. They banked millions, and Victoria inherited it all. Harry came from a prominent Chicago family before he met Victoria at Yale, and now he managed her fortune, buying manufacturing and food businesses throughout the country and in Europe.

The couple drove matching Cadillac convertibles, new every year, that differed only in color. His was dark green, like old money, and hers was brilliant yellow to match her flamboyant personality. He was the stereotypical Yale stud who never cracked a smile in public and would not be spotted without a hand-tailored pinstriped suit and designer shoes. Victoria must have used a putty knife to apply makeup, and her lips glowed in the dark with brilliant red. Her dyed jet-black hair looked as though it had been in a tornado, the way it was spun and piled high. Jenny spent hours every day shaping and pasting Victoria's twisted mound of hair with truckloads of hairspray. The hair helmet made the diminutive woman appear larger than life.

Their home was an incredible contrast to the neighboring houses, not only because it was at least twice the size but because of its strange design. Victoria would tell anyone willing to listen that it was designed by Frank Lloyd Wright. Jason had no idea who that was, but he feigned excitement.

Unlike its two-, three-, and four-story-tall neighbors, Villa Cunningham was only one story tall, although that single story stretched out across three lots and stretched upward at least sixteen feet with even taller archways in the glass-covered hallways. The place was more like a series of buildings tied together by glass tubes, perhaps modeled after a gerbil cage.

It boasted a flat roof, possibly the only one in town. Jason wondered how they dealt with snow. In fact, the whole home was something pulled right out of Arizona, with earth-tone exterior walls and a massive sun porch overlooking their sprawling private gardens. Libby felt right at home with the Southwestern atmosphere.

"Gee," Victoria said to Libby, "it's been so long since our days in elementary school. And we haven't gotten together for coffee in a long time either, perhaps since Ernie died. I've been meaning to call—with all that stuff in the paper about your son-in-law. Terrible. Terrible. What an awful time you are having. How can I help?"

"Actually, we're here because we're wondering if you can help us with another matter. I know Mrs. Harris next door is quite ill. Her son, Lloyd, is one of Jason's Boy Scout leaders. We're concerned about how they're doing, but we don't want to bother them with prying questions. Plus, it was a good excuse to come see you. What can you tell us about them?"

Jason almost grinned as he marveled at how convincingly his grandmother lied.

"Uff da," Victoria said. "Well, if Harry were here, he might be able to tell you more than I can. But he's in Tuscany checking out a vineyard he bought last week. I wish he'd stop buying things so we could just enjoy retirement like normal people."

Somehow, Jason doubted the Cunninghams could be normal under any circumstances.

"Ah, let me think," Victoria said, drumming a manicured finger on her cheek. "You know, I kinda like Lloyd, even if he is a tad strange. He's very friendly and an outstanding pianist. He often entertains at my parties."

"What do you mean, a tad strange?" Libby asked.

"Well, he's nearing thirty, he still lives in the second-floor apartment in his mother's home, and he never shows any interest in getting married or even dating. I guess that qualifies as strange in my mind. He seems to spend most of his time with young boys. I suspect he's a bit light in the loafers, if you know what I mean."

Libby closed her eyes momentarily and spread a field of

wrinkles across her extra high forehead. "I think we do. What do you know about his parents?"

"There was always a lot of yelling when he was there. Then Marjorie got polio about ten years ago. She spent nearly a year in an iron lung at Mount Washington Sanatorium, then came home in a wheelchair. I guess Leroy couldn't handle it. Apparently, he found a young, able-bodied woman and left Marjorie and Lloyd to fend for themselves as he moved to California. Lloyd said at least Leroy gave them his retirement checks."

"Does he ever visit?" Libby asked.

Victoria shook her head. "Not that I know of. But we don't have a lot of contact with them anymore. Marjorie used to come over for coffee before the polio, but I haven't seen her since the day she came home from the hospital—unless you count spotting her roll past a window now and then in her wheelchair. She lives on the first floor, and I don't think she's left that house one time. She doesn't even go to the doctor. Ol' Doc Farwell stops by now and again. I suppose I should go visit her, but it's been so long now it would be awkward. And to be blunt, I never cared for her that much when she was healthy."

"Anything unusual you ever notice around there?" Jason chimed in, trying to make the question sound casual.

"Not really." Then Victoria paused and pursed her ruby-red lips. "Well, yes. It's not much, but the lights are on in the basement just about every night, and sometimes it's very late. I mean two, three in the morning. But it's not like the lights are left on all the time, because other times, it will suddenly go dark. Sometimes I can't sleep, and I see the lights on. It makes me wonder what is that boy doing down there."

Jason remembered the time he stopped by Lloyd's house after a Boy Scout meeting. He was convinced the aging two-story white clapboard house was the ideal setting for a horror movie. Being in

Lloyd's upstairs apartment had been horrible enough. Every time Lloyd's name came up, he was forced to relive the nightmare.

Victoria waved her hands and shook her head. "As I said, it's probably nothing. I do like Lloyd, even with his quirks. He cuts our lawn and shovels the snow and never wants a penny. But I always have Jenny give him pastries and a cold drink in the summer or hot cocoa in the winter. As a matter of fact," she added, "he just finished cutting the lawn right before you came. Well, he didn't actually finish. It's too hot today. I told him to come in and have some treats and lemonade." She pointed at the dishes still resting on a colorful china platter almost out of sight atop the piano. "Jenny hasn't even had time clean up yet. Sorry—we usually aren't this messy, but it's been a busy day."

As Jason stared at the glass, an idea suddenly struck him. "Is that the glass he used?" he inquired.

"Yes. Again, we're usually not this messy."

"No, no. That's fine," Jason assured her. "Would you mind if I took his glass? You see, I'm working on fingerprinting for a Boy Scout merit badge," he fibbed, surprised at how convincing he too sounded. "Lloyd's our assistant scoutmaster, and it would be fun to identify his prints. I'll clean it up when I'm done and get it back to you."

"Sure, that's fine," Victoria said with a shrug. "And don't worry about returning the glass. It's nothing special."

"Please don't say a word to Lloyd. I want to surprise him." Jason gave a big, fake smile.

Victoria had Jenny dig a brown paper lunch bag out of the pantry, a room about the size of Jason's bedroom, maybe bigger. Jason deftly lifted the glass using a Kleenex and dropped it into the bag.

Libby rose to her feet. "Victoria, we don't want to take any more of your time, and I better get Jason to work. Thank you so, so much."

"Libby, it's always good to talk with you. You are one of the most interesting people I know. Please don't wait so long to come see me again. Heck, what am I saying? How about if I stop by your place next week?"

With a stout laugh, Libby gave her old friend a warm hug. "Wonderful. Please do come. I'm always there. If you come on Wednesday, we can have fresh pie and ice cream with our coffee."

Victoria's face lit up as though she had won the Dinner Bell Jamboree, the most popular show on WEAU Radio. Of course, it was Libby who usually won it.

"It's a date," Victoria exclaimed. "See you Wednesday."

Libby and Jason were feeling pretty good as they waved good-bye and headed out Victoria's eight-foot-tall redwood door—until their eyes fell on Lloyd pulling up right next to Libby's Plymouth in his sparkling clean '56 white-over-black Ford hardtop convertible.

"Oh crap, it's Lloyd," Jason whispered.

There was nowhere to hide the brown paper bag. Putting it behind his back would only draw more attention. Jason held it casually at his side, hoping Lloyd would ignore it.

Lloyd popped out with a Cheshire grin. "Hey, Jason. Long time, no see. Man, we really miss you on the dance team. So, is this your mother or your sister?" he said with a wink. He was so focused on Libby that he gave no attention to the bag—much to Jason's relief.

"Hey, Lloyd." Jason tried to be as cool as possible, which was nearly impossible. He just hoped Lloyd couldn't see him quivering. "This is my grandma Libby."

"Hello, Grandma Libby. Wow, you must have been a very young mother." He turned his back on Jason and stepped right up to Grandma Libby, projecting his ear-to-ear smile.

I've got a powerful urge to kick that grin off that overconfident asshole, Jason thought to himself. Immediately, he hoped his grandmother couldn't hear his thoughts, or he'd be in for another language lecture.

"Thank you for the kind words," Libby said with a fabricated laugh. "But I'm probably not looking so young today. I was up early working in my garden."

"So, whatcha doing at the Cunninghams'?" Lloyd inquired.

"Oh, Victoria has been one of my good friends since we were in grade school so many, many years ago. We still get together for coffee now and again."

"Strange—I've never seen you here before." Lloyd maintained his focus on Libby but swept his head around momentarily to draw Jason into his inquiry.

Libby didn't skip a beat. "Oh, maybe you've been at work when I've stopped by. And mostly she comes to my house for fresh pie." She laughed, then started rummaging around in the colorful canvass bag she brought back from Mexico and called a purse.

"Do you know Mrs. Cunningham too, Jason?" Lloyd asked, narrowing his eyes just a bit as he slowly turned around.

Before Jason could speak, Libby glanced up from her purse for a brief second. "Victoria wanted to show Jason her signed first editions from Hemingway, Fitzgerald, and Steinbeck."

Jason nodded enthusiastically, thankful Grams was quick on the uptake.

"Well," Libby said, still up to her elbow in the bag, "I suppose we should get going. Now where are those keys?"

"It was good meeting you, Grandma Libby. Maybe I'll come by for some of that pie one of these days," Lloyd said with a smirk that would seem innocent enough if you didn't know how vile he was. "And it was great seeing you, Jason. You should be proud of him," he said to Libby. "He's the best Scout in our troop. As I said, we really miss him on the Indian dance team. He's very, very talented and was always the star of the show."

Libby continued to fumble incessantly in her bag. It was beginning to annoy Jason. Finally, her arm shot into the air clutching her keys. They climbed into the car without glancing in Lloyd's direction, although Jason was certain he felt a stare burning into the back of his neck.

As she turned the corner at a faster than usual speed, Libby's bag tipped over on the car floor—and Jason spotted it.

"Grams! What are you doing with a *gun*?"

The little pistol looked like something from a museum—except nowhere as clean. It was rusty and in severe need of cleaning.

"We were heading into enemy territory, and the enemy himself showed up. Did you really think I couldn't find my keys?"

"I mean, where did you even get that?" he exclaimed.

"Oh. My dad gave it to me years ago when I had to ride through the woods to school. I never needed it, but I did a lot of target practice in the gravel pit. I got pretty good. That's where your grandfather asked me out, you know. I had almost forgotten about the gun until now. It probably won't shoot, and the bullets most likely are no good, but it might scare somebody."

"Scares me," Jason said while he cautiously moved her purse and the gun into the back seat. "That thing is in worse shape than some of my old toy guns. If you pulled the trigger, you'd get hurt worse than the guy you were shooting. It'd explode in your hand."

As they left the neighborhood, heading for home, Jason couldn't help but symbolically pat himself on the back. Maybe this detective work wasn't so hard. He had real evidence now that might just blow the case wide open.

What was next? That was simple: talk to Detective Stroud.

CHAPTER 23

MAY 26, 1959

Detective Stroud's car was nowhere to be seen when Jason arrived at the police station first thing in the morning. He would wait, then. There was no way he would walk in there to talk with anyone else. Stroud barely believed his story about Lloyd, and anybody else would just laugh.

When Stroud drove up an hour later, there Jason sat on the back steps of the library, behind the station, rereading the same page for at least the tenth time in whatever book he happened to have in his hands. The brown paper bag was safely stored in the backpack next to him.

"Jason, what's up?" Stroud said, strolling over to him.

Jason hurriedly put his book away in his backpack. "So, Grams and I went to visit her friend Victoria Cunningham, who just happens to live next door to Lloyd Harris, and—"

"Whoa, whoa," Stroud interrupted. "You did *what*? My God. Don't be doing that. If you're right about this guy, he could be very dangerous. You need to be careful. And tell your grandma to lay off the Miss Marple routine."

"But I think you'll want to know what we found," Jason said, undeterred.

Stroud flashed a blank stare that said "Aren't you listening to me?" louder than any words. When Jason just stared back at him with eager, earnest eyes, Stroud sighed.

"Okay. Tell me what you have. But please, please, *please* do not go anywhere near him again."

Jason pulled out the lunch bag and explained the whole story about their visit with Victoria and the things she said about him being an odd duck and leaving the basement lights on at strange hours.

"This is a drinking glass with Lloyd's fingerprints," Jason said, holding the bag out to the detective. "I was careful not to touch the glass, and I maintained continuous custody of the bag—just like Sergeant Joe Friday does on *Dragnet.*"

After a few more warnings, Stroud grabbed the bag and disappeared into the station. As he walked, he pulled from his pocket a crumpled scrap of paper ripped earlier from his small spiral-bound note pad.

"Gordon, I need you to dig up anything you can find on this guy."

Without breaking stride, Stroud dropped the paper on Detective Sergeant Gordon Richardson's desk and moved quickly toward his office.

Gordon unfolded the paper to see "Lloyd Harris" scribbled in lightly smeared blue ink.

"Does this have anything to do with the Boy Scout murder?" he slowly asked.

"Absolutely."

"Then I can't touch it."

Stroud spun about, poised to dive across the sergeant's desk. "What are you talking about?"

"Chief Schmidt said Milbrandt directed him to not waste any more tax dollars 'chasing shadows' when we already have the killer in jail. It's a direct order that came down once Milbrandt caught wind of us looking into that choir director. You need to talk with the chief."

Stroud spewed a poisonous concoction of frustration, anger, and disappointment over his sergeant, who looked away in obvious embarrassment, wishing he were anywhere else.

"That's pure bullshit. Then I'll handle it myself. Damn it, Gordon—I thought we were cops, not political puppets." He stomped into his office.

Five minutes later, Gordon stood in Stroud's open office doorway. If he had a hat, it would have been crumpled in his hand as he slumped into the chair beside Stroud's desk. Humiliation spilled from his face.

"Hey, boss. You're absolutely right. We're cops, not politicians. And we need to do this right. Plus, the more I look at it, the more I think you may be right about Korsen not being our guy. How can I help?"

Stroud nodded his approval, then spoke in a hushed voice. "I got a tip from a citizen at the church that night. He claims Lloyd Harris is somebody we should check out. He's the assistant scoutmaster and was at the Scout ceremony that night. He was very close with the victim. From the sounds of it, the guy maybe likes boys a bit too much. It may be nothing, but we better take a look. See what you can find out about him. But do it quietly. Don't make any waves. We don't need anybody getting their nose out of joint just yet."

"I'm on it, boss. Caution is my middle name."

Gordon started for the door, but stopped when Stroud called

out to him again.

"One more thing, Gordon." He handed over the brown bag. "There are some prints on this drinking glass. Can you pull them off and have Dempsey check 'em against the one on the boy's belt buckle?"

"Sure thing. Where did this come from?"

"My informant collected it, and he said he maintained the chain of custody."

"Wow," Gordon said with a laugh. "Sounds like we found your replacement."

Stroud snorted. "Not a bad thought. I'm ready to start packing."

As Gordon exited, he all but collided with Olberdorf, who was entering.

"We got a report back from the Stoughton Police Department on your choir director," the desk sergeant said, handing Stroud a report. "Looks like he just might have some explaining to do."

"Really? Let me take a look."

Finally alone in his office, Stroud settled in to peruse choir director Martin Goodrich's police report. Goodrich, a twenty-two-year-old University of Wisconsin student, worked as a teacher aide at Stoughton High School two years before he moved to Eau Claire. He had been arrested and held overnight for allegedly having inappropriate relations with a student. There was no conviction, and all charges had been dropped, but Goodrich's employment ended not long after.

Doing the math, Stroud realized Goodrich had been just a tad bit older than the Stoughton high school students at the time of the arrest. Even now, he was still not much older than Sonja Drake and the other choir members at Saint Luke.

Stroud slumped back in his desk chair. So much was happening with the case. After imploring people to come forward,

Stroud suddenly found himself buried under a pile of leads—no matter what the mayor thought. Stroud pulled out his notebook and scribbled the name of each possible suspect across the top of a separate page.

The choir director posed a new angle that couldn't be ignored. Roy's brother, Batshit Bart, and his degenerate pals appeared to be in the clear, but he couldn't totally put them out of mind. And just maybe it was that simple—maybe Peder did do it. Still, that old cop's gut was barking at him, telling him the cases in La Crosse and Eau Claire were connected. Plus, he had to deal with this Boy Scout leader Lloyd before Jason and Libby got themselves into serious trouble.

Olberdorf again poked his head around Stroud's doorway, breaking his train of thought.

"Hey, Stroud—grab line three. Some gal says she has information on the Boy Scout murder."

"Super. We didn't have any leads for the longest time. Now everybody has one. Well, maybe this is the one," Stroud said without conviction as he picked up the phone. "This is Detective Joe Stroud. With whom am I speaking?"

"My name's not important," said a young woman. Her voice quivered a bit. "All you need to know is I'm the one who called the night that boy got killed."

"Okay. And how am I supposed to know it's really you?"

"It said in the newspaper last week you want to talk to me," the girl continued. "But I never called because there isn't anything to talk about. I guess that's why I finally called today—just to let you know I don't know anything else."

Stroud could hear the tension in her voice, unlike all the other callers who were doing nothing more than using the murder case to cause trouble for an unlikeable neighbor or a cheating husband. This caller sounded legitimately upset. If she was the witness, as he was beginning to believe, Stroud knew she undoubtedly had more information than she realized. He needed to tread softly—ease it out of her carefully and gently.

"Well, how about you just talk me through what you saw? How did you come to find the body? Was anyone else in the area?"

"We were quite a ways away, closer to the pond, back in the tall grass. We saw the body later, when we were leaving."

"*We?* Who was with you?"

"Not important," she said quickly.

Stroud knew this touched a nerve. If she had been in the tall grass in the park that night, it didn't take a detective to assume she'd been with a beau. A beau she seemingly didn't want anyone to know about.

There was a pause on the other end of the line before the girl continued. "But now that you mention it . . . there was somebody else in the park at first. He was right by the picnic table, but we were too far away to see what he was doing. I'm pretty sure he saw us when we stood up. He seemed to freeze for a minute, he looked at us, then he bent down, doing something by the table, before he shot off into the cemetery. We didn't think anything about it then. But later, when we walked out in that direction, that's when we saw the Boy Scout. It really scared me. I'm still terrified to death." She let out a long breath to settle herself.

Stroud scribbled as fast as he could in his note pad. "That's really good information. Exactly why I wanted to talk with you. You know more than you realize. Next, tell me what this guy looked like."

"As I said, he was way off. We didn't really get a good look. I have no idea what he looks like. I wish we'd been closer."

Stroud could hear willingness in her voice now. She was eager to help but overwhelmed by it all. He just needed to guide her with the right questions to unlock her memories.

"Okay. Then tell me this: Was he a big guy?"

"Oh, not at all," she said. "He was short and skinny. Heck, it might have even have been another kid. But probably not. I can't explain why, but something about the way he moved—I just don't think he was a kid. Does that make any sense?"

"Yes, absolutely. It does indeed. Thank you. This is really, really helpful. If you and your friend could meet with me, we might be able to get even more details."

The young woman hesitated. "I can't do it right now. Not until we figure out some stuff . . . Just tell my parents I didn't fall into Half Moon Lake."

"*Sonja?*"

The line went dead.

Stroud wasted no time.

Louise Drake opened the door to their opulent mini-palace and stood there bathed in the fear of bad news, showing a level of sorrow no amount of wealth could ease. She greeted Stroud with a sad smile and red eyes that didn't even attempt to look confident. She was almost reluctant to speak, for fear of what she might learn.

"Did you find her?" she finally managed.

"I may have some good news," Stroud said cautiously, "but I don't want to give you false hope."

As though flipping a light switch, her face ignited with an enormous smile. Stroud thought she might kiss him. "Any hope is not false." She turned to shout down the foyer. "Jeremy! Come quick! Detective Stroud is here and he has news!"

Leading Stroud, Louise retreated into the house that could have been taken straight from the pages of *Better Homes and Gardens*. Her husband raced out from the kitchen with great expectation painted on his face.

"What's going on, Detective?"

"A short time ago, I received a phone call from a young female who claimed to be the anonymous caller who found the dead boy up at the pond. She refused to identify herself by name, but just before she hung up, she said, 'Tell my parents I didn't fall into Half Moon Lake.' While I can't be certain, I believe it was Sonja."

"Then what?" Jeremy demanded.

"Then nothing. The line went dead, and I immediately drove out here to tell you."

"So you lost her?" Jeremy scowled and dismissively turned to leave the room.

"Not exactly," Stroud reassured. "I think she'll call again. She may have witnessed that boy being killed or at least was at the scene when it happened. She seems eager to help, but she's just terribly confused and very frightened."

"Oh my God." Louise didn't know whether to cry or scream with joy. "If she's frightened, why doesn't she just come home, where she'll be safe? What's going on? I don't understand. Did somebody kidnap her?"

"I think it may be a bit more complicated," Stroud said. "During our conversation, she said 'we.' She was in the park that night with another person, possibly a boyfriend."

"That's bullshit," Jeremy spit his words with a sudden flash of anger. "She's headed to the university. I strictly prohibited her from getting entangled with some guy and messing up her life." Then he glared at his wife. "Did you know about this?"

"Jeremy, all that's important is that she's alive," Louise prefaced. "And yes. She may have said something about a boy from school. I don't know his name, but she thought he was pretty special. Don't forget that we met in high school, and I don't think you ruined my life."

"That's not the point here."

"I'm not a social worker or psychologist," Stroud interjected, "but I think this may be part of the challenge here." He subtly nodded toward Jeremy, who was still fuming. "She may be just as worried about talking to you about this boy as she is about the danger she faces from witnessing a murder. She just doesn't know where to turn. My biggest concern is that both she and her friend may be in grave danger if they saw the murderer and he discovers who they are."

Louise reached out to her husband and took his hand. "Jeremy, we can't worry about this matter with the boy right now. All I care about is that she's alive. You can't drive her away when she desperately needs our help. We're her parents. She needs us. Everything else will work out. Why, that poor boy is probably even more scared than she is."

Stroud stood, nodded politely, and moved toward the front door.

"Folks, if you hear from her, please call me immediately. I don't care if it's the middle of the night. Here's my card. I put my home number on there too. I'll let you know if we learn anything."

Stroud excused himself, leaving the Drakes to deal with their issues.

As Stroud came through the door into police headquarters, Olberdorf called out to him.

"Hey, Stroud," he bellowed. "You're the most popular guy in town today. Rick Otteson is on line two—says he needs to talk with you right away about the body at Half Moon."

Stroud slipped into his office and grabbed the phone. "Stroud here."

"Hello, Detective. It's Rick. I just pulled up your body."

"And?" Stroud asked but didn't want to hear.

He was convinced now that Sonja was okay. But perhaps another girl or boy had met an unfortunate end there in the lake.

He thought of Danny White and the three boys who had presumably drowned in La Crosse.

"The body is nothing more than a department store mannequin with some fishing line wrapped around one arm."

Stroud breathed an audible sigh of relief.

Otteson continued. "The good news—well, aside from the fact that it's not some kid's body—is that I also retrieved that boy's rod and reel, good as new."

"That's great. If you can drop it by the station, we'll give him a call," Stroud said with delight. They finally had a positive development, even if it didn't lead to Roy's killer.

"Okay. I'll swing by there on the way home," Otteson said, his tone much more buoyant as well.

Stroud hung up but didn't have time to lift his hand off the receiver before it rang again.

"Joe, it's Randy Olson," the La Crosse detective greeted his friend. "We got a new wrinkle down here in our missing boys' cases."

"Hey, Randy. Can you hold just a second?" Stroud held the phone at arm's length as he yelled at his open door, "Gordon!"

"Yeah, boss?" Gordon said, coming to the door.

"Have somebody talk to Sonja Drake's friends again. Find out her boyfriend's name. We need to talk to him too. It looks like she's alive—just a runaway lover. She and the boy may be witnesses to our murder."

Gordon sprang into action, and Stroud pulled the receiver back to his ear.

"Sorry, Randy. Things are popping here too. We have some potential leads on the murder, we've heard from the missing girl, and we just found out the body in Half Moon Lake is a mannequin. Whatcha got on your end? I was just thinking about your cases."

"Toby's mother came in yesterday with quite a tale. We've

arrested his old man. She had enough bruises to fill in for the tattooed lady at the carnival. The hospital backed up her story about seven visits there in the past few years, including two broken arms, a fractured left cheekbone, and a ruptured ear drum."

"Holy shit. What a bastard."

"Yeah, and it just gets worse."

"How's that?"

Olson took a breath. "She said he's been raping their fourteen- and sixteen-year-old daughters for years, but she was afraid to say anything until now. After a strong push by the mother, the girls confirmed that as well. Apparently, that was the spark that may have lit this whole episode to explode. The day Toby disappeared, he came home from school early and found the old bastard screwing his sister Judy. He whacked the old man in the head with a baseball bat, then split. A neighbor confirmed she saw him heading toward the river with his fishing gear."

"So, what do you think happened?" Stroud asked, leaning forward in his chair.

"I don't know. It's possible Toby's been on the run this whole time. But Toby's mother thinks the old man might have chased him down to the river. Maybe it got out of control, and he dumped the kid in the river. We got sworn statements from Toby's mother and sisters that will put the old man behind bars for a long time, whether he did anything to Toby or not."

"Well, at least that's some good news," Stroud offered.

"Whatever happened to Toby, it's starting to look like an isolated case," Olson concluded. "There may not be a connection with the other two boys from La Crosse or the boy from your case."

Stroud was quiet for a moment. "Yeah, well, I'm not quite ready give up on the connection yet. I need a little time to digest all these changes. Let's keep in touch."

CHAPTER 24

MAY 27, 1959

Stroud headed out in the unmarked squad car. His first stop was the junior high. His second stop would be the high school.

At the junior high, Stroud found a private place to speak with Martin Goodrich. With Sonja now alive, the suspicion that she'd been involved in foul play with the Saint Luke choir director was no longer valid. Still, Stroud had a dead Boy Scout who'd been raped, so anyone alleged of having inappropriate relations with minors needed to be checked out.

Goodrich turned out to be a very pleasant sandy-haired Irishman with a handsome face full of freckles. Stroud knew appearances could be deceiving, so he cautiously explained that he had received a call from a mother who was concerned about his history in Stoughton and his interactions with the church choir girls.

Goodrich deposited a tall stack of sheet music he had tucked under his arm onto a nearby desk, jammed his hands in his pockets, and gave Stroud a look of resignation.

"Wow. Some things just don't go away, do they, Detective? And the stories seem to grow with each retelling." He sighed. "Yes, there was an 'issue' at Stoughton High School. I was not quite twenty when I worked there part-time as a teacher aide for a semester. I guess someone thought I was too friendly with Sarah, a senior who was seventeen, almost eighteen. Rumors started flying. No one wanted to know the actual truth then or now, but Sarah and I never did more than flirt a bit. One of the mothers reported me based only on the rumors. It wasn't even Sarah's mom."

"Ah," Stroud said, starting to see the big picture. "Did you get fired because of it?"

"No, not at all. The arrest happened near the end of the semester. Once the charges were cleared, I finished the last few days, then went back to the university as planned."

"What about the new complaint from one of the mothers at Saint Luke?" Stroud asked. "What do you make of that?"

Goodrich shook his head. "All I can guess is with a Boy Scout murdered and our own Sonja missing"—his eyes clouded with sadness—"perhaps people are grasping at anything they can. I know how easy it is for a young guy like me to get people whispering and wondering. But I've learned from the Stoughton situation that it's so important to maintain professional distance with my students and choir members."

Stroud nodded. He was nearly certain now this was a dead-end lead, as so many of them had been. The caller had most likely been some overreacting mother who found this young choir director too handsome for his own good. Or who knows—maybe the mother was upset her kid didn't get the solo last Sunday. The station had been flooded with all sorts of "leads" fueled only by people looking to cause trouble for someone else.

"Okay, well, it sounds innocent enough," Stroud said. "I'll still need to check some more, perhaps with the girl and her family."

Goodrich nodded. "If you want to talk with Sarah, she's at home—our home, that is. We ended up getting married. And her mother's here this week helping with our new baby, if you want to speak with her too. Again, it's fine. I understand you need to do your job—especially with everything that's happening right now. We're all just so worried about Sonja. If there's anything I can do to help, please let me know."

Stroud did his best to keep a poker face about Sonja. "Thank you," he said. "I'll be in touch if there's anything else."

Stroud made his way outside. Next stop, the high school.

Jason slipped out the side door at Memorial High. He'd been back at school for only about a week. After the newspaper article started turning the tide away from Peder as the likely suspect, Jason decided it was safe to return to school. Still, he tried to keep a low profile. The students, like everyone else in town, were on edge as the days stretched by with a killer on the loose.

Jason headed to the parking lot and did his best to avoid everyone. Then he spotted Detective Stroud leaning against his unmarked squad car.

"Jason, the more I look at this case, the more I need to know what you know about this Lloyd Harris. He may just be our strongest suspect right now. But I can't even talk with him unless you give me something to go on."

Jason looked the other way. "I don't know what else I can tell you. It's probably nothing. I'm sorry I said anything."

"No. I think you're on to something. But you gotta tell me what you know. I got a feeling you know something important." He managed a tired smiled. "Got time to run over to the Dairy Queen? Treat's on me. We can sit in my car and talk, where no one will hear a thing."

Jason checked to make sure no one was looking his way, then

quickly yet nonetheless reluctantly climbed into the car. They drove to the Dairy Queen, where he ordered a hot fudge banana malt. Stroud settled for two large coffees.

Normally, malts lifted him. But this time, the treat seemed to burn as it slid down his throat as he struggled with what and how much to tell Stroud.

"I don't know if I can talk about this." Jason hesitated, his breath quickening. "If I tell you something bad, can we keep it just between us?"

"Jason, you gotta remember—I'm a cop. If you tell me something that's a crime, I may have to do something about it. But I promise I'll do everything possible to keep your secrets."

Jason began at the edges of the story, partly to provide context and partly to delay or maybe even avoid the difficult details. Even out there on the periphery of the story, he felt as if he were trapped in a nightmare, watching himself. It was so real he could see, feel, and smell the pain again.

He began by explaining that without a man in his life, he had buried himself in school, church, and Boy Scouts. His scout troop had a particular fascination with Native American culture, and Lloyd was especially knowledgeable in the art of Indian dance. Lloyd selected a team of boys to learn Indian dancing, and Jason made the cut.

Lloyd was a jovial, very likeable, but unattractive guy who mostly overcame his physical deficiencies with a giant smile and smooth banter that charmed every Scout's mother. He was the troop's lone Eagle Scout.

"My uncle is married to an actual Ojibwa Indian, Emmy Korsen," Jason said, eager to talk about anything but Lloyd. "She offered to help me create an authentic costume."

Jason deliberately strayed off course as he described in rich detail how he and Emmy collected feathers for a headdress and how she taught him to weave brightly colored beads onto his deerskin jacket and loincloth. Emmy told him how her father was a shaman, a highly respected elder among the Ojibwa people. He was a healer with a success rate as good as or better than any white doctor. His methods and herbal medications had been passed down through the Ojibwa people for centuries.

Jason also expounded on how he asked Emmy why she never attended Korsen family events. He was sad when she said it was because many white people didn't like Native Americans, seeing them as savages. The Korsens didn't want her in their homes to avoid the ridicule from anyone who saw her there.

"I told her, 'But I never think of you as different than us,'" Jason said. "And she said, 'Jason, I wish everyone saw things as you do. Hopefully, they will one day.'"

Stroud desperately wanted to move the conversation along. But long years of experience interviewing people told him to just keep his mouth shut and listen, no matter how long it took. So he sat back and popped the lid on his second cup of coffee.

Jason paused to take a difficult sip from his malt. He realized he was just stalling. He had to get back on track—even though it only led him to the darkest part of the nightmare.

"Us guys in the Indian dance troupe spent hours practicing with Lloyd," he slowly said, much to Stroud's relief.

Jason explained that the troupe first performed at the Court of Honor awards program for Scouts and parents. Soon they were visiting nursing homes, schools, and churches. A big story and photo in the *Eau Claire Telegram* only built on their popularity. The boys were becoming young celebrities, and Lloyd was the town hero for his remarkable skill leading the troupe.

"One night after practice," Jason said, his mouth dry, "Lloyd offered me a ride home. I was thirteen. He said he had just gotten an authentic Obijwa chief's headdress. He asked if I'd wear it at the next performance. He said we'd stop at his house to try it out."

With that, Jason disconnected, though his voice continued.

Lloyd led Jason up the creaky wooden stairway to his apartment, with little more than a frayed green couch and a well-worn cherry wood table with two black bentwood chairs. The apartment was dark with heavy gray curtains over every window.

Why bother with windows if you're just going to cover them? Jason thought.

"The headdress is in here," Lloyd said, leading Jason into the bedroom, which was even darker.

Lloyd handed Jason the magnificent headpiece crafted from dozens of authentic eagle feathers, black porcupine quills, multi-colored beads, and long deer hide strips. The sheer weight of the massive headdress instantly transformed Jason into a chief.

"Wait—you need to get the full effect," Lloyd said. "Here, put on this loincloth and some war paint."

Without thought or hesitation, Jason stripped off his clothes and got into costume. He stood before a smudged antique-framed mirror, while Lloyd snapped photographs with his Brownie Hawkeye camera.

Fixated on the amazing headdress, Jason failed to notice when Lloyd disappeared into the bathroom and emerged moments later dressed in his own Indian dance costume. They did a couple of Indian dances, laughed, then collapsed on the bed to catch their breaths.

Suddenly, Jason felt Lloyd's warm hand on his left leg. It slithered like a slimy serpent across his thigh into his crotch. Jason was too stunned to move when Lloyd then ripped his loincloth away. Jason lay paralyzed in a state somewhere between fear and guilt. Lloyd kept at it until the most amazing sensation Jason had ever felt ripped through his groin.

When it was over, Jason was breathless and totally conflicted. It scared the living hell out of him, yet it was such an electrifying sensation that he didn't want it to stop. He wasn't totally naïve, but pretty close. He struggled to understand what had happened. Guys talked, but no one ever talked about an adult guy doing this to a younger guy.

"Now, it's your turn to do me," Lloyd said, startling him to attention.

Even when he smiled, Lloyd was not an attractive person—about five feet five, nearly anorexic, and with pocked and crimson-stained skin that seemed stretched too tightly across his gaunt cheeks. At that moment, though, he was a monster leering at his prey with that sickening smile pasted across his face, standing completely naked, and pointing his monstrous penis at Jason's mouth.

"I can't do it," Jason managed to say.

"You liked what I did for you. Now, it's your turn to do me."

"I can't."

Jason grabbed his clothes and bolted for the door. Despite his stature, Lloyd was still too fast and too strong for Jason. He flung Jason onto the grungy bed. This time, he didn't ask, and it wasn't Jason's mouth he entered. The ripping pain was far worse than any pleasure Jason had received.

When it ended, Lloyd rolled over, flashed a demonic smile, and exhaled.

"Thanks," he said, as though Jason had done him a favor.

Did I? Jason thought.

Jason raced for the door again. His monster didn't bother following him. Jason pulled up his pants as he stumbled down the stairs. As he ran through the dark hallway, his mind suddenly flashed to a time when monsters once stood in his own hallway. Somehow he knew those monsters had led to this monster.

He raced for home as fast as the burning pain would permit. He didn't even remember traveling the first mile into downtown until he found himself sitting on a bench in an idyllic little park in the midst of the city.

He was too angry to cry. Angry at Lloyd. Angry at himself. Angry at God.

Jason recalled Reverend Russell admonishing their confirmation class to remember that "God is always with you."

Well, I don't see God anywhere in sight.

A plump gray squirrel almost ran into Jason's foot.

"What are you doing out here so late?" he asked.

The startled little fur ball scurried across the sidewalk into a giant oak tree—probably in big trouble for being out too late.

Then another creature appeared. An orange monarch butterfly settled gently on Jason's right arm. It crept slowly across his arm hairs up to his shoulder, creating just the slightest tickle. He appeared to be staring into Jason's eyes.

"And what are you doing out here? I thought you were supposed to be heading south. Grams said you fly all the way to Mexico to get away from winter."

I need to get away from here too. Far, far away.

The butterfly just sat there staring into Jason's eyes as though he understood. Then, with a whisper of wings, he lifted silently into the night and was swallowed by darkness. For some strange reason, Jason felt just a little bit better.

Once at home, he told Grandma Libby he was tired and escaped into his bedroom. It took a long time to fall asleep, only to be awakened by a terrific boom in the middle of the night. The blast was followed almost immediately by a blinding burst of lightning, which was in turn accompanied immediately by another thunderous boom. The bolt must have struck very close to home.

As the storm slid eastward, a melodic percussion concert

225

began. Gentle rain tapped on the roof like a chorus of snare drums. It was interrupted periodically by the deep bass of thunder retreating in the distance. It was comforting.

Suddenly Jason thought about his little orange friend. *Where do butterflies go when it rains? I hope he's safe. Do lightning and thunder scare him? I wish I could be there to tell him it will be okay.*

Then he slept.

The physical pain endured two weeks; the guilt never stopped. An overwhelming sense of shame constantly whispered to him: *You enjoyed what he did to you, so it must have been your fault.*

Jason considered telling someone what happened. Compounding matters was the fact that everybody admired Lloyd. Who could he tell? Who would believe a kid?

If there ever was a time in life when Jason needed a dad, this was it. He didn't have that option, though. Jason's mother did more than most parents could ever do as she filled in as both mother and father. Yet Jason could never talk with her about Lloyd—or any sexual things, for that matter. They had never even had the birds and bees seminar.

So Jason just caged this monster away in that special dark corner of his brain. He was able to keep it chained up most of the time. He mostly forgot about it. Perhaps imprisoning the memories of his monster was an effective coping mechanism. Or perhaps dealing with his father's issues had just numbed his brain to further trauma.

Nevertheless, this monster still occasionally managed to break free and jump out at the most unexpected moments. It often roused him in the middle of the night, when Jason would come to life sweating, out of breath, and shaking uncontrollably.

Jason quickly learned that his best friends were reading and writing—far more pleasant distractions to possess his little brain with positive thoughts. Reading was the perfect travel machine that carried him anywhere in the world to meet the most intriguing people. And writing about even his darkest memories was somehow cathartic, especially when he devised clever ways to slay his monsters on the page. He always destroyed his monster stories in fear that Grams or his mother would discover them.

Jason stayed in Scouts but dropped off the Indian dance team to avoid his monster as much as possible. Lloyd was always still there, though, smiling like a moon creature in Jason's living nightmare.

Fortunately, Lloyd didn't approach Jason again until one night three years later, when he asked if Jason wanted to come to his house for a party. But Jason was no longer a scrawny thirteen-year-old.

Throughout grade school, he had been one of the shortest kids in class. But between ages fifteen and sixteen, he shot up nearly a foot. He was in the throes of such a massive growth spurt that his knees hurt constantly. Though still skinny, he was suddenly six feet tall and in great condition from basketball and cross-country. His newfound size gave him the courage to stare down at that puny rat Lloyd and tell him he despised him. He warned Lloyd he would spill the beans if he ever talked to him again.

Determined to keep his distance, Jason even gave up the chance to achieve his Eagle Scout award before his eighteenth birthday. There was no way Jason would stand before his monster to complete the Scoutmaster Conference and Eagle Scout Board of Review.

Then Roy was found dead.

As if a movie screen had gone to black, Jason turned to Detective Stroud. He blinked and wondered what he had just said out loud while his nightmare played in the theater of his mind.

Stroud was still for a long moment. "My God, Jason. I was hoping against hope that this wasn't the story you had to tell."

Jason felt true warmth from the big guy. He wasn't a cop; he was friend. God, how Jason wished he had a father just like him. One to share ideas and fears with.

"As awful as this is for you," Stroud said gently, "together maybe we can make something good out of it by getting this guy off the street. At the very least, he needs to atone for what he did to you."

"No." Jason looked as though Stroud had just put a pistol to his head. "I don't want to deal with anything like that. It's still my word against his. You can't tell anybody about this."

"Jason, like I said, I can't guarantee anything. I promise to keep your story as secret as I can. But if you don't want to press charges, then know we'll be looking really hard at this Lloyd character for Roy's murder. Based on what you've told me, he sure seems like a good candidate. I'm eager to see what that fingerprint from your glass reveals. At the very least, maybe you've given me enough information to convince the district attorney to seek a search warrant for Lloyd's home. Who knows what we might find there." He sighed. "As I said, I'll do everything in my power to keep you out of it. But I don't know what details may shake out here."

They drove back to the high school, where a handshake and quick good-byes ended the session. Jason got into his own car and just sat there with his keys in his right hand, poised to turn the ignition. But he froze as his mind tumbled into darkness.

Would Roy still be alive if I had said something about Lloyd sooner? Is this all my fault? And now Dad is in the middle of it just because he wanted to show me he cared—on the night my friend happened to get murdered.

Jason longed for someone to talk to. A dad. Yes, Stroud was a friend—in a way. He seemed like a good guy, and they could talk. But still, he was cop. And that trumped being a friend.

The more he thought, the more Jason convinced himself he

could not go public about what Lloyd had done to him. Instead, he had to tie Lloyd to Roy's murder. That was the only way this would end right for everybody. He owed that to Roy. After all, Jason talked Roy into joining Scouts, and he never did anything to stop Lloyd from going after other boys.

Jason had come forward with his theory about Lloyd being the killer. He'd delivered Lloyd's fingerprint to Stroud. And now he'd shared an incriminating story about him. Hopefully it was enough to get Stroud an arrest or search warrant or something.

Jason had done everything he could—and would—do.

CHAPTER 25

MAY 28, 1959

Arriving at the station that morning, Stroud didn't bother to hang his jacket on the hook behind his door. Half asleep from a restless night, he just dropped it into one of the guest chairs and then flopped himself into the chair behind his desk. Once again, he had to sort through the ever-growing stacks of reports, notes, and phone messages.

The more he replayed his conversation with Jason, the more convinced he was that Lloyd was the one. But he had to remind himself not to be foolish like the city council president and get fixated on one suspect. Yet this guy sure seemed to fit the mold far better than any other. He pulled out his notepad and paged through it, trying to find enough pieces to pull it all together.

Suddenly, his office door flew open, smacking into the wall. Gordon bolted through.

"Holy crap, boss—where did you get that glass? The thumb-print is a perfect match with the print on the boy's belt. You got him."

Stroud even surprised himself as he leapt to his feet, sending his chair crashing against the wall. "Outstanding!"

But then Stroud held out his hands to temper his own enthusiasm as well as Gordon's. "Well, we don't actually have him yet. We need evidence that will hold up in the long run. But at least we now know who he is." Stroud stood. "C'mon. Let's bring down the hammer."

The Third Ward was in its quiet daytime college mode. A few students chattered as they meandered throughout the neighborhood. The only significant sound came from the lawnmower gliding across Victoria Cunningham's vast green lawn, tinting the air with the sweet fragrance of newly mown grass. Attached to the mower was a short, thin man who smiled, waved, and cut the power as Stroud and Gordon approached.

"Lloyd Harris?" Stroud asked.

"Yes, sir. How can I help ya?"

"We're doing a new round of interviews for everyone at the Boy Scout event at Saint Luke Lutheran Church the night Roy Pettit died. Do you have a few minutes to talk?"

Lloyd grinned. "Oh sure. I'm just finishing up the mowing I didn't get done on Monday—boy, it was a hot one that day, wasn't it? But I'm always happy to help the police."

As they slid around to the back of the Cunningham mansion, Stroud realized what Jason meant when he said Lloyd was good at charming people.

They settled into three lawn chairs overlooking a garden complete with a pond full of active goldfish and three ornamental dancing water fountains imported from Tuscany. The Cunninghams' maid, Jenny, appeared to ask if anyone wanted tea or coffee. Stroud politely declined for the group.

"Okay, Lloyd—let's talk about the Boy Scout meeting. Or I

should say, after the Boy Scout meeting. Tell me where you went, who you saw, and what you did."

Lloyd shrugged. "Not much. I just drove around town a bit and went home."

He paused and glanced quickly between Gordon and Stroud, who both stared at him with hard eyes.

"Wait—wow. Am I a suspect? That's not right. I loved that boy. Would never harm him." His voice edged higher.

"Really?" Stroud asked stone-faced. "Then what would you say if I told you two people saw you at McDonough Park after the meeting?"

"But they weren't close enough to see—" Lloyd froze at the realization of his own stupidity.

"They weren't close enough? Ah, so you *were* there." Stroud let a smirk curl up.

"Yeah," Lloyd quickly corrected, "but just for a minute as I passed through. I left my car at the cemetery after work—I'm a grave digger—and I walked over to church for the Scout meeting. Maybe somebody saw me walking back to get the car, but I wasn't in the park."

Bingo. There comes that moment in every successful interrogation when the guilty guy starts coming apart. Now Stroud saw it in Lloyd's blurred eyes; heard it in his faltering, confused voice; and could smell his sour odor of guilt.

"Come on, Lloyd. They saw you at that picnic table where we found Roy. Stop playing games." This was it. Stroud leaned in, almost touching foreheads, and barked, "What happened to Roy?"

Lloyd stiffened, stared into his hands, and sat motionless. He sat so still it was difficult to tell he was breathing.

Stroud, in turn, folded his hands and sat there in absolute silence too. He knew he had him, and he was willing to sit there as long as it took. The only sound was the constant splashing of the fountains.

Lloyd suddenly sat up straight. "Roy was a wonderful boy." He spoke without emotion, as though reading an economics textbook aloud. "I can't believe this happened. I would never hurt him. I loved him so much. I don't know what to tell you. I don't know what happened. He just went limp. Maybe something just happened to his heart or something."

As if waking from a trance, Lloyd snapped back to life. Words streamed out quickly now.

"I mean, it was those two kids. I bet they did it. They must have raped him and killed him. I would never hurt Roy. This is just awful."

"Who said the witnesses were kids?" Stroud asked, raising an eyebrow.

Once again, Lloyd realized he'd ratted himself out, but he tried to backpedal out of it. "I just assume it was kids—who else would be at a park in the evening?"

"Lloyd, this is bullshit," Stroud replied. "Why would two kids jump out of the woods and kill Roy?"

"I don't know. You'll have to ask them."

"Well, I did," Stroud said. It was partially true. "And they say he was already dead when they got to him. What I can't understand is why you were there at the park with him. Why did you take him there?"

Lloyd glanced into the goldfish pond, probably searching for a quick story. "It was a beautiful night, and we went to the park to talk. Roy is working on his astronomy merit badge, so I brought my telescope to check out some constellations."

"That sounds like a good time," Gordon chimed in. "What galaxies were visible?"

"Wow. I don't know. I don't remember. I can hardly think straight—I'm so nervous with all these questions and hearing all this awful stuff about Roy. It's just so sad. Terrible. And you're just trying to get me all confused. I can't think straight."

"Well," Stroud said, "what would you say if I told you it was cloudy that night and you would have needed an awfully powerful telescope to see any stars?"

Stroud actually recalled it was clear that night, but it was immediately obvious that Lloyd didn't remember. Stroud pressed on.

"And by the way, what happened to that telescope, anyway? It wasn't at the scene, and you surely didn't take it with you when you ran. Where is it?"

"I don't know. Those kids probably stole it. That's what they were doing there. Just looking for somebody to rob."

"I don't think so, Lloyd. They were just a couple of lovers. They don't seem like the kind of kids to rob anybody. In fact, they had just left choir practice at the church. They know you."

This last part was a stretch for effect. Maybe Sonja or her beau knew him. Maybe not. Regardless, they weren't close enough to positively ID him.

Lloyd went quiet again. Stroud was ready to give him a Scout badge for creative thinking—this was a bizarre tale he was spinning. But he also saw that Lloyd was digging himself deeper and deeper into a very dark corner.

"Okay, Lloyd. First you tell me you weren't at the park. Then you say, 'Well, yeah, I was nearby, but not right there.' When I tell you people saw you there, you change the story again and tell me about looking at stars on a cloudy night with a telescope that magically disappeared. You know, I'm having a really tough time believing anything you say."

Lloyd was drenched in perspiration, and his voice had become little more than a whisper. He shook his head and uttered, "I don't think I should say any more. You just twist everything to make me look bad. I want an attorney."

Stroud nodded at Gordon, who reached to retrieve the handcuffs.

"Lloyd, I'm arresting you on suspicion of the murder of Roy Pettit. We're going to take your fingerprints, find you some jail clothes, and get you settled into a nice, warm jail cell. You can talk to an attorney in the morning."

Back at the station, Stroud handed an even paler than usual Lloyd over for processing, then he and Gordon stepped into his office.

"Way to go, boss," Gordon said, clapping him on the back. "You sure nailed that slimy rat's ass to the wall. Fingerprint. Eyewitness. All his lies. He's dead meat."

"Well, we know this is the right guy, but I fudged a little on the details when we talked to him. The eyewitnesses weren't close enough to positively identify him. It wasn't cloudy that night either, so we can't use that. Even the fingerprint he might be able to explain away from the Indian dance bit. Everything we have is very circumstantial, and any good attorney will jump all over it right away. Hell, even a mediocre mouthpiece might put up a good defense."

Gordon's face fell. "So you're saying he'll walk?"

"No. I'm just saying we've got some work to do. Hopefully this is enough to get a search warrant for his house. The woman next door says strange things go on in that house, especially at night down in the basement. Who knows what we'll find. We need to take a good look at the place before he can get back there and clean up. But we just can't get ahead of ourselves with this guy, Gordon. Milbrandt already did that to Korsen, and you see what happened there."

"Speaking of," Gordon said, "what ya wanna do with Korsen? We haven't actually charged him with anything other than walking away from the asylum, and now that Lloyd has taken up residence, we'll sure need all the jail space we can clear out for drunks this weekend."

"Before we release him, let me check with his family. Maybe they want to see him before he heads back to the asylum."

Stroud picked up the nearest phone and called Libby's number. He was pleased when Jason answered, as Ginger, Libby, and Sidney were out.

"I doubt Mom will want to see him, but I'd like to," Jason said. "When's a good time?"

"As soon as possible, because we're about to send him back to the asylum."

"I'll be right there," Jason replied

Stroud hesitated a moment before suggesting Jason stop by the A&W Drive-In and grab a large cheeseburger and quart of root beer for his dad.

Almost in laughter, Jason said, "Yeah, he used to take me there all the time when I was little. I guess it's only fair that I return the favor."

Thirty minutes later, Jason walked into the lower level of the police station to find Stroud and Peder sitting at the visitors' table in the lounge area outside the jail cells.

Jason displayed joy that hadn't shown on his face for weeks. He held up a large bag and a jug. "Good thing I bought extra burgers and a gallon of root beer!"

Stroud gathered three clean coffee cups from the break room, and Jason filled them to the rim with root beer. Olberdorf and two other cops strolled by with empty cups waving in the air, and he treated them as well.

There wasn't much conversation, but just sitting there with his father and his new best friend, Detective Stroud, gave Jason a good feeling. The feeling that somehow everything would be okay.

Almost by design, they ate very slowly and savored every sip of root beer, dragging the impromptu meeting out as long as possible.

When they finally finished, Stroud stood, saying, "Peder, it's time to get you back to your bakery. People are getting hungry for those pies."

Jason and Peder exchanged a long, awkward handshake until Jason felt an overpowering compulsion to just wrap his arms around Peder and squeeze. It was the first time he could ever recall having hugged his father, but it said more than any words.

They separated and exchanged a prolonged warm smile. Then Sergeant Olberdorf and Sergeant Paul Middleton escorted Peder back to the asylum in their squad car. Under the order of Detective Stroud, they broke protocol and did not handcuff Peder.

As he entered the kitchen at home, Jason was greeted by Ginger, who appeared none too happy as she sat at the table waiting for him.

"Tell me you didn't go see your father without telling me." Ginger rarely displayed emotion, but Jason could almost feel flames blasting from her eyes as anger boiled inside her.

"Sorry, but I did," he replied. "There was no time to wait for you to get home before they took him back. Detective Stroud thought it would be a good idea."

Ginger seemed to mellow slightly. "I know. He called a few minutes ago. But he had no right putting you in that position. I'm still terrified just having your father so close, and now you're making things worse by seeing him."

Her words stung Jason as he slid into a kitchen chair across the table from her. He could see Grandma Libby dusting furniture in the living room, clearly planning to stand clear of the fireworks.

Jason always tried to please his mother. This time, it was proving difficult. He looked at her with sincerity.

"Mom, I'm sorry if you think it was wrong, but I feel good

about it. He has become very calm. Jessie, his nurse, assures me he's no threat to us. Seeing him was something I felt I should do. Besides, I'm old enough to join the army, so I should be old enough to make my own decisions."

His comments did little to ease her fears, but somehow she felt good that he was becoming a man. A man she was proud to call her son.

Peder couldn't have been happier to see his own room—his own bed—when he arrived back at the asylum. He was home. At last.

Little did he know the asylum would remain his home only until 1977. Then, after twenty-seven years in state mental hospitals, he would be released. Not because of any miraculous cure but because the federal government would start shutting down most of its mental institutions to cut state and federal expenses.

Further cuts would come as well. By the early 1980s, most of the half million mental patients across the country would melt into society. Many would just relocate into prisons. Some would roam the city streets as homeless shadows. The elderly would be deposited in nursing homes ill-prepared to deal with either the volume or scope of the job.

Fortunately, a few patients would survive with the help of family willing to accept them. This would be the case for Peder. He would get a small apartment near his daughter, Sidney, where she could keep close watch on him. He would live three years in freedom before the cancers deposited in his lungs by his Chesterfield cigarettes and those nightly card games at the asylum would snuff out his life. Jason and Sidney would be at his side.

But that was a future Peder couldn't envision. Today, he was just happy to be back where he belonged.

CHAPTER 26

MAY 29, 1959

Stroud pulled together every detail he could muster, focusing on the fingerprint match, and strolled over to the county courthouse to meet with District Attorney Riley McDermott III.

McDermott, a one-time star quarterback at the University of Wisconsin, was a brilliant lawyer who could easily make ten times the income in private practice as a defense attorney. But he thrived on punishing lawbreakers. No one could imagine the law-and-order zealot ever being comfortable as a defense attorney, no matter how much money it paid. Besides, as heir to the McDermott Mining Company fortune, money was no worry.

McDermott wore reading glasses as he carefully scanned Stroud's report. He hesitated frequently to peer over the top of his black-rimmed half-lens spectacles, grunt, and smile broadly like a man who had just landed a world-record muskie. Right there in his hands, McDermott felt the biggest case he had ever touched coming to life and throbbing with potential. This would catapult him high into the upper branches of Wisconsin's political tree. Maybe attorney general. Or maybe he could follow his grandfather into the governor's chair. That would silence everybody in the family who thought he was nothing but a dumb jock.

"So what do you need from me, Detective?" he asked as he removed his glasses.

"We need to search his house."

"Why? What are you looking for?"

"Neighbors say Lloyd is a bit strange. They think he entertains young boys and that something unusual goes on late at night in his basement. We're also looking for any connection to the boy who was killed. His story about his activities that night is sketchy. He admitted to being with Roy that night at the park. At the crime scene, we collected some feathers. We have reason to believe they came from the Indian headdress he wore at the Boy Scout ceremony that night. The headdress belongs to Lloyd. Perhaps there's other evidence connecting him to Roy."

"You do realize that while this is definitely titillating stuff, you don't really have enough here to keep him in jail more than a couple of days."

"Absolutely. That's why I need to get into that house before he can get home and clean up."

Stroud considered mentioning that a juvenile had reported being sexually assaulted by Lloyd Harris in that house. But he wanted to keep his promise to Jason that he wouldn't get him involved unless it became absolutely necessary.

McDermott eyed Stroud, sensing he had more to say.

"At the very least," Stroud offered, "I have good reason to believe we'll find evidence at the house if we can just get in there soon."

McDermott scowled under the realization that getting the search warrant would be a challenge with so little to go on. But he was convinced Stroud knew what he was doing and that they were dealing with a sadistic killer.

"I'll take it to Judge Albertson. He's usually a bit more liberal in granting search warrants, especially when it involves danger to children. I'm going to play it that way—make the assertion that this guy poses imminent danger to young boys. Who knows, maybe he'll kill again. Or possibly he's done it before." He nodded. "I'll give you a call when I get back from the judge's office."

Two hours later, Stroud had the search warrant in his hand as he and Gordon headed back to the Third Ward to Lloyd's house. After ten minutes banging on doors, circling the yard, and peeking in windows, they were preparing to force the front door. Then it opened ever so slightly.

"What do you want?" a frail voice inquired.

"Police, ma'am," Gordon said. "We have a search warrant for your residence. Please open the door."

"I don't know," Marjorie said slowly. "Lloyd isn't here right now. You come back when he gets home."

"Lloyd is the reason why we're here," Stroud said. "He's in jail. Please open the door or just slide back out of the way. We're coming in."

Marjorie rolled back and sat in shock. She was as thin as someone who had just escaped from a Nazi death camp. Stroud hated this part of his job, knowing this woman's sad life was about to get far worse.

"Is there anyone we can call to come stay with you?" he asked her. "Lloyd won't be coming home for a while."

"There's only my daughter, Claire, and she's in New Mexico."

"All right. Why don't you give me her phone number in New Mexico? I'll give her a call. She needs to know what's happening."

Marjorie slowly turned her wheelchair to face Stroud.

The frail woman held up her fragile hands, as if imploring his understanding.

"Claire is a famous scientist, you know. She works for the federal government in Los Alamos along with her husband. He's a nuclear physicist. They're very important people. I don't know if you should be bothering them. Lloyd can handle things. Lloyd takes good care of me—has been ever since Leroy ran off with his whore and left us."

She mustered what energy she had in a vain attempt to demonstrate confidence. Stroud thought of his own mother, who had spent her final years navigating in a wheelchair and how frustrated she had become. He was convinced that when she died, she had just given up. Looking at this tired old woman, he knew she wouldn't be able to cope with what was happening.

"We'll take care of it, Mrs. Harris. I'm certain she'll want to know you need some help here. Like I said, Lloyd is not going to be coming home for quite a while. We're just going to look around now. We'll be very careful not to harm anything."

Marjorie rolled into the nearby living room. Clearly, she had no handle on what was happening, and Stroud didn't want to make her life any worse until he knew the daughter was there to help.

"Gordon, you check out Lloyd's apartment upstairs. I'll look around on the first floor. We'll tackle the basement together." His face was taut. "My gut tells me there are some dark secrets down there. I don't really want to go down there by myself."

Gordon couldn't help but smile. "What's the matter, boss? You getting jumpy in your old age? Think there's a monster locked up down there?" He climbed the stairs, still chuckling to himself.

Stroud didn't discount the monster theory.

As expected, the main floor revealed no potential evidence. It was clearly Marjorie's domain locked in time from the day she fell ill with polio. It was coated with years of accumulated dust. Soiled gray curtains blocked out the outside world.

Gordon came back downstairs with a box of condoms, a massive Indian chief's headdress, and a wooden crate that had been stuffed under the bed.

"There's at least a dozen photo albums in here and a huge pile of negatives," Gordon said of the crate. "Really sick stuff. I just thumbed through it all quickly, but every photograph seems to be of a young boy. Some are just random shots that appear to have been taken without the boys' knowing. But then there are some where the kids are naked. I thought I was gonna puke."

Stroud's expression was a mixture of disgust, sadness, and relief. The photos were just what they needed to nail Lloyd.

Gordon lifted the headdress. "Don't these look like the feathers we found at Roy's murder scene?"

"They surely do. Put all that in the bags and stick it in the car. Then let's check the basement."

The basement was just as haunting as Stroud had feared. Small half windows were black with dust, grime, and spider webs. In fact, the entire basement was something of one enormous spider den. At least the arachnids had cleaned up all the other bugs, digesting the tasty innards and dumping what wasn't edible in tiny piles of insect parts throughout the musty cellar.

Other than digested bugs, there was little else in the room except some dirty storm windows stacked against the wall and a big cabinet full of paint cans, garden tools, a couple of cardboard boxes, and some miscellaneous hand tools.

"Maybe we were wrong," Gordon said, looking around. "There isn't much of anything down here."

"Just a minute," Stroud said, flicking on his flashlight.

He swept the light across the floor. Every inch was caked in thick dust—except for a relatively clean, shiny path from the bottom of the stairway over to the cabinet.

"The lady next door says he spends hours down here," Stroud said, squinting at the floor. "So why would he come down here every night and walk only between the stairway and that cabinet? Yet the stuff on the cabinet hasn't been touched for years. Doesn't that strike you as a bit odd?"

"I see what you mean," Gordon replied, turning on his own flashlight. "Yeah, that's definitely odd."

They took a tentative step toward the cabinet.

"And look over there on the floor." Gordon moved his flashlight onto an arc pattern in the dust. "It looks like something's been sliding across there—maybe that cabinet. Boss, what's the chance that cabinet moves and there's another room back there?"

"I'm thinking there's a damn good chance," Stroud answered. "Let's see if we can move that thing."

They tugged and pulled on the cabinet, but it wouldn't budge. They tried pulling it from both sides. Still no movement.

Then Stroud spotted a latch near the top. He flipped it open, and the cabinet heaved forward. It seemed to be on wheels or rollers as it slid easily away from the wall, revealing what appeared to be a four-foot-tall door with a circular handle.

"It looks like a fallout shelter," Gordon said. "But why hide it behind a cabinet? And why come down here at all hours of the night?"

Stroud turned the wheel left and felt the door give inward. Cautiously, he pushed forward. Gordon pulled his gun and held it in his right hand with the flashlight in his left.

Lying on the bed reading the newspaper for about the twentieth time, Toby was starving, weak, and white as baby powder. As much as he hated Digger, he was excited to hear the door move. And as much as he hated himself for giving in to his new life, he knew he had to cooperate at mealtime. He needed food if he ever wanted to crawl out of the dungeon.

Toby sat up only to be blinded by two flashlights aimed right at him.

"Who are you?" a strange voice inquired from behind the light.

Toby dropped the newspaper and scrambled back on his bed against the wall. As an unfamiliar head poked into the bomb shelter, Toby feared Digger may have sent someone to check on him.

"I—I'm Toby," he stuttered. "What do you want? Did Digger send you?"

"Relax, son. I'm a policeman. What are you doing down here?"

A cop? Toby wasn't certain whether he was in trouble or being rescued.

"Digger brought me here and he won't let me go."

"Wait—did you say Toby? Are you Toby Swartz from La Crosse?" Stroud asked in disbelief.

This was Randy Olson's alleged drowning victim. The pair of old detectives had been right—their cases were connected.

"Yeah. Toby Swartz. You know who I am?" Toby slid off the bed and hurried over to the door. "Oh my God—are you here to take me home?"

"Yes. Absolutely. You're safe now."

Stroud reached into Toby's cage and led him out into the shabby basement. But then Toby's initial excitement turned to renewed fear.

"Where's Digger?" Toby asked, frantically looking over the policemen's shoulders, expecting his monster to suddenly appear. "You gotta get me out before he comes back!"

Gordon shook his head in confusion. "Who's Digger?"

"That must be the name Lloyd told him," Stroud said. "He's a grave digger."

"That's right. That's him," Toby said excitedly. Words came flooding out now. "He choked me unconscious when I was fishing, then he brought me here. My parents think I drowned. He said he was going to keep me here for a long time and that he loved me."

He looked away, too ashamed to tell them everything Digger had done to him. He had a feeling they had already figured it out anyway.

"He's had other boys down here too—Terry and Danny and Rodney. Their names are written on the walls. He said they 'left.' I don't know what that means. I think he killed them. I think he was gonna kill me too. You gotta get me outta here."

"It's okay," Stroud said gently. "Digger's in jail now, and that's where he's staying. He's not going to hurt you or anyone else. Let's get you out of here."

As they sat in Stroud's office, Toby sucked down three Milky Way bars and two bottles of 7UP. Along with the sweet taste of sugar came the burst of relief that he would live.

He had survived being raped then locked away like a caged animal, but he didn't die. After reading about those other guys in the newspaper and seeing their names etched on the wall in the bomb shelter, he knew Digger killed them and planned to kill him too. Now he was safe.

"Toby," Stroud said, "I called my friend, Detective Randy Olson in La Crosse. He never gave up looking for you. He didn't believe you—or Rod or Terry, for that matter—had drowned. He says your mother and sisters are on their way from La Crosse. They'll be here soon. But before they come, I need to talk to you about your father."

After handing Toby another bottle of 7UP, Stroud carefully explained how Toby's mother and sisters had gone to the police when they feared his father was somehow behind the disappearance. Once there, they had opened up and revealed the whole sordid story about how the old man was beating his wife and sexually assaulting his daughters.

"The La Crosse police grabbed him and threw him in jail," Stroud said. "Thanks to your mother's and sisters' testimony, he's awaiting a trial that will most likely send him to prison for a long time."

Toby set his pop on Stroud's desk, sat back, and mulled over how this might affect his life. Truthfully, he saw it as nothing but good. He hated his old man and wouldn't miss him. He finally got what was coming to him.

Then it struck him—Toby's own ordeal, as gruesome as it had been, had saved his mother and sisters from their life of torture. They were all safe now.

Maybe there really was a silver lining behind the blackest of clouds.

CHAPTER 27

MAY 30, 1959

Stroud sat paralyzed in thought with his back to his desk. He stared into the open space outside his second-floor office window as he relived one more time the horrors of what he and Gordon had uncovered beneath the Harris home. He was so deep in thought he failed to hear Gordon enter.

"Stroud, Lloyd's sister is here."

Spinning about, Stroud was taken aback as Gordon led a woman into the office. He didn't know what he had expected Lloyd's sister to look like, but she definitely didn't fit into any of the options. She bore no family resemblance to Lloyd or their mother, nor did she fit any image he might have of a scientist.

Claire Spielberg was stunningly attractive. She was tall and slim with jet-black shoulder-length hair framing a strikingly sculptured face with high, pink cheekbones, a button nose, brilliant red lips, and a square chin. She radiated refined beauty and the confidence of a Jackie Kennedy look-a-like stepping off the cover of the 1959 spring *Vogue* fashion magazine. Her perfectly tailored Turkish blue tweed day suit accentuated her shape. It was subtly set off with a single string of pearls, gold earrings, a petite gold wristwatch, and black high-heeled pumps.

Stroud almost forgot to speak.

"Mrs. Spielberg, thank you for coming so quickly," he said, regaining his focus. "I realize this is shocking, but your mother really needs you right now. And I guess your brother does as well."

"It's Dr. Spielberg, but please call me Claire." She stepped forward with deliberate strides and descended into the side chair before his desk. "Shocking doesn't begin to explain this. Our family has been dysfunctional as long as I can remember, but this is beyond insane. Have you notified my dad yet?"

In less than two minutes, this distinguished woman had nearly tossed Stroud off track—which didn't happen often.

"We have no idea where your father is, actually. Lloyd said somewhere in California, but police there can't find any record of a Leroy Melvin Harris in any official records after 1948, when he separated from Camp Pendleton. I was hoping you would have his address."

She gently shook her head. "No. I have no idea either. I really don't want to know, truth be told. His memory haunts me every night. I know he's my father, and maybe I shouldn't feel this way, but I absolutely despise the man. And I don't feel much better about my mother. She sat there and said nothing about what he did to me or how he brutalized Lloyd. When I left for college, I told Lloyd I didn't care if I ever saw our father again, and nothing has changed my mind. I still feel guilty about leaving Lloyd alone to face the Beast, but I just couldn't take it anymore."

She gazed out the window as she spoke. "I have a wonderful husband and two beautiful children, but I do not want them to even know my father's name. As far as they know, he never existed.

Died in the war. I fear that just knowing about him or seeing him might contaminate their lives. I will not risk that." She turned back to Stroud. "And now you tell me Lloyd has become a monster too. It's almost too much to take in."

Stroud stood, walked around his desk, and sat in the other guest chair facing her.

"I can't imagine how terrible this is for you, but we need your help," he said with as much compassion as he could muster.

"Help? What could *I* possibly do?" For the first time, the tiniest crack appeared in her stoic demeanor.

Stroud had seen powerful men break down in battle. He'd seen strong cops crumble in horrific cases. Claire was living the worst crisis anyone could imagine, yet she was somehow holding it together with little emotion. He needed her assistance now, but he didn't want to push her over the edge to get it. He had to tread lightly. He looked into her eyes and pleaded more like a father than a cop.

"As you know, we rescued a boy from the bomb shelter beneath your mother's house. We have reason to believe Lloyd abducted and kept at least three other young men down there over the years. But we have no idea what happened to them. He won't say a word to us." Stroud sighed. "Look, he's definitely going down for kidnapping and molesting Toby, so he's already spending life behind bars whether he talks or not. We're just hoping you can convince your brother to tell you where the boys are. That's all we need."

He leaned in closer. "You're a mother. Imagine how you would feel if your kids were missing and someone could find out what happened to them. Please help us get some answers for these parents."

Claire's eyes betrayed her as they became moist. Stroud hoped he hadn't pushed too hard.

"I can try," she said, taking a deep breath to recompose herself.

Jail clearly did not agree with Lloyd. He'd barely been there forty-eight hours, and already he appeared emaciated and weak. He shuffled into the interrogation room with the staggering gait of the living dead. His skin was more ashen than the pallid gray uniform that hung on his bones like a tablecloth. He didn't seem to recognize the woman seated before him.

"Lloyd. It's me—Claire."

He snapped his head up and glared like some Hollywood monster, a monster she did not recognize.

"Yeah. I see ya. What do you want?"

"Oh, Lloyd. I feel so badly for you." She struggled to find her brother in this creature. "What happened to you?"

"Like you care. You abandoned us."

"No. I never stopped praying for you, Lloyd." She realized now how hollow that must have sounded to Lloyd. She looked at her hands. "I guess I did let you down, but I was just too terrified of letting him back into my life. I couldn't risk it. Surely, you must know the terrible things he did to me."

They went silent as the ghosts of Claire's memory floated to the surface. Her father had never physically assaulted her, but she wondered if that might not have been easier to handle. His constant insults, berating, and disgusting, baseless accusations inflicted unending pain. And once he realized the level of her intelligence, his campaign of intimidation only ramped up.

She wondered how her parents had ever met. Had there ever been love? He was so imposing that she became immune to sexual attraction—something of a benefit during her early years in college.

Then she met Anthony Spielberg. Through incredible persistence, lots of flowers, and gentle words, the future nuclear scientist eventually convinced her that not all men were beasts. Even after they married, she sometimes hesitated during moments of intimacy, only to have her husband soothe her pain with kind words and loving caresses. Gradually, over the years, she relaxed and almost put it all behind her. Until today.

A sly smile spread across Lloyd's face, snapping Claire alert in her daylight nightmare and sending chills through her spine.

"Yeah, well, you don't need to worry about him anymore. I took care of that."

"What do you mean? Is that why he left for California? Did you get him to leave?"

"He didn't actually leave," Lloyd said matter-of-factly. "He was beating on Mom one night. Imagine—there she sits in that damn wheelchair, and he's pounding away on her. I tried to pull him off, but he just punched me in the face and laughed when I fell on the floor. So, I went downstairs, grabbed his hatchet, and stuck it in the back of his head before he could slap her again."

Claire's breath escaped her.

"Funny thing," Lloyd continued, "when he fell down, he turned and looked at me with shock and fear. It felt good. *He* looked at *me* with fear. I just smiled and said, 'Who's worthless now?' I couldn't believe how tiny he looked lying there on the floor. He always seemed so big when he was the Beast. But now he was just a little dead rodent swimming in his own blood. It took me weeks to clean up. I bet some of it probably is still there in the cracks."

Lloyd gave a menacing smile, then a stomach-turning chuckle, amusing himself with the memory.

"Dad had knocked Mom out. She didn't come to for hours. When she did, I told her Dad had taken off with some mistress. She totally bought it. We told the government he was in California so they'd still send his retirement checks. We just kept cashing them. Nobody seemed to care. Yep," he stated, "I took care of him all right. And he never hurt me or Mom again."

Claire was without words. Bile rose in her throat. This was not her brother. She just wanted to get out of this tiny space she shared with this awful person. Nevertheless, she struggled to maintain her poise. She had to keep him talking.

"What did you do with him?" the refined scientist forced herself to ask.

Lloyd rocked back in his chair and beamed as if describing some heroic accomplishment.

"Well, I wrapped him up in the shower curtain and took him out to the cemetery. It was too cold to bury him, so I hid him in the storage shed and kept him frozen. I used his crosscut saw to cut him into little pieces. In spring, I buried some and threw the leftovers into that outdoor latrine at the park next to the cemetery. He was nothing but crap in life. That seemed to be a fitting final resting place for the old bastard. I sure wasn't going to give him a proper burial, like I did my boys."

Claire was shocked—even though she shouldn't have been. The boys—this was why Detective Stroud had sent her in to speak with Lloyd.

"Your boys? What boys?"

Lloyd was beginning to relax. He finally appeared to be enjoying his sister's company as he described his murderous deeds as though he were talking about a baseball game.

"My wonderful little boys—Danny and Rodney and Terry." He shook his head. "It was always so sad when they had to die. I loved them."

Claire was not certain how much more she could stand, yet she needed him to reveal the grim details.

"Where did you bury them?"

"They're buried below other people in the cemetery. It was simple. I mean, that's what I do—I dig graves." He gave her a little glare. "I didn't get to go to college and be a big-shot scientist or anything important. I just dig holes. And sometimes I dig them a little deeper, then put my lovely little boys in there before the other bodies arrive."

Lloyd began to smile. He seemed to come to life, taking extreme pride in his demented vision of love. It scorched Claire's brain as she wondered who he was. How did this happen? Inside she knew—the Beast did this. The Beast destroyed Lloyd, just as he had tried to destroy her.

"Every day, I go to my boys' graves. I say a little prayer for them and put flowers on their graves. I visit Roy's grave too." His faced clouded a bit. "I don't know what happened—all I wanted to do was love him. It didn't have to happen. Those damn kids popped up in the woods, and he started to call out to them. I couldn't have that."

Claire needed all the restraint she had to frame a false smile and speak calmly amid his delusional discourse.

"Lloyd, if something happens to you"—surely he realized he was going to prison—"there won't be anyone to pray at their graves. Why don't you let Detective Stroud take you to the cemetery so you can show him where they're buried? He'll make sure they get their own graves, where their families and other people can visit and pray for them."

Lloyd sat straight, as though he suddenly had some level of control. "Yeah, I can do that. With one condition: I won't show him the Beast's grave. He can rot in hell. I don't want the police or you or anyone else bringing him up and giving him a private grave."

That was it. Claire couldn't take any more.

"Lloyd, I need to go. But I'm going to talk with your lawyer and make certain you get help. And I'm going to take good care of Mother. She can come live with me and Anthony and the kids in New Mexico."

Before Lloyd could say another word, she rushed out of the interrogation room. She was on the verge of vomiting. She needed to get away from her brother. This was not somebody she knew.

All along, she'd worried that her father would contaminate her children's lives. Turns out, she should have worried about Lloyd. Now she only hoped he hadn't just contaminated her.

A few hours later, Stroud walked through the cemetery as a handcuffed Lloyd identified the graves where he'd buried the boys' bodies. Stroud noted that although Lloyd's job was to dig graves in each of the five cemeteries on Omaha Street, he had buried his victims only in the Lutheran cemetery—and always beneath men.

Stroud also made mental notes to obtain court orders and notify relatives that the three caskets would be brought up briefly so the young murder victims' remains could be removed and reburied.

As for the Beast, Stroud was sure no one would make a great effort to locate his grave nor retrieve his bones from the outhouse.

Later that evening, Stroud was more than ready to head home, but he had one last thing to do. He made a quick call to Libby's house, then gathered a few things in a large evidence envelope. By the time he walked out of the station, he found Jason, as planned, sitting on the library steps. It had only been four days since Jason had sat in that very spot with the glass that provided Lloyd's fingerprints, but it sure felt like a lifetime ago.

"Jason," Stroud began, "I wanted to tell you this myself: we got him. Thanks to you, we had enough evidence to get a search warrant. We found a boy from La Crosse trapped in his basement. Lloyd eventually confessed to everything—to killing Roy, killing his father, plus killing three other boys. One of them was Danny White. We're gonna put Lloyd away for good."

Jason sat back. He wasn't sure if it was okay to be proud, but he was. As much as his heart filled with sorrow thinking about Lloyd's victims, Jason also felt as though he'd just won a year's worth of Grams' newspaper jackpots.

He had set out to prove Lloyd was the killer, and he had succeeded. Had he not taken action, his dad would have been sent to prison. There would have been no justice for Roy—nor Danny and those other boys. The kid from La Crosse would have been killed too. And Lloyd would have been free to continue his sick campaign.

But now, Lloyd would pay for everything. Jason hadn't been this happy since Mary Wright said she'd go to the prom with him.

Yes, this truly was a proud moment.

Stroud beamed with his own burst of pride. "And through it all, I was able to keep my promise to not implicate you at all. No one knows a thing."

With that, he handed Jason the evidence envelope.

"Inside are six photographs I found at Lloyd's. I thought you might want to burn them yourself. I also included your fingerprint cards and the report from the burglary you helped me solve last fall. I thought you might want them. Maybe you could use them as a front to explain our visit to your mother and 'Detective Libby.'"

"Photographs?" Jason asked.

Then that ugliest of all days—there in Lloyd's bedroom—exploded in his head once more like a living movie. The Indian headdress. The loincloth. Lloyd's camera. The attack. Jason shut it down as quickly as he could. He wondered if it would ever truly go away, though.

Stroud seemed to read his mind. "Jason, for your own benefit, you should think about talking to your family about Lloyd at some point. It would be good to get that off your mind."

Jason smiled and nodded, but he knew that wouldn't happen. He simply planned to burn the photographs the minute Stroud left.

"Bette and I are heading south. Our new address is in the envelope too. Stop by if you ever get down there." Stroud placed a hand on his shoulder. "Have a good life, Jason. You are an out-standing young man."

As Stroud removed his hand, turned, and walked away, Jason felt a strange pain in his chest. He had really grown to like the old detective—the man he needed in his life. It was a sad note to real-ize that Stroud was moving away, out of his life just as they had become friends.

Then it occurred to Jason that he was eighteen. He was vir-tually an adult, heading off to college in the fall, ready to see the world. Florida sounded like a great place to see.

He'd put it at the top of his list.

PART IV

CHAPTER 28

SEPTEMBER 4, 1961

Joe Stroud sat on the white sandy beach outside of Breakers restaurant in New Smyrna Beach, Florida, savoring an ultra-thick Hawaiian cheeseburger and watching kids run across the silver beach sand and dive into the frothy blue Atlantic Ocean. A sailboat slid across the distant horizon. Screaming seagulls edged close to his chair, begging to sample his burger. Somebody tumbled into the sea after trying to mount a tall wave with a colorful surfboard.

It was Labor Day, and Stroud had a snow-white frozen coconut margarita chilling his hand. For a moment, the biggest question on his mind was, *Why a Hawaiian cheeseburger in Florida?*

He glanced at his wristwatch. It was almost 3:00 p.m.—time to stroll up to Treats on the Beach for his afternoon cup of coffee and maybe a scoop of rum cherry ice cream in a freshly made waffle cone. Bette had meandered up Flagler Avenue to check out all the swim shops, antique stores, and gift shops in search of just the right postcards and souvenirs to send back to the grandkids.

They would be starting school tomorrow. When she was done, she'd come join him at Treats on the Beach for her daily ration of sweet tea.

You gotta love seven-day weekends, he thought. Time no longer mattered. Life was good.

Yet Stroud couldn't clear his mind of the evil he had encountered in his final weeks as a cop over two years ago. How could he survive five battles in World War II plus thirty years as a cop, yet have so much shit rain down on him in just one month?

Thankfully, Stroud left for Florida right on schedule as planned once the case wrapped. But that didn't mean he escaped the case. The aftermath followed him—a call here and a letter there kept him in the loop for months.

At least justice had been served. Lloyd's confession plus the evidence against him swiftly convinced Judge Orrin Forester of Lloyd's guilt. In addition to abducting and molesting Toby Swartz, he was charged with five counts of murder.

In court, the photo albums retrieved from Lloyd's bedroom revealed he had been secretly photographing Boy Scouts and schoolchildren for years, often from a great distance. Most of the photographs were harmless candid shots. But two albums contained graphic pictures of Boy Scout Indian dancers, many of them naked. There were several close-ups of young genitals. Among the most explicit photographs were those of Toby Swartz, Terry Fullmer, Rodney Smith, Danny White, and two unidentifiable boys. Strangely, six photographs appeared to have been removed, though Lloyd denied removing them.

Considering that the first suspect in the case was an insane asylum patient, Stroud found it ironic that Judge Forester declared Lloyd criminally insane and unfit for trial. He committed Lloyd indefinitely to Mendota State Hospital to live out his life alongside fellow murderer and graverobber Ed Gein.

Stroud was stunned when he read that City Council President Milbrandt had won his reelection. The old detective may have been an expert in solving crime, but he was a neophyte in the smarmy cesspool of politics. Lloyd's confession had barely left his lips before Milbrandt, the consummate politician, had called a press conference to proclaim victory in the arrest and confinement of Roy Pettit's killer.

He even had the audacious temerity to claim he had assisted the investigation. His spin was that he had turned the public focus on another suspect so Lloyd would not realize he was being investigated. He never bothered to apologize for what he had done to Peder and his family—after all, Peder was just that crazy guy anyway.

Surprisingly, Milbrandt did heap praise on the police, citing the "outstanding work of Joe Stroud, the finest detective I have ever known." Stroud had to smile to himself. *Did Milbrandt know another detective?*

Lloyd's mother never made it to New Mexico to live with Claire. Three days after learning her son was a sadistic killer and pedophile, Marjorie suffered a massive stroke and died. Claire buried her mother in a grave overlooking Dells Pond—at the opposite end of the cemetery from where the Beast's parts were said to have been stashed in the latrine.

As the sole heir, Claire wanted nothing to do with the family home. She had the bomb shelter sealed off and the house sold. She gave the money to the families of the four boys her brother had kidnapped.

In a letter accompanying the gifts, she apologized for the horrible acts her brother had committed. As a mother, she said she realized there was no way to compensate the parents for the loss of their sons, but she wanted to express her profound sorrow and offer the money so the boys might have proper memorial services.

From Toby, she asked for forgiveness and hoped he could put the money to good use.

Rodney's mother returned the money with a nasty reply. But Danny's and Terry's parents each wrote back thanking Claire for her kindness and absolving her of any guilt for what her brother had done. Terry's mother even paraphrased, "You are not your brother's keeper."

Toby wrote back to Claire, saying he would use the money for college, where he planned to study law enforcement. He added that, in some small way, he felt sorry for Lloyd.

Sonja Drake had a tearful reunion with her parents. Jeremy Drake was much relieved to see his daughter but not happy to see a diamond ring on her left hand. Jeremy cautiously shook hands with Michael Brand, her boyfriend, but neither man totally sold the greeting. Undaunted, Sonja and Michael vowed to make it work while they headed off to their respective colleges—she to the University of Wisconsin in Madison and he to Harvard.

Back from his outing, Stroud settled into a yellow-cushioned lounge chair on the deck of their fourth-floor condominium overlooking the Atlantic Ocean. Stroud didn't miss much about Eau Claire, just his friends—especially his new young friend, Jason. He thought how strange it was that they had bonded so quickly. He decided a phone call to Jason was needed to ensure that he knew the invitation to come visit was more than idle conversation.

He was happy and glad to be done fighting crime, but even the calming effect of ocean waves slapping against the beach couldn't completely obliterate thoughts of evil. He thought briefly about Lloyd sitting in a padded room in Madison.

Sure, he solved the case and won great praise. But he only wished he had retired a month earlier. Maybe he wouldn't see those vacant, bottomless blue eyes staring through his nightmares.

Miles away, Jason was enjoying his Labor Day. His junior year at Wisconsin State College started tomorrow. He was looking forward to getting lost in textbooks and lectures, forgetting about murder. He was particularly anxious to see Jessie Simonson. He had signed up for her Psychology 301 course.

It was a perfect day. The yard had been scrubbed clean by overnight rain, and the air tasted sweet and clean. A vast floral rainbow wrapped around the house in an explosion of color and sweet aromas from his grandmother's phlox, begonias, daisies, and brilliant red canna. A chorus of robins, chickadees, nuthatches, and an angry blue jay added audio.

Mr. Radinski, their next-door neighbor, was slashing through his heavily fertilized dark-green lawn with his big red mower, blending the aroma of fresh-cut grass into the already fragrant air. Two houses away, Mrs. Warren was singing along with the birds as she pinned her extra-large white undies on the clothesline.

And there was Grandma Libby already busy collecting tomatoes and green beans from her garden.

"Jason, come quick," Grandma Libby said. "The monarchs are here."

Sure enough, her garden was ablaze in a pulsating sea of orange with dozens of butterflies draining nectar from her field of flowers and milkweeds. (She swore that the monarchs especially loved milkweeds.)

"They're fueling up for the long flight south," Libby explained. "Many of them won't make it through the challenges of nasty storms and hungry birds—not to mention the chemicals farmers use to kill off weeds and unwanted insects."

Watching the beautiful bugs flit about, seemingly oblivious to the world around them, Jason reflected on how far he had come in two years. His life had flipped 180 degrees from desperate and hopeless to delightful and full of potential.

But the past still came to visit at inopportune moments. It would never go away. He laughed to himself, thinking about those people who prattled on about the concept of closure. Why were they so consumed with "closure" from traumatic life events?

Closure? Are you kidding? Jason thought to himself.

He realized closure wasn't possible when dealing with great trauma. Hollow chatter pressuring people to achieve closure just makes life even more difficult when you're caged in your own nightmare.

The best anyone can hope for is acceptance. Jason had accepted his situation, and that freed him to live. To enjoy life, finally.

With the precision of a Bolshoi ballet troupe, the clusters of little butterflies suddenly rose up in a cloud of orange. Their wings stirred the air with a strong whisper. One broke away and dropped onto Jason's shoulder for just a moment, then gently kissed his cheek with a flap of her wing as she jumped up to rejoin the vanishing orange cloud. Together, they rose higher and higher until they disappeared into the southern sky.

Jason knew then that his world was filled with many more butterflies than monsters.

Happiness in life is like a butterfly.
The more you chase it, the more it eludes you.
But if you turn your attention to other things,
it comes and sits softly on your shoulder.

—Henry David Thoreau

AUTHOR'S NOTE

Monsters in the Hallway is fiction, but it draws heavily upon my life experiences. Just about everything—except the murders—is some version of the truth. Some characters may have been inspired by real persons, but this is fiction based on my memory and perspective.

I was motivated to write *Monsters in the Hallway* when I realized my "normal" was not so normal to most people. In 1951, a voice only my father could hear told him aliens had invaded the bodies of his family members. He set fire to our home while we slept. Fortunately, we escaped. I was ten. My father was then declared mentally ill and institutionalized.

It threw our family into poverty. If you think life in the workplace is difficult for women today, you have no idea what my mother endured just to feed my sister, Sandee, and me. Somehow, she did it—so well Sandee and I didn't realize we were poor until we were older.

The monsters of my father's institutionalization spawned other monsters as well. Our situation provided ammunition for some bullies to make my life miserable. Then when I was twelve, my Boy Scout leader sexually assaulted me, leaving me with more mental than physical scars. He preyed on single-parent boys, which put me right in his sights.

I faced many monsters in my early years, yet I somehow managed to beat them. Thanks to my mother and grandmother, Sandee and I both obtained an excellent education and succeeded in business and life. My wish is that through this fictionalized account, my experiences might reassure others that they can beat their monsters too.

My other wish is that this book will provide a glimpse into mental illness and how it impacts patients, care providers, and families—especially families, then and now.

My father was released after his first hospitalization, but he was hospitalized again in 1953. He ultimately languished for twenty-seven years in mental asylums in Madison, Eau Claire, and Whitehall, Wisconsin.

Then in the 1970s and 1980s, Congress discovered it could save a lot of money by closing the nation's mental hospitals and tossing the mentally ill out onto the streets. Dad was one of the few with family willing to support him when he was released in 1977. Many others curled up under bridges, found their way into prisons, or just melted into society—hiding in plain view.

Forty years later, we're still fighting the same stigmas, the same public perceptions, and, sadly, the same lack of adequate treatment. Yes, positive strides have been taken, successful medications are helping, and some facilities are introducing exciting treatments. But millions of people are impacted daily by mental illness—progress is far too slow and grossly underfunded.

Even with family willing to help, my dad still faced the daunting challenge of being dumped into an unwelcoming society that looked nothing like the one he had departed twenty-seven years earlier. Dad turned sixty-five the day he left the hospital. He no longer showed significant evidence of mental disorder, but he was a hollow shell of his former self. Occasionally, he stared into space with that glassy, vacant look that identifies those who have experienced extended institutionalization. Otherwise, he was some version of normal, as long as he stayed on his medications.

Sandee, an ordained minister and college educator, lived nearby and could keep an eye on him. I lived in Chicago at the time, working as assistant communications director for the American Medical Association. I visited Dad on holidays.

Dad exercised his newfound freedom walking the streets of Eau Claire, logging many miles every day. On his walks, Dad often visited his childhood church, First Lutheran. He entertained Pastors Bob Esse and James Homme with lively biblical repertoire, a skill rooted in his devout Norwegian Lutheran childhood and reinforced through years of intense Bible study in the hospital. The pastors saw him as something of an intellectual and biblical scholar; they assumed he was a retired businessman. They were stunned and saddened to learn of his lost life due to mental illness. They too wondered what might have been.

Sandee quickly discovered Dad had trouble integrating the present with the past. He constantly addressed her daughter Sonja as "Sandee." He still envisioned our mother, Virginia, as the young, slim beauty she had been the day they married. Mom may have retained her beauty in her sixties, but she was no longer that ultra-slim young wife imprinted on his memory.

The past and the present came together, however, on Sandee's birthday in 1978. "Come right over," he said on the phone. "We're going to have a party."

On arrival, she saw him sporting a huge smile, perched atop the stairway. Inside his apartment was a party for two, intended to span decades of missed opportunities. Employing the baking skills he perfected over years working in the hospital kitchen, he had spent at least a week creating enough sweet rolls, cakes, and fruit pies to cover two four-by-four card tables.

"You and I are the party," he said.

As they embraced, thirty years of missed birthdays, Father's Days, and holidays melted together.

Three years after leaving the hospital, Dad was diagnosed with intestinal and liver cancer, thanks to years of inhaling cigarette smoke. I had just returned from a business trip to Norway and proudly told him, "Dad, Norway is exactly like you always told me. I visited that big ski jump in Oslo you talked about, and I felt right at home."

Then it occurred to me he had never seen and would never see the Norway he seemed to know and love so much from his father's stories. Because of his illness, Dad never had a chance to experience the world.

He died peacefully with me and Sandee at his side.

I hope *Monsters in the Hallway* sheds some much-needed light on mental health. Studies suggest that at some point in life, one in five Americans suffers some form of mental illness. If that statistic is even close to accurate, this is a topic that demands our full attention.

Progress has been made, but it is woefully slow, tremendously inadequate, and grossly underfunded. We no longer put people in mental hospitals without hope for release, but we may have gone too far. Today, per capita, the United States has less than 10 percent of the mental health hospital beds it had available in 1950. In that same timespan, the US population has more than doubled. Care for the mentally ill has not kept pace with the population growth, making it extremely difficult for families to get extended-stay hospitalization for someone in desperate need.

No one advocates a return to permanent long-term institutionalization, but there is great need for extended-stay intensive residential treatment services. Congress has slowly begun to recognize the need for many more crisis beds, long-term inpatient mental health beds, assisted outpatient treatment, adult foster care, transitional housing, day treatment, affordable therapists, skilled nursing facilities for the rapidly expanding population of mentally ill seniors, and improved services for veterans.

Dealing with a condition that impacts an estimated

forty-three million people—8.1 million of whom are classified as severely mentally ill—will be incredibly expensive, but not nearly as expensive as the impact of ignoring them.

Here are some important numbers to keep in mind pertaining to those 8.1 million severely mentally ill citizens:

- 5.4 million have severe bipolar disorder (3.3% of population), and 51% are untreated.

- 2.7 million have schizophrenia (1.1% of population), and 40% are untreated.

- 169,000 are homeless, living on the streets.

- 383,000 are in prisons and jails (ten times more than are in psychiatric hospitals).

- They commit 90% of suicides (44,193 total suicides in 2015).

- They commit 29% of family homicides.

- They commit 50% of mass killings.

- They are victims of 50% of police shootings (approximately 500 annually).

(Sources: Treatment Advocacy Center, 2017; National Institute of Mental Health, 2016; 2015 Annual Homeless Assessment Report)

For additional information on this topic, please visit my website. I am also available to speak to your book club or other organizations.

www.JimKosmo.com

LESTER GOES TO PRISON

A s *Monsters in the Hallway* was completed and ready for the printer, I met Eric Larsen, retired deputy chief of police in Eau Claire, who agreed to read my manuscript to ensure accuracy of police procedures. I also mentioned my monster, Lester Hanson, the seventeen-year-old who assaulted me when I was twelve.

Eric offered helpful hints on firming up some procedural details in the story. But he also enlisted Eau Claire police officer Todd Johnson to search the records for information about Lester. As it turned out, Todd uncovered a mountain of stunning information.

In January 1953, Lester and I were both listed in the newspaper among a group of thirty Boy Scouts signed up to attend the National Jamboree in Santa Ana, California. By July, following the assault, I tried to avoid Lester like the proverbial plague. I quietly withdrew from the Jamboree. About that time, Lester left Troop 44 at Our Redeemer Lutheran Church and transferred to Troop 115 at Black Elementary School in the nearby town of Seymour.

There is no documentation, but Detective Larsen postulates that someone in authority discovered that Lester liked little boys too much and sent him away. "That's the way they dealt with it in those days," he told me. Obviously, the Catholic church wasn't the only institution with such issues.

I never spoke a word about my assault. In particular, I feared no one would believe me, given Lester's reputation as a respectable young man from a prominent family. Looking at the files now, this fear was reinforced. Not only was Lester celebrated as Troop 44's first Eagle Scout and Indian dance instructor but he was also president of his class at Regis High School, member of the Chippewa Valley field archery team, and a leader of the ham radio operators' club.

He left Eau Claire in 1957 after joining the air force. He was stationed in North Carolina as a ground communications repairman. He later told police that he served less than six years in the air force—he was most likely discharged early for some offense.

He then vanished from public records for a few years until he was charged with sexual misconduct with a minor in Alabama. He underwent involuntary commitment at a mental hospital. In 1973, Lester was put on probation and was permitted to return to Eau Claire, where he began psychiatric treatment with Dr. John Berg.

Very adept at finding ways to connect with children, Lester became coach of the Eau Claire Fencing Club and created the Academy of Safe Scuba, a scuba-training club headquartered at his home on Starr Avenue.

In March 1979, parents of a seven-year-old boy told police officer Mary Beth Berg of an assault by Lester. During an interrogation with Eau Claire detectives Ed Sturgal and Richard Meyer, Lester confessed to sexually assaulting that boy as well as eight other juveniles, including three girls, in Eau Claire and Fall Creek. He didn't identify any of his victims in Alabama nor those of us who had the misfortune to know him in the 1950s.

The seven-year-old boy was apparently Lester's youngest victim. The boy's parents had delayed notifying police when Lester told them he would get psychiatric help. When that didn't happen, the family went to the police.

Lester told the judge, "I want treatment. It's a problem. It's a problem that I want to take care of any way I can."

Judge Thomas Barland accepted a plea agreement, sent Lester to Mendota State Hospital for psychiatric examination, and put him in prison for twenty years. Lester was scheduled for release from prison in 1998, but he died in 1994 at age fifty-nine. There is no information available on his cause of death.

Whether Lester was sincere or disingenuous about wanting treatment is immaterial. The question is, what penalty is appropriate for a monster who repeatedly rips away children's innocence, destroys their opportunity for a normal childhood, and condemns them to a lifetime of gruesome memories? I may have been Lester's first victim in 1953, when I was twelve and he was seventeen. As a compassionate person, I probably should forgive Lester.

Maybe I will, someday.

PHOTOS

Eau Claire County Asylum, a 446-acre working farm and mental health treatment center from 1900 until 1999, when it was torn down to make room for a housing subdivision.

Author Jim Kosmo inspects the fire damage in his family home following the fire his father set on November 23, 1951.

Lifesaver Award— Steve Andrews, advancement chairman of the Old Abe district of the Boy Scouts, presents a life saving award to Scout James Kosmo at the annual court of honor Monday night. The award, given by the national court of honor of New York City, was the first ever won by a scout from the Chippewa Valley council. James received it for going back into his burning home and carrying his sister to safety about a year ago.

The *Eau Claire Telegram* announces Jim's Lifesaver Award in an article published on February 10, 1953.

The author's parents, Palmer and Virginia Kosmo, were a striking couple on their wedding day on September 1, 1937.

After graduating from high school in 1959, Jim drove his 1952 Chevrolet to visit his father, Palmer Kosmo, at the asylum. His mother was not pleased.

ALSO FROM AUTHOR JIM KOSMO

Still Standing: The Story of SSG John Kriesel continues to sell very well. Jim and John also appear throughout the country speaking to audiences from school children to senior corporate executives. The message from John's story is particularly popular with corporate sales and training meetings and national management conferences.

To purchase books or reserve a speaking appearance, visit:
www.jimkosmo.com

ACKNOWLEDGMENTS

Writing can be a lonely disease. My wife, Shelley, will attest to this. There were days when I wasn't "present" even though I was right there in the same house. When I retired in 2010, she expected it to be more than just a change of vocation for me. Fortunately, every day she would drag me out from my writing and back to the present for afternoon tea at Caribou Coffee in Stillwater.

A big thank-you to my sister, Reverend Sandee Kosmo, who dug into our father's past with me, filled in some blanks, and served as a sounding board. One of our most interesting revelations was how we often remembered events differently—nothing significant, mostly just little variations in the seemingly mundane details that form our memories.

A posthumous thank-you to Pearl Landfair, my English teacher at Eau Claire Memorial High School. She encouraged my passion to write when she said my stories made correcting papers bearable. She added, "But you better get yourself a dictionary."

Thanks also to those wonderful people who shared their stories and gave so much of themselves to my dad and all patients at Eau Claire County Mental Hospital: Jim Schuh, Verna Gunderson, Betty Hacher Klohs, Sharon Dahlby Bestull, Anita Blaeser, Arletta Rud, Stan Olsen, Jean Jirovec, and Jim Christianson. Very special thanks to Arletta Rud for bringing the others together.

Thank you, Dr. Steven Weiss of Mayo Clinic, for retrieving my father's hospital records from Mendota Mental Health Center in Madison.

And thank you to Gretchen Prohofsky and Keevan Kosidowski of the mental health department at Regions Hospital in Saint Paul, and Tim Burkett, PhD, former CEO of People, Inc., for sharing your thoughts.

Tip of the cap to Eric Larsen, retired deputy chief in the detective division of the Eau Claire Police Department. Chief Larsen provided valuable insight and clarification of process for criminal matters involving police and the court system in Eau Claire County.

Thanks to Erin Hart, a highly successful author, who stomped on my ego, ripped my early draft to shreds, and gave me direction to craft a coherent novel. (www.ErinHart.com)

My loudest Thank You goes to Angela Wiechmann, development editor. I dubbed Angie my Max Perkins in honor of the guy who put Ernest Hemmingway and F. Scott Fitzgerald into print. She truly was my Max.

And, of course, I cannot forget the wonderful folks at Beaver's Pond Press, who once again gave me support: Tom Kerber, Hanna Kjeldbjerg, Athena Currier, Mark Jung (Itasca Books), designer Jay Monroe, and editor David Rochelero.

SUGGESTED DISCUSSION TOPICS FOR BOOK CLUBS

Bullies are not new—only their methods have changed with the advent of the internet. How did Jason deal with his bullies? Do you think his strategies were effective? Why or why not? How has attention to the bullying issue changed? What can individuals do today to help?

Jason endured sexual assault, bullying, and the loss of his father, leaving him with many "monsters" to cope with. Was Jason right to lock his monsters away in that dark corner of his brain? What could he have done differently? How did other characters deal with their monsters? How have attitudes changed about trauma and personal demons? What tools do we have now for such challenges?

Just as monsters represent evil in the novel, butterflies represent good. What were the butterflies in his life? Did Jason have more butterflies than monsters, as he contends at the end? Do you feel there are more butterflies than monsters in your own life? How do you focus on the butterflies in the face of your monsters?

Mental health is the background for much of this book. How has the way we treat those with mental illness changed over time? What are we doing right? What can we do better? Do you have a loved one with mental illness, or have you yourself experienced mental illness in your life? What was your experience?

When someone was diagnosed with mental illness in the 1950s, the individual's family was shunned and offered virtually no assistance. What has changed for families dealing with the mental illness of a loved one?

RECOMMENDED READING

The Insanity Offense (2012) and *American Psychosis* (2014) by E. Fuller Torrey, MD

Torrey, a research psychiatrist specializing in schizophrenia and manic-depressive illness, is founder of the Treatment Advocacy Center and executive director of the Stanley Medical Research Institute. Unlike many books on mental health, Dr. Torrey's books are readable, extremely well researched, and beneficial. Check him out at TreatmentAdvocacyCenter.org.

Mad in America (2002) and *Anatomy of an Epidemic* (2010) by Robert Whitaker

These are two of several books by Robert Whitaker, an award-winning and Pulitzer Prize–nominated journalist. His exhaustive research, insightful eye, and excellent writing style put him high on my list.

A Mad People's History of Madness (1982), compiled and edited by Dale Peterson

A Mad People's History of Madness provides the complete history of madness, or mental illness. Peterson once worked as a nursing assistant in a psychiatric hospital and later taught writing at Stanford University.

The Mad Among Us (1994) by Gerald Grob

Written by a professor of medical history at Rutgers University, *The Mad Among Us* delves into the history of mental illness in

America with a comprehensive view into hospitals.

Madness: A Very Short Introduction (2011) and *Madness in Civilization* (2015) by Andrew Scull

These are, respectively, the shortest and longest books about mental illness that I own. Andrew Scull is professor of sociology and science studies at the University of California, San Diego. *Madness in Civilization* provides an amazing history lesson and includes many photographs and drawings.

Circle of Madness (1974) by Robert Perrucci

Perrucci spent a year inside a mental hospital observing how patients and staff interact, how the ill were treated, and what needed to change. It's a story that helps explain where we have been and how we got where we are today when it comes to the treatment of mental illness. Author of several books, Perrucci was a professor of sociology at Purdue University.

My Lobotomy (2007) by Howard Dully

When Dully was only twelve in 1960, he was hospitalized because he irritated his stepmother, who then convinced Walter Freeman, MD, the noted "ice pick lobotomy" advocate, to operate on the boy. It is a difficult memoir about how he overcame unfathomable medical treatment. Somehow, Dully survived, eventually married, and now lives and works in San Jose, California.

The Lobotomist (2005) by Jack El-Hai

This is a well-written biography about Walter Freeman, MD, the father of lobotomy in America. He performed more than 3,500 lobotomies, including Howard Dully's and Rosemary Kennedy's. With words, El-Hai draws a picture of a very complex man who destroyed more lives than he healed yet was revered by many, including some patients. Freeman thought he could save the world from mental illness and felt he should have received the Nobel Peace Prize.

HELPFUL WEBSITES

NAMI.org
The National Alliance on Mental Illness website provides facts, opinions, and news as well as local resources in every part of the country. NAMI is an excellent place to start for anyone wanting more information or needing assistance in dealing with mental illness.

TreatmentAdvocacyCenter.org
This is an outstanding resource for all information pertaining to mental illness. Founded by author E. Fuller Torrey, MD, the Treatment Advocacy Center may well be as close to a twenty-first-century Dorothea Dix as we can find.

MakeItOK.org
Developed by the mental health unit at Regions Hospital in St. Paul, Minnesota, the "Make It OK" campaign seeks to foster public understanding and support for those who deal with mental illness.

ABOUT THE AUTHOR

In 2010, Captain Jim Kosmo retired as a Mississippi riverboat pilot and partner with the Padelford Riverboats Co., of Saint Paul, Minnesota, to spend more time writing and working with new authors through his company, Author's Advocates, LLC. He wrote the national-award-winning *Still Standing: The Story of SSG John Kriesel* and helped Lieutenant Colonel Mark Weber self-publish *Tell My Sons*, which was then acquired by Random House Publishing.

Kosmo is past president of the Rotary Club of Saint Paul, member of the Minnesota National Guard Senior Advisory Task Force, and former mayor of Bayport, Minnesota. He spent twenty years as a newspaper reporter and editor and as a public relations manager in Minneapolis and Chicago. After joining the family riverboat business in 1980 as president, he was licensed by the US Coast Guard to operate hundred-ton commercial passenger vessels as a US Merchant Marine officer.

Kosmo and his wife, Shelley, have a blended family of eight adult children and twelve grandchildren. He resides in Bayport.

www.JimKosmo.com